Knights of the Octagon:
QUAKE

Colleen Snyder

ISBN: 978-1-962168-42-7

THURSDAY

They heard the crack from beyond the treeline. Almost like an explosion but deeper. More resonance. Micah jerked his head up and looked around the yard. He stood from his lounge chair by the fire pit. Mialma, the black lab, jumped from her cot to the grass and barked frantically. Another clap sounded almost immediately after. It came from the hills. Micah stared hard, looking for movement, smoke, anything that would tell him the cause of the noise. Neither the plants nor the trellises vibrated. The ground remained solid beneath his feet.

Two air-reverberating crashes and nothing else. What did it mean?

Micah calmed Mialma. "Shh, girl. It's okay. Whatever it was is over now. Shh."

Mialma quieted but paced around the yard. The lab sniffed air anxiously, then lapped water at the small pond. Finally, she settled down at Micah's feet, laid her head on her paws, and watched her master.

BB slid the screen door open, sticking his head out of the kitchen. "Did you hear the noise?" The lanky teenager leaned against the doorframe.

"Yeah. Weird. Not an explosion. It came from the hills." Micah continued to survey the area for the source of the noise. Trees in the neighborhood swayed with the wind, but as they always did, not in an unusual pattern.

"What do you think it could have been?" BB's voice carried more curiosity than concern. He looked at his thumb and chewed a hang nail.

"I don't know. Check the news. See what the buzz is about." BB disappeared back into the house to comply. Very little rattled BB. Adopting him had been an easy call despite the only eight-year age difference between them.

Micah pulled out his phone and scanned the news sites to see if anyone else heard or knew anything. Nothing. No mention of the sound at all.

Local neighborhood sites mentioned it but dismissed it as construction blasting. Not that there was any in the vicinity, but what else could it be? Had to be construction. Yeah, we'll go with that.

Micah's senses all said no. This had to be out of the ordinary. He didn't know what, but he would catalog it for more research.

Nine-year-old Ben came out of the house. He tiptoed to his dad's side and stepped in front of Micah. The boy reached out for a hug. Micah gave him one. Ben didn't let go. Micah held Ben until the child released *him*. Ben looked up at Micah searching his face. Micah smiled. "It's okay, buddy. Just loud noise. Like thunder. It comes, it makes noise, it goes. Can't hurt you."

Ben hesitated, then nodded. He hugged Micah one more time, then went back inside the house. Too thin. Even after two years with Micah as his adopted son, the boy still hadn't put on enough weight. Not to Micah's mind. But the doctors all agreed the boy was fine. Let him grow.

Micah followed Ben in, along with Mialma. BB sat at the kitchen table surfing the news on his phone. "So far, it's construction, it's the quarry blasting, it's the aliens, it's a precursor to an earthquake, it's the government, it's rifles, it's jet engines backfiring…pick your theory."

Micah nodded. "Aliens. Has to be the aliens."

BB snorted. "That would be my guess, too." He laid the phone down and stretched.

Micah chuckled. "Unless something more happens, I say we forget it and move on. What have you got planned for tonight?"

"Kenmore and Lutz are coming over to jam for a while if that's okay with you."

Micah eyed his eldest son. "Sure. Long as you keep it street legal, and everyone goes home at midnight."

BB grinned. "Sure thing, Dad. We'll keep it down to the dull roar you're always telling us about."

Micah put a hand on Ben's shoulder. "Ben and I will go bowling for a couple hours." He knelt and asked, "Would you like that tonight?"

Ben bounced up and down on his toes. "Yes."

Micah smiled. "Should we invite Tav and Jen to come, too?"

More bouncing on the toes. Beaming face. "Yes!" Ben loved Tav. Tav loved Jen, so Ben loved Jen as well. Worked well.

"And should we invite Wendy?"

Ben's head dropped, and he stood still. He didn't move, but Micah read the emotion. And heard the voice. "No."

"You don't want Wendy to come?" Micah kept his tone soft. Even. Avoid the frustration.

Ben turned his body left, then right. Once.

Micah sighed. Quietly. He needed to break through this wall. "Okay, buddy. This time, it's just you and me. Next time, we'll invite Wendy, okay?"

Ben continued to hang his head. Micah looked into Ben's eyes. "Wendy is Tav's sister. Tav loves her. So does Luke. And Addison. It's not fair to Tav to say we don't want Wendy around. That will make Tav feel bad. He won't want to come around, either. Do you understand?"

Ben nodded, then shook his head again. Micah

squeezed Ben's shoulder. "We'll still invite Tav and Jen." Maybe if Tav talked to Ben, it would help. Nothing Micah had to say mattered.

The boy loved Wendy in the beginning. Last year. But as Micah and Wendy spent more time together—making sure to keep Ben in the picture—Ben had become jealous of Micah's time. And less tolerant of Wendy. Micah wanted to give the boy time to "work it out." But after six months, they were no closer to resolving Ben's issues with Wendy. Counselors, teachers, pastors…no one had the magic answer to Ben accepting Wendy as anything but a rival for Micah's attention. Just "give it time."

He made the text. *Bowling? Kensies? Seven?*
Jen out. Luke okay?
Micah grinned. *Your date. I got Ben.*
No Wendy?
Not yet.
Bummer.
Yeah. I know.
See you.
BB passed in the hall. "You want me to keep the little guy so you and Wendy can go out?"

"Thanks, but no. Jen is out, so it's Luke and Tav. Ben will be fine with us." Micah tapped fists with BB. "I appreciate the thought, my man."

"You got it. I may need the favor one day."

"And I'll remember it."

BB grinned and went to the back to set up the gear for his friends.

Micah looked at the clock and pointed it out to Ben. "We will meet Tav and Luke at seven. What should we do until then?"

Ben grabbed a menu from the drawer. "Pizza."

"Maybe not pizza since they have it at the bowling alley. Maybe a different meal?"

"Pizza."

"Ben…" *Pick your battles.* "Pizza it is." Nothing said Micah couldn't have a salad. Not everything had to be a test of wills. Not yet.

* * *

FRIDAY

Micah sat in his office chair and stared at the accounting book. Mialma lay curled up under his desk. Micah knew this stuff. Backward and forward. So why was he having so much trouble with the questions? Maybe he needed a break. That would do it. A nice, long break…

Except he'd only been studying ten minutes. And he'd blocked out an hour for his homework. Focus. Focus. *A credit to an asset is a liability.* The words jumbled together.

His phone dinged. Message from Quinn. *Video Conference 6 a.m. All call.*

He groaned. Mialma groaned in sympathy. BB called from the kitchen, "I thought I heard a discouraging word."

"Smart alec. Quinn wants a video conference at six tomorrow morning."

BB walked into the home office. "Really? Why?" The teen leaned against the doorframe.

"It's an all-call. You'll find out the same time I do." Micah shoved his books away.

"But tomorrow's Saturday. I wanted to sleep in." BB kicked the frame.

"Yeah, well, guess what? None of us are sleeping in. When Quinn calls, we respond." Knight's code…one for all and all for one. Calling the conference at six in the morning guaranteed everyone would be available. Maybe not coherent, but available. Micah responded, *3K.* It let Quinn know all three Knights at Micah's house would be in attendance. Even Ben would be included in the call. Another part of the code. Leave no man behind.

Micah sighed. Except he'd been forced to leave Wendy behind. Tav had talked with Ben last night at the bowling alley. What effect it would have would be known the next time Micah wanted to include her in any activity. He'd see.

BB flipped pages in Micah's textbook. "I don't see a lot of notes in here."

Micah took the book from him. "Go do your own homework."

BB grinned. "I will if you will."

Micah buried his head in his desk. "Go away. I don't need another voice telling me what to do and when to do it."

BB sat on the side of Micah's desk. "Talk to me, Dad. What's going on? You're really struggling with this class, aren't you?"

Micah sighed. "It's not the class. It's the subject matter. I'm tired of working with numbers." He stopped. "That's not true. I love numbers. I'm tired of figuring them for people who only want to make the fastest buck in the easiest way possible. I want to do something that matters." He rubbed Mialma's ears with his foot.

"Like what?" BB folded his arms in his best "fatherly" pose.

Micah laughed. "I don't know. Research. Analysis. Number crunching. But not financial accounting."

"You talked with Quinn?" BB raised an eyebrow.

"About this? No." Micah squinted. Talk to Quinn?

"What if you could use your accounting to catch the bad guys instead of helping them escape? Would that matter?" BB cocked his head.

Micah thought about it. Thought about it hard. Looked at BB. "Why are you my kid, and I'm not yours?"

"Because you had a rough start, and I at least knew I was capable. Uncle Petey wasn't much, but at least he believed I could do things. Your mom never gave you any credit."

Micah grinned. "Counseling's paying off, isn't it?" Micah tapped knuckles with his son.

"About time, but yeah."

"Okay, I'll stick with accounting. And I'll see it through this class. Maybe when I get to statistics, it'll be better." Micah flipped the pages back in his book.

BB laughed. "That's next year. Maybe we can learn it together."

Studying with his son? What a concept. "You've got a deal." BB turned and left the room.

Micah went back to work. *A credit to an asset is a liability. A credit to a liability is an asset. A debit to an asset...* Mialma settled under the desk once again.

* * *

SATURDAY MORNING

Six a.m. The video conference began. Five pictures came up on the screen in the living room. All five locations were accounted for: Quinn and Grace. Micah, BB, and Ben. Wendy and Jen. Tav, Luke, and Addison. Chay. She was still the group's outlier, being off in Santa Clara at school. Micah grinned at her video background: the beach in Monterey. Yeah, they all wished they could be there.

From his office desk, Quinn opened with, "God, guide everything we're about to think, say, or do. In Your Name, amen." He looked into the camera. Grace sat beside him. "Who heard the explosion yesterday?" Quinn leaned forward to be more "present" on the screen.

Micah, BB, and Ben all raised their hands. Luke semi-raised his, giving it the palm flutter to say, "Mostly." Tav and Addison shook their heads. Jen heard it. "I thought the house would collapse." Wendy didn't. Chay didn't.

Quinn nodded. "If you didn't hear it, you heard about it, correct?"

Now, every head nodded. Chay's face froze for several seconds, then came back online.

Quinn grunted but waited until everyone was live and listening. "We've got a guy here. Geologist. Says the noise is usually a precursor to an earthquake. No telling how soon or how big, but a quake."

Quinn scowled. "That's the party line. The private scuttle is we're looking at a big one within three weeks." He sat back in his chair.

Tav whistled. Addison clapped his hands. "No finals!" The youngest Vaughn threw a fist in the air.

Quinn glared. "This isn't a joke."

Addison sobered. Sarcasm—respectful sarcasm—tinged his voice. "No one can know precisely. Seismologists have been trying for centuries to get within the same year, much less the same month. It'd be like finding the holy grail. If there was such a thing. Which there isn't."

Quinn nodded. "I'm aware of the science. I'm also aware of science to which you have no access." He let that sink in a moment.

And it did. Everyone got serious. Quinn had access to many things no one else did. No one asked how or why.

Quinn looked at the camera and tapped his desk. "I'm proposing a little camping trip at the end of the month. A week, maybe two, in the hills. Table Mountain." He stopped. "I'm not going to say, 'God told me' and sit on the mountaintop waiting for a disaster. I'm saying I'd like to play a hunch, backed by intel I have, and be out of the city.

No one spoke. Quinn continued, "Let me tell you about my other nightmare. Combine an earthquake with an old dam. Can you understand my concern?"

Tav voiced the thought. "Table Mountain Recreation Area puts us above the dam, away from the valley if there's a break."

"Exactly."

The tinge in Addison's voice deepened. He dropped onto the couch visible in the small space reserved for the three brothers. "And we'd do what, exactly?"

"My plan is to discreetly purchase supplies to stockpile up in the hills. If the worst happens, we're in a position to come down and help survivors before the official recovery teams arrive. We would have food and medicines and necessities to share with others." Quinn glanced to the left. Micah knew he would be looking out his window at the park on his right.

"How do we do that without looking like a cult calling for the end times?" BB spoke Micah's question. His son's face appeared drawn. At least he took it seriously.

"If we all purchase a few cases of food at the warehouse store, two or three times during the week, no one will think anything of it. We slip up in the evenings, drop them off at a designated location, and we're good. In ten days, we all go camping for two weeks."

Quinn stared into the camera. No one doubted he would be looking into each of their eyes. "That's my proposal. The floor is open for discussion."

Jen raised her hand. "How solid is your intel? Solid enough to go on the nightly news and warn everyone?" The young woman sat on her bed, a laptop computer balancing on her lap.

Quinn shook his head. "Not my call. I've talked with my source, and he says he fears a panic."

Luke snorted. "How much more panic can there be than the dam letting loose? At least this way, people could get organized."

"I agree. But I can't make that decision."

Wendy raised her hand as well. She sat beside Jen on the bed. "What about warning friends? Family?"

"If you can convince them, bring them. I think you'll find no one will be as convinced of the science as I am." Quinn grimaced. "I'm the crackpot of the group."

"Who's saved our lives more than once." Micah voiced the reality. "I feel like Lot in Sodom. Trying to convince people to flee before the coming apocalypse."

Quinn nodded. "I think you'll get about the same level of response. There are those who may believe but will want to wait to see it. Others won't want to leave home for fear of looters."

Tav threw his hands in the air. "The whole area will be destroyed in the flood. There won't be anything left to loot!"

"Understood. But people are people. Look how many never evacuate when a hurricane is coming. And those, they can predict down to the day and hour. People still don't leave."

"Right." Tav looked away from the camera. Micah could only guess his thinking. Until he asked, "Why not just leave? Why not simply go someplace many miles from here? Why hang around in the hills?"

"So we can be in a position to help others if the quake happens. We're all going to be leaving friends and family behind. If we can't convince them, we can at least act as a readiness team, as it were. That's my plan."

"And you think Table Mountain is the place to do that?"

"It's a plateau. Not a lot of trees, and not a place where boulders are going to come crashing down on us. It's got showers, indoor plumbing, running water for the campsites. Playgrounds for the kids."

"Kids? What kids? There's only Ben."

"Of us. There might be others who think like we do. Who want to get away but not too far away."

BB nodded. "Yeah, I'd want to come back and help. Maybe that would be a way to get others involved."

Micah asked, "Do you have a suggested list of supplies we should all get?"

Quinn shook his head. "I thought we could put a list together now if everyone is in agreement on going."

Addison asked, "What if we're not?"

Luke glared at his brother. "One for all and all for one, Addison. We go as a team."

Quinn held up his hand. "I think we can agree if anyone is adamant about not going, they can be excused. No one should be forced to go." He smiled, straight-lipped. "As for me and my house, we're going."

Micah looked at BB and Ben. He raised his eyebrows at BB. "Thoughts?"

"Two weeks camping?"

Quinn nodded. "At the most."

"I'm in." BB began scrolling through his phone. Singling out friends to warn?

Micah turned to Ben. "Buddy. You get to vote, too. We're going to go camping with Quinn and Grace and the others. You'll come with us."

Ben kept his eyes on the floor. He whispered, "Wendy come?"

"Tav and Luke and Wendy and Addison and Jen and Chay, yes."

"No. Not go-ing." Micah caught Wendy's grimace. Jen shook her head. Tav muttered under his breath. Quinn's eyes narrowed. Grace put a hand on his arm.

Micah looked at Quinn. "We're three in."

Tav glanced at his brothers. "We're in."

Jen nodded. Wendy nodded. Chay nodded.

Quinn smiled. "Thank you. It may all be a false alarm. If it is, we donate supplies to the food bank. And we've had a good time camping." Relief on the older man's face was palpable.

Grace held up a yellow legal pad. "I'm taking orders for camping meals. What do we need?"

"Pancakes and syrup."

"Ready-cooked bacon and potatoes."

"Rice and beans."

"Canned milk."

"Cereal."

"Jerky."

The ideas came in fast. Followed by the needs for the stash: rice. Proteins. Vegetables. Rice. Fruits. All canned varieties. Rice. Baby formula. Diapers. (For after the flood, of course. No one in the immediate group needed them...) First aid kits. Bandages. Water. Water purification tablets. Dog food. Lots of dog food. Mialma reminded them they would need an equal amount of dog treats. Leave no dog behind.

They settled it. Each member of the Knights would purchase a pallet of supplies: one of fruit, one of beans, one of canned meat…not enough to raise suspicion. Different stores, different days. They would take the goods to Table Mountain, to a cavern Quinn would mark for their use. If they could talk friends or family into coming, great. If not, they could pray all their preparations were for nothing.

Once they disconnected the video call, Micah turned to BB. "Who do you want to talk to?"

BB shook his head. "I don't know. This all sounds so out there. We're going to look like idiots."

Micah nodded. "Yes, we are. If others know about us going. We could always slip off without saying anything and have to regret the ones we left behind to die." He paused. "I'm going to call Dad."

BB stared off to the side of the room. "Do you think if the city officials knew about this, they would do something?"

"Like, get out of Dodge?"

"Like warn people?" BB had more faith in his elected officials than Micah.

"I would hope they would. I would hope they have a disaster preparedness plan that takes into account evacuating the area. There should be plans for where the water would go in the event of a break. The city and county governments should have all this in place. But you have to have time to execute it. If the dam breaks catastrophically, there won't be time."

BB walked over to Micah. "I need a hug, Dad."

"So do I, bro. So do I." And they did. Ben even joined them. Mialma gathered close to her humans. Micah's gut curled and tightened. All the people. All the loss. All the death. He kneeled and prayed. "God. Lord in Heaven, please. If there is room in Your will, prevent this. You hold all things in Your hands. You can orchestrate a flood and move it away from the city. You can bring an earthquake and not have it hit the towns. You can do all things. Please."

Micah stopped. He knew. He knew. "But You are God. I am not. Whatever You bring is because You know the end. You know what You intend to do with this storm. Have Your way, Lord. Be in me, in us. Make us instruments of Your will. Your hands and feet. Help us be what You want us to be. In Jesus' Name, amen."

BB added his own prayers. "God, You know I'm scared. I'm scared for me, and I'm scared for my friends. If this is really going to happen, show me what to do. Who to speak to. What to say. I don't want to be silent when I should speak, even if I look like an idiot. Make me brave, Lord. In Jesus' Name, amen."

Ben prayed, "Jesus loves me. Jesus' Name, amen."

* * *

SATURDAY

The call to Dad went as expected.

"Kurt Andres."

"Dad. Mick. You up for camping for a couple weeks?" Micah walked in circles around his office.

His dad's voice came back quickly. "Did Quinn talk to you?"

"Yeah. How much—"

Dad cut him off. "I'll stop by the house tonight to see the boys. Will they be home?"

"Sure, Dad." Micah would check with BB. He suspected it wouldn't matter if the teen was home or not. Dad wanted to talk without being overheard by anyone at the office.

"Great. I'll see you about seven."

"We'll be here." Micah hung up. He grumbled, "Where else would I be?" Who should he call next? Pastor Fulton? How would the older man react? One way to find out. Micah dialed.

Mrs. Fulton answered. "Micah! How lovely to see your name pop up."

"Good to talk to you, too, Mrs. Fulton. Is Pastor around and available?" Micah held his breath. Keep it cool. Keep it friendly. Nothing wrong here. Nothing wrong…

"He's at the hospital. Trevor Bills fell and broke a hip. They're doing surgery this morning. Can I give him a message for you?"

"I'd like to talk to him when he has time. I've got a situation that's heavy on my heart. I could use his wisdom." Micah doodled on a notepad. Two bikes and their riders passed his office window. Kids on the street. Would they be ones left behind?

"I'll certainly have him call you when he's free. In the meantime, I'll keep you in prayer. This isn't about the boys, is it? They're doing well?"

"They're doing fine, ma'am." *And I want them to stay that way.* "I appreciate your prayers. Thanks."

Micah ended the call. Should he have told Mrs. Fulton?

Talk to Pastor Fulton first. He might not appreciate Micah spreading rumors and panic among the flock. No sense in a wild stampede over nothing.

But was it nothing? Micah and his people were acting on the information. He kicked the table. Lightly. Why wouldn't Quinn's source go public with the news? Avoid panic, right? But with two weeks to prepare, there wouldn't be panic. Like before a hurricane…people had time to get ready. How do you get ready for an earthquake?

You leave the area. And leave your home for the looters and criminals? Should the police or National Guard be ordered to stay behind and protect what they left behind? So, the police die in the process?

Micah shook his head. There were no good answers to this. He knelt by the couch. "Lord, direct every thought. Every action. I need You like I've never needed You before. I feel lost, Lord. Help me."

He rose and walked into the kitchen. The whiteboard on the fridge had a list of grocery items. He would add his survival products: canned meat. First Aid kits. Flashlights. Batteries. Power bars. Dried fruits. Evaporated milk. All in bulk. That would be enough for the first trip. The others were purchasing varied items. At least he didn't have to buy diapers and formula. Jen and Wendy drew the short straw. They would tell people they were supplying the pregnancy center. If anyone asked. And no one would. It would be just another purchase from the warehouse store. No one asked. Customers might wonder about combinations of items, but no one asked. Not even when the carts were full of liquor. Don't ask. Don't tell. Today's society.

Micah walked to BB's room and knocked. The teen opened his door. His face appeared drawn, down. Micah asked, "What's going on, bud?"

"I talked to Lambert. He thinks I'm nuts. Wouldn't come even if he knew it was real. Rather stay here and die with his people." BB scowled deep.

"You tell him his people were invited, too?"

"Of course. But he says none of them would believe it, so they won't go. And if they don't go, he won't."

Micah put a hand on BB's shoulder. "I understand. You think he's going to tell anyone else?"

"No. He said he respects me too much to tell anyone I've gone over the edge. He thinks we're becoming a cult."

Micah squeezed his son's shoulder. "We believe in the Lord Jesus. We follow Him. We're not saying the world is ending or sitting on a hill waiting for Him to return. We're up about our Father's business. No cult."

BB nodded. "No cult. Got it." He smiled. "Did you need something besides to encourage me?"

"I'm going to run to the warehouse store. Do you want to come, too?"

"You'll need help loading stuff, right?"

"Always preferable to doing it alone, yes."

"We'll come. I'll get Ben." He grinned. "He doesn't argue with me as much as you these days."

"Wait until you get a girlfriend."

"Could be a long time coming."

"I doubt it. I've seen looks from the girls at church."

"Yeah? Who?" BB cocked his head. His eyes sparked interest.

"I'll never tell. Yet. I'll give them first shot at telling

you themselves."

"Don't want too long. They might lose interest."

"Doubtful." Micah grinned. "All right, let's get moving. We have a lot of supplies to buy."

"Donations to the food pantry, right?"

"We'll look at it that way for now."

BB went to get Ben. Micah retrieved his keys and wallet. Together, the three males climbed into the van and drove to the store.

The warehouse had its usual Saturday crowd. Vendors stocked up for the night's activities. Families sampled the freebies at the ends of the aisles. The food court already had a group of early bird munchers. Life moved at its normal rhythm. Micah grabbed a stock cart and headed up the aisle. He forced his mind to focus on the task at hand. Ignore the growing urge to yell, "Grab what you can! Get out of town!"

No panic. Do not panic. Do not cause panic. We're shopping for the food pantry. That's all.

How many of these people's deaths would be on his head?

Micah gritted his teeth and moved to the canned goods aisle. Rice. Potted meats. Stews. Baked beans. All full of protein. And salt. Yeah, well, sacrifices had to be made. His blood pressure was already through the roof.

They got their supplies and exited the store before Micah lost his nerve. BB walked beside him, repeating, "We're buying for the food pantry. We're going camping. That's all we're doing. Going camping. And buying for the food pantry. We can do this."

Micah exhaled. "Thanks, BB. I'm not sure I could go any further."

BB sighed. "I hear you. This is tougher than I imagined." Tears filled his eyes. "He's wrong, right? Quinn's source. He's got to be wrong. I mean, we'll go up in the hills like we planned, but he's going to be wrong about the quake. Or the dam breaking, anyhow. God won't let it happen." He looked to Micah, his eyes pleading. "He won't. Right?"

Micah closed his eyes. "He is God. I am not. I want to tell you, 'No, God would never do anything like this…let a whole town drown.' But I can't, BB. I'm not Him. I don't know. I know He is Good. I know He loves every soul in this town. And I know He sees things I will never be able to understand this side of Heaven. I have to trust Him. I have to. I have to believe He is God, and He is in control. Beyond that, I can't say."

BB quieted while Micah talked. The young man nodded. "Right. I know. He's in charge." They loaded the car and headed home.

Unloading took time to plan where to keep everything until they could deliver it to the mountain. Empty shelves in the garage made the perfect receptacle. Out of sight, out of mind. Away from prying eyes and pointed questions. BB went to find a pick-up game. Ben went to the neighbor's house to play with their son. Micah went to his office.

He sat at his desk and reminded himself the world wasn't ending. It still mattered what he did between now and their camping trip. People still had expectations he would perform his accounting services. He would file their taxes. Move their money. Look out for their best interests. He had a job to do. He would be faithful. He could do it.

Mialma jumped up on the couch. Micah's phone rang. Pastor Fulton.

"Micah. What can I do for you?"

"Thanks for calling me back, Pastor. I have a dilemma." Micah outlined the situation for the man. "I don't know what to do. I feel like Lot before God destroyed Sodom and Gomorrah. Trying to get people to believe me. But I don't want to start a panic and be responsible for creating an incident if nothing happens." He paused. "What would you do? And what do you say I should do?"

Silence. "How credible is your information?"

"The one who told us is very reliable. He doesn't cry wolf." Micah rocked back and forth in his chair. He couldn't sit. Not and be still.

"And he's acting on this hunch?"

"Yes, sir."

"I would follow your gut, get your family and as many friends as you can convince to come with you, and go camping for the week."

"Will you come?" Micah sat forward in his chair.

Long pause. Long pause. "No. I have members of the congregation who either can't or won't leave. I'll stay with them."

"Should we stay, too, then?" Micah's shoulders slumped. He crossed off the name "Fulton" on his yellow pad.

"No. Absolutely not. That's not your job. Your responsibility is to your family first."

"Will you tell the church?" His voice choked.

Long pause. "I don't know. I'll pray about it." He hesitated, then added, "I would send Mrs. Fulton if I believed she would go. But she won't without me. No sense arguing over it."

Micah smiled. "I understand, sir. Thank you for listening."

"Thank you for trusting me, Mick. We'll both pray the Lord averts this tragedy."

"Amen."

Micah hung up. Mialma jumped from the couch and took up residence under Micah's desk. Closer to her fretting master.

Hours passed. Micah continued to add to the lists. One of people to call. One of items to bring. Both lists filled pages. BB came home. Ben returned also. Micah left the office and prepared supper. They would grill out. Brats and sweet corn and baked beans…well, no beans. There would be beans enough while they were camping. Maybe potato salad and chips. Enough for tonight.

The brats were sizzling when Kurt Andres' silver Tesla pulled into the driveway. Micah waved at his dad, put down his oversized fork, and went to greet him.

They hugged. Micah smiled. "Good to see you. Been a couple weeks."

Dad nodded. "Yeah, I've been out of town. On business."

Which became Micah's cue not to ask where or why. He motioned to the grill. "We're fixing dinner. You have room for a brat or two?"

"Always. Where are the boys?"

"Inside. Ben's setting the table."

"I'll go tell him to set one more." He clapped Micah on the shoulder and went into the house, petting a panting Mialma. She would not be ignored forever. Guard dog that she wasn't.

Micah continued to grill the meat, placed it on a plate, and carried it into the house. He set it on the dining room table. "Food's up. Let's eat."

Ben, BB, and Dad all came from the game room. They took their places at the table. Mialma took her place under the table. Clean up crew member. Micah said grace. They passed the food, and the first mouthfuls were consumed. Only when the chewing finished did BB ask, "So what about the camping trip?"

Dad pointed to his food. "Let's finish eating, then we can talk business. I want to enjoy a home-cooked meal."

Ben nodded. "Pop-dad eat first. Then talk. Chew your food."

Dad laughed. "That's right, Ben. Chew, swallow, then talk." His eyes held a note of concern, which made Micah uncomfortable. Something bothered his father. Something deep.

The men ate, cleared the table, put the dishes in the dishwasher, then retired to the living room. Everyone had a drink of choice. Micah offered to prepare coffee, but Dad refused. "I need to sleep tonight and again tomorrow night. Your coffee will prevent that."

Micah snorted. "Lightweight."

"Call it what you will." Dad stretched on the couch next to Ben. He looked across the room at BB sitting in the rocker. "What do you think about this 'camping trip?'"

BB shook his head. "I don't know. It scares me. The idea anyone knows when a disaster will happen but won't tell the general public bothers me. I want people to know. I don't want to be one of few survivors. Especially if people could be warned."

Dad nodded. He addressed his gaze to Micah. "What exactly did Quinn tell you?"

"He has intel not otherwise available saying an earthquake is coming, and the dam is vulnerable. He suggested we could save people after the fact by storing food and supplies and using them for the survivors."

Again, Dad nodded. "So I've heard. Let's talk about his intel. Did he say who it might be?"

"Of course not. I wouldn't expect him to." *I probably wouldn't know him anyhow.*

"When Quinn talked to you, did he give any supporting information to say this event would actually happen?"

Micah shifted in his seat. "What are you driving at? Quinn said it, and we trust Quinn. His suggestion to camp in the hills for a couple weeks isn't outlandish. Maybe he has information. Maybe he doesn't. We talked it over, and we're going to follow him." He stared hard at his dad. "Can you give me a reason not to trust Quinn? After all this time?"

Dad glanced off to the side of the room before turning back to hold Micah's eyes. "Some people have noticed a distinct shift in Quinn's behavior. Since marrying Grace Painter, he's become more controlling. More...okay, let's say it, more paranoid. In this business, we are all careful. But he's going beyond the norm. I can't give you all the observations. But a few coworkers have expressed concern Quinn is starting a cult with himself as the supreme leader."

BB slapped the table. "That's insane. Quinn?" He jumped to his feet.

Micah added to BB's outburst. "Quinn is the reason I'm here, Dad. Without Quinn, I would have no house, no sons, no freedom. I wouldn't even have a relationship with you if it weren't for Quinn's intervention. Quinn a cult leader? Who makes up the cult? Who are his followers?"

Dad lifted his eyebrows. "You. The Knights of the Octagon."

BB laughed but harshly. "We are. We're a cult. We follow Jesus. If that makes us a cult—"

Dad held up his hand. "Hang on. Just hang on. Step back." He motioned for BB to sit down, then shifted in his seat again. "From the outside looking in, Quinn controls you boys. And girls."

Micah shook his head. "What do you mean controls? We do what we want. We go where we want. Quinn doesn't tell us what to do or how to think."

"Doesn't he? He's got you all heading for the hills for a calamity that might happen. A calamity only he knows about. Based on secret intel only he holds. That's the definition of a cult, son."

"No one has suggested we sell everything and give the money to him. No one is suggesting we form a secret society to live away from the rest of the world. We're going camping. We're storing supplies in case of a natural disaster. If it happens, we'll be prepared. That doesn't make us a cult."

"But you're stashing supplies in the hills? What kind of supplies? For who?"

"Food. Emergency equipment. Things to have on hand if the earthquake happens. If, Dad. If."

"And if it doesn't?"

"Then the food banks get a healthy donation. And

everyone wins."

"Are you inviting others to this camping trip?"

BB answered. "Yes, we are. I've already called a friend."

"And what did he say?" Dad leaned forward and stared hard at BB.

"He'd rather die than look like an idiot. His words, not mine." BB held his grandfather's gaze.

Dad sat back. "Your friend said that?"

"Yes." BB's voice carried heat.

Micah tried to rein it in. "Dad, we're aware we look like a cult. That we think there's going to be a disaster, and we're going up in the hills to wait for it. I understand how that looks and sounds. But we're inviting others to go with us. I called you. First. Doesn't that say we're not a cult?"

"Are you going to knock on doors?"

"Would you?"

Dad nodded. "Yeah. If I was convinced this thing would happen, I would knock on every door in this town."

BB threw in, "And get arrested as a nut case. Or for disturbing the peace or causing a panic. We've talked about it. We'd love for Quinn's source to go on TV and tell everyone. Give an interview. Do something to warn people. But until he does, we're going to prepare." BB stopped. "Sir."

Micah leaned forward. "What is it you're worried about, Dad?"

"How long are you going to wait for this disaster? A week? A month? How long will you live in the hills?"

Micah shook his head. "We're not planning on a long siege, Dad. We're going up for a week prior. And staying a week after. Two weeks. Three at most."

"Now you're hedging."

"I'm giving it the benefit of the doubt." Micah lifted his hands palms up. "I'm convinced there's a real threat. I want to protect my family. Why does that make me a cult?"

"I'm concerned about all the food you're stockpiling. With what you've told me, you plan to stay a lot longer than three weeks."

"The food is to distribute to others if the worst happens. It's not for us to hoard. We're followers of Christ, Dad. We don't think of ourselves first. We're thinking about what we can do to help others if the worst happens. And if it doesn't, we help others with food donations."

Dad shook his head. "You're determined to do this. All I ask is you watch yourselves."

Dad stood. Ben rose and hugged his grandfather. "You come cam-ping. We leave Wendy. You come in-stead."

Dad patted the boy on the back. "Wendy is a good friend. She will go for me."

"So, you're not coming? Not even just to camp? Eat brats and beans and s'mores?" Micah smiled to take the sting out.

"I may come up one night for the campfire. But I won't stay."

"Fair enough. We'll let you know where we'll be." Micah eyed his dad. "That's all it is, Dad. Camping. Unless a disaster happens, we're only camping."

"I hear you." He hugged BB and Micah, patted Mialma, and exited.

BB gritted his teeth. "You think it's going to be like this with everyone?"

"I hope not, bud. I hope not."

* * *

SUNDAY

Tav Vaughn laid his phone down carefully. Precisely. With incredible control. He whirled, grabbed a pillow, and chucked it across the room with all his might. "AARRGGHH!!"

His younger brother Luke came in from the back bedroom and asked, "Another rejection?" He sat on the floor beside the trophy case. His helmet, "Team Captain," emblazoned on the back, sat front and center. A game ball sat below it. Mini helmets flanked the football. Plaques for "Outstanding Student" with Tav's name on them graced the wall above the case. Tav had done well in school, as Luke had done well in football. But none of the honors made any difference when trying to talk friends and family into heading for the hills.

Tav snorted. "What was your first clue?"

"The missile." Luke leaned against the couch. "How many acceptances do you have? Let's talk about those."

"Three. Belcher. Diamond. Widloe. They all think being prepared for a disaster, being ready to help after, is a good idea. That's all I got." Tav collapsed on the couch beside his brother.

"That many? You're doing good." Luke nodded in approval.

Tav glared at his brother. "Three out of fifteen? I don't call that good."

"I got two out of twenty. Face it, this town has gotten

jaded about earthquakes and dams breaking. Every ten years or so, someone sets a date, and nothing happens. People aren't going to jump for the dog whistle anymore." Luke stretched out his legs to get comfortable.

"Is that what you think this is?" Tav leaned back on the couch.

"If it were anyone but Quinn, I might say yes. But it's not. It's Quinn Magary, and that says we have to take it seriously." Luke looked up at his brother.

"Even if we're joining or forming a cult?" Tav's voice darkened.

"Even then." Luke curled his legs in front of him. "I'm right there with you, Tav. I've never wanted to look like a fool or an idiot, but for this, I'll take it. I hope we're wrong."

"But…" Tav waited for the answer.

"But I'm going to act on the information." He stood up. "You want to go shopping first? Or go together?"

"I think we can go together this first time." Tav looked at their list. "Have we checked the gear? Is there anything we might need for the camping trip?"

"Bigger tent?"

"Widloes and Belchers have their own. I think the Diamonds are going to bring their pop-up trailer."

"What about a gas griddle? One that will feed ten people at a time?"

"And a few foldable water jugs."

"Sounds good. Let's do this."

Tav started for the garage, then stopped. "What about Addison?"

"He can get his own tent."

Tav grimaced. Luke ducked his head. "Okay. I don't know where he went this morning. I know he's not one hundred percent on board with this idea. But that's because he doesn't know Quinn like we do. We've got to convince him. Or knock him out and drag him."

Tav pointed at his brother. "That works. Come on."

They headed to the store.

* * *

Wendy Smothers threw her hands in the air. "We're getting nowhere. Mom, you can't care for the babies if you drown in the flood. There won't be any babies to care for. If you come with us to the hills, you can care for everyone who's left. It makes sense."

The argument they had started in the bedroom moved to the kitchen. If Quinn was right, the dedicated chef's kitchen, with its array of pots and pans and crockery stuffed with spatulas, serving spoons and forks, potato mashers, and other essential kitchen cutlery, would soon be destroyed under billions of gallons of water. A lifetime of marital bliss wiped out in a day.

Mom stared at the floor. "But if I stay here, I can care for the ones left behind."

Jen laid her hand on her mom's arm. "Wendy is saying there won't be any babies here to care for, Mom. They'll all be washed away. It's only if you come with us you can help anyone."

Wendy ached for her mom's confusion. The early-onset Alzheimer's made it hard for her to make rational decisions. Losing her husband—Wendy and Jen's father— just last year also severely affected her cognitive abilities.

Finally, she looked at Wendy and Jen and smiled. "If you two think this is the right thing to do, we'll go together."

Wendy wanted to shout, "Hallelujah!" but didn't. If convincing Mom had been tough, how hard would it be to win her siblings? Maybe she would save that fight for another day.

If there would be another day. How much time did they really have? The expert said three weeks. What if he was wrong? What if the quake happened tomorrow?

What if it never happened at all?

Wendy sighed. She nodded to her mom. "That's great, Mom. We'll call it a camping trip with a bunch of close friends. We'll have fun and pray that's all it is."

Jen led Mom back to the living room. Wendy bowed her head, then hit her knees. "Lord, this is heavy. You have got to guide me every step, every word. In Your Name, amen."

They went off to the warehouse store for supplies. Diapers. Wet wipes. Formula. All for a catastrophe no one wanted to happen. Ever.

* * *

WEDNESDAY

Micah took the call. "Quinn."

The older man's voice came across as curt. To the point. "Watch the local government channel tonight at six." Quinn hung up.

Micah stared at the phone. That's it? That's all he got? The local government channel. The city council, the county officials, the preparedness…

Preparedness. Had Quinn's source decided to go public? Micah alerted the rest of the Knights via text. He would be watching. And hoping. Hoping it made a difference. Hoping more could be convinced. Sitting in his office, he stared at the original Knights of the Octagon, silhouetted against a setting sun. Tav, Jeremiah, Luke, and Micah. Full of laughter, full of promise. Micah cast his eyes to the floor. "We miss you, Jere. You were always the one to convince others. If only by your size." He ducked his head and smiled. But the smile reflected the pain of Jeremiah's brutal murder. "You convinced me more than once. Save our seats, brother. If this goes bad, we could be joining you sooner rather than later." Micah went back to his work. He had to force himself. Be faithful to the end. Even if the end looks closer than it did before.

At six that evening, Micah gathered BB and Ben and sat in the living room to watch the town council meeting. Micah tore his eyes away from looking at the pictures of BB and Ben on the wall. This wasn't the end of the world. Just a portion of it. Just the immediate surroundings and all the boys had known since coming down out of the hills. All the "good life" they'd experienced. How many times can you start over?

As many as needed. Life—settled and easy—wasn't a promise. Change was the constant in life. They would survive. They would prosper if Micah had his way. If the Lord allowed.

On the grainy TV broadcast, Professor Maynard Orton approached the podium at the city council meeting. He stuttered slightly but started with, "I was invited to speak by Councilman Avery."

The moderator nodded. "So we were told. How can we help you, Professor Orton?"

Orton shifted his feet. "Without wasting time giving you all my credentials and all the research and factors going into my conclusion, I want to warn this council and the city there is an imminent threat of a 6.0 earthquake in the next three weeks. You should also be warned the dam will suffer a catastrophic failure and flood the town to a height of four feet or more."

Murmurs, complaints, and yelling ensued. The moderator slammed his gavel down and cried for order. Only when the council chambers became quiet did he address Orton. "Perhaps you better give us information on who you are and where your predictions come from."

The screen froze. BB groaned. "When will this town spring for a better broadcasting network?"

Micah grimaced. "When a hot place freezes over."

Ben cocked his head. "What hot place?"

BB grinned. "Never mind, buddy. Dad is making a joke." He raised his eyebrows at Micah. "A poor one, but he tried."

Micah sneered at BB and pointed to the TV. "Just watch the meeting."

Orton's dialogue rushed to match the scene. "I

prepared a paper with all the facts. Pass them around, please." More muttering but subdued. Papers were distributed around the room. Silence came over the chambers as men and women read the sheets they were given. Orton spoke. "The critical data is the timeline. You can see the build-up to the release of seismic pressure. From my calculations, this event will happen in three weeks' time. The quake will shatter the dam, and the town will flood. Structures west of the I-95 freeway will escape damage. Everything east will be destroyed. We need to begin evacuations."

Micah looked at BB. BB's eyes narrowed. "Finally. It's out there." The teen's tone sounded triumphant. Micah relaxed on the couch. He hadn't realized how tense he had been.

A council member stood. "Professor Orton. We see your qualifications and appreciate your work on this projection. Can you tell me who else has participated in your research?"

"If you mean, are there others who agree with me, the answer is no." Mutters and mumbles and sighs of relief. "I have had my calculations reviewed, and my colleagues will vouch for the numbers. They agree the build-up is correct. They agree with the conclusion of the release of the pressure and the size of the eventual quake. They disagree with my timing."

"How far off do they think this event is?"

"Anywhere from three weeks to three years." Orton looked around the room. "The explosions you heard last week were the first warnings. The precursor to the quake that is coming. I'm convinced, and the data backs me up, there will be a major quake in three weeks." He looked around the room. "What do you plan to do about it?"

The council president stood. "We have contingency plans for any natural disasters, Professor Orton. Our first responders and emergency preparedness teams practice for just such events. We will be adequately equipped to handle any contingency."

"Does that include a catastrophic failure of the dam?" Silence filled the room.

The president cleared his throat. "We have our own scientists and experts who do not share your doomsday predictions, Professor Orton. We've been assured the dam can withstand an 8.5 or higher. Your calculations only put the possible quake at 6.5. Well below the maximum."

"Your experts aren't allowing for the depth of the quake. My research—"

"What would you have us do, Professor? Gather in the hills and wait for three weeks for your quake? Who guards the hen house while we're waiting?"

Councilman Epp stood. "We've heard predictions like this before. Nothing ever comes of it." He glared at Orton

"Tell me, Professor. What others have you told about this outside of your scientific community?"

"What are you referring to?"

"I'm hearing rumors on the wind that you have followers who are preparing to hide out in the hills. Followers who are trying to recruit others to stock up on food and supplies and squirrel it away. Friends of friends are telling me about phone calls they are getting to that effect. Preparing for an apocalypse, are you? Are you hiding money as well?"

"I can't speak to any rumors you might have heard, Councilman. I can tell you what I know. Maybe there are some people who believe me and are making contingency plans to get out of the city. Is that who you're referring to?"

"I'm referring to you establishing a cult with you as the head, sitting on top of the mountain waiting for the end to come. Your appearance here is nothing more than a proselytizing attempt to recruit more followers."

Orton glared at Epps. "I wouldn't call people who follow my science cult members."

"Oh? And what would you call them?"

"Wise."

Before a fight could break out, the moderator slapped his gavel against the podium. "Your plan is to evacuate the town into the hills for three weeks. That is hardly possible. We do not have the jurisdiction to empty the city for a possibility. Thank you for your time, Professor, but this council has other more pressing concerns." He looked at his agenda. "The matter of the roundabout at Fifth and Market. Mr. Leeds, you were to bring the environmental impact statement."

Micah watched Orton stalk away. Several people approached him to speak with him. Micah hoped they would listen. He shut the TV off and looked at BB. "What do you think?"

"I think we have more politicians than humanitarians." He looked at Micah. "What do you think?"

"I think no one will listen more than they have now. Maybe we'll get a handful that want to come. But I bet the majority will hang back and wait for concrete proof." Micah shook his head. "If the dam goes, there won't be any second chances. It'll take out everything around here."

He sighed. "We'll see what the fallout is in the morning. Once this gets out and around, we'll see who listens and who doesn't."

BB scowled. "We're not a cult. We're not. Why do people want to think that?"

"It's easier to ridicule groups. If we were a hundred people, that might be a hundred people who've seen the evidence and made up their minds. That's powerful. But if it's a cult, there's only one person, and everyone else goes along with him. No one thinks for themselves. Easier to dismiss that way."

"But we haven't seen the research. We're going on one man's word."

"We're going on faith in one man, son. We've put our

trust in Quinn Magary. Who's always been trustworthy and faithful in all his dealings with us. He says Orton knows what he's doing. He's at least willing to ride out three weeks in the hills. We're going on faith." Micah shrugged. "And a lot of prayer. I've never set myself up to be a fool before and prayed fervently it would come true. I want to be wrong. But I'm not willing to sacrifice you, Ben, or others if Orton is right."

BB nodded. "I'm with you, Dad. I'm going to prepare like it will happen and hope I look like an idiot when it doesn't."

"We need to think about packing and taking everything we can't readily replace. Think about things you have you don't want to lose. The essentials. Pictures. School notes. Birth certificate. If it can be replaced, leave it. If it can't, pack it."

"And pray we get to come back."

Micah put his arm around BB's shoulder. "You got it. Let's get dinner."

* * *

MONDAY

"How many do we have?" Tav looked around at the tents and campers dotting the area in the hills. Tents were set up on the flat below the crest of the hill. Sturdy saplings had been left to use to attach guy lines and the occasional clothesline for drying towels. And other assorted unmentionables. The motorized campers had the high ground. Tent campers had metal fire rings in the dug-out fire pits. Motor campers brought their own fire pits. Uptown, downtown. Satellite dishes marked the motor homes. All the comforts of home. For what might be their homes in the long run. At least they were prepared.

Micah took stock of the surrounding crowd. "Maybe a hundred." He shrugged. "I think a lot of them don't have any other place to go. They don't want to get too far from home if the quake doesn't hit. They want a place to wait it out." He stared at the campers and admitted, "There's more than I thought, but less than I'd like to see." He tightened the guylines on his tent. Mialma snuffled around the base of the tent. All the wildlife aromas excited her.

The Knights set their tents in a circle so as to be close to one another. A central fire pit marked the epicenter of their friendship. And interdependence.

"We'll take what we can get," Tav agreed with Mick. "Maybe more will come later."

"I don't know which to hope." Micah dropped the ropes. The four-man shelter would stand. Unless Mialma was teased by a squirrel tunneling under it. Then, all bets were off.

"I hear you." Tav watched children running around, obviously happy to be pulled out of school. Who doesn't want an extra vacation? Especially when you get to go camping in the hills. Eat hotdogs and s'mores? Heaven.

Micah stretched. "If we get any more tremors, we'll probably see a few extra come up."

Tav shook his head. "I think the rest are dug in. They've been convinced we're the crazy ones. I hope they're right."

He'd never been more conflicted. If they were wrong, they'd be a laughingstock for years. Their testimony would be damaged, maybe irreparably. If they were right, thousands of people would die. *Lord? Make this make sense. Show us what You expect. What You want.*

Faithful. That's all he had to be. Faithful to what he knew, what he'd always known.

By mutual consent, no one tried to organize the camp. Porta-potties had been brought in for easier access to facilities, but that was the most anyone had suggested. This wasn't a cult. They weren't one integrated body. They were individual families who believed the data and wanted to protect their loved ones.

As with any state campground, however, there came the borrowing of supplies, the cookovers, the occasional sing-a-long. For the children. The sizzle of hot dogs, the smell of flaming marshmallows, the chocolate-covered faces and hands...all of it for the children. No one wanted the youngest crowd to be afraid. Adults were afraid enough for everyone. The public campground, although hardly state-of-the-art, would provide both a safety net and fun getaway. There were outdated playground areas with the requisite swings and jungle gyms and metal sliding boards. Merry-go-rounds and scattered disk golf baskets. A couple of pavilions along with barbeques. Areas for both tents and motor camping with water access points for hose hook-ups, but no electricity. Limited picnic tables and modest facilities.

Tav moved to his tent and his books. He'd brought all his textbooks to study for the finals. His last year of college. Finally. He wasn't sure if bringing them was a sign of faith or the ultimate denial. The same with all the other irreplaceable items they'd brought. Photos of Jeremiah when they had been the Knights Four. Financial records. Items of sentimental value. A dress outfit. The award plaque from the Magary Chase. Extra clothes. Medicines. Doctor's records. What else?

Tav sat at the fold-up desk and pulled out his notes. Maybe repeating the year wouldn't be a bad thing. It might make—

A sharp tremblor rattled the desk. Tav grabbed it and held on. Just as quickly, the motion rolled away and dissipated.

Bodies everywhere came out of tents. Those in the open moved away from standing trees. Yells, calls, frantic whistles for kids and dogs sounded all over the camping area. People rushed to the center of the campground and demanded a million variations of, "Did you feel that?"

Professor Orton waved his hands to settle the crowd. "We all felt it. Only a tremblor. Gone and done."

"But what does it mean? Is that the whole quake? Can we go home now?"

Orton shook his head. "It wasn't the quake. It was another precursor. The little ones before the major one hits. It's what I've been saying and why you're here."

Someone called out, "How do you know it's not the big one releasing pressure a little at a time? We'll feel a bunch of little ones, but nothing big will happen?"

Angry voices joined the protestor. Quinn stepped up. "Everyone is here by choice. If you want to go back to the city, no one is holding anyone captive. You're all free to use your best judgment."

People grumbled, but most returned to their tents and settled down. The buzz of voices didn't stop. Children were called in to stay close. It would be a tense night.

Luke entered the tent five minutes later. He pointed to Tav's books. "You need some alone time? I'll go visit Chay and the others."

Tav grinned. "You mean the women's tent?" Chay, Wendy, Jen, and Mrs. Smothers were all camping together. Two of Wendy's younger siblings had agreed to come, but they set up house separately.

Tav shook his head. "No, you're good. This was a time-killer, anyhow. I'd rather walk around and see if the quake left any signs."

Luke held the tent flap open for his brother. The two Vaughns hiked up to the top of the hill. The flat top of the area had been reserved for those with campers and fifth wheels. Gas generators provided electricity for the less-than-hardy among them. Or the privileged, however you wanted to look at it. A few of the units had satellite TV set up. Tav wondered what the local news would have to say about the tremblor. Would more campers appear? Would many go home? Hard to know.

They found a crack in the ground. A crevice that hadn't been there before. Not huge. But still, evidence of the passage of the quake. Tav pointed out the damage. "I wonder what happened in town?"

"Probably a few broken windows. Maybe tiles down from ceilings. I don't think there'd be too much destruction."

They hiked back to the tents. The Andres boys—Micah, BB, and Ben—hung around the entrance. Mialma had decided the fire pit needed inspection. Tav smiled. "What brings you out?"

"Bible study. I thought it would be good if we stayed in our normal routine. We have study on Monday nights. It's Monday." Micah pointed to Luke. "And you're leading."

Luke groaned. "I forgot all about it. I'll get my notes."

He stopped. "Did you tell Chay?"

"And Quinn and Grace. Since we're all here, we may as well all be invited. We can have co-ed Bible study."

Tav chuckled. "Did you tell them to bring their own chairs? Otherwise, we'll do this the New Testament way and sit on the ground."

Micah pointed. "New Testament church. The ground is easy."

"Until you get my age and have to get back up." Quinn snipped at the younger men as he arrived with Grace.

Tav wasn't having it. "You're in better shape than any of us, except maybe Luke. And that's because he's still on the football team."

"Nothing keeps you from exercising." Quinn took a place on an overturned bucket. Grace sat in a chair. Chay, Wendy, and Jen wandered in from their tent. Wendy and Jen's mom must have decided to sit this meeting out.

Luke opened in prayer. He gave a short devotional, then opened the ground to discussion of the week's events. "Who has the Lord challenged this week?"

Hands went up. "What have you done about it?"

BB grumbled, "Besides argue and avoid it?"

Luke grinned. "There is that. What positive steps have you taken?"

Tav narrowed his eyes as he watched outliers move closer to the group. People he didn't know were coming in to listen. To participate? Always welcome. To argue and mock? Always expected. Micah directed Mialma to their tent in order not to frighten any visitors.

One man had an earpiece with a wire running to his top pocket. Hearing aid? Or did he plan on recording? He held up his hand to speak.

Luke smiled. "I appreciate the hand gesture. It keeps things in order. What would you like to add?"

"Is this meeting open to anyone?"

Luke nodded. "Sure. Anyone who wants to hear the

Word is welcome." Tav studied his brother closely. He dropped his hand to his side and motioned. *Watch.*

Luke smiled at the newcomer. "What's your name?"

"Craig. What is this group about?"

Luke leaned forward. He flashed a sign to Tav. *Heard.* He addressed Craig. "We're a loose bunch of friends who do Bible study together on Monday nights at Micah's house." He motioned to Micah. "Been going on for about four years now."

"Who are you affiliated with?"

"My brother and I attend Wilmont Avenue Church. Micah and his sons go to the Ninth Street Mission."

Quinn spoke for himself. "My wife and I attend New Press."

Wendy threw in, "Belling Heights."

Jen held up her hand. "I attend Wilmont Avenue with Tav." She smiled. "We're dating."

"Is this all of you?"

Luke went back to being lead. "All who are here at the moment. We have a few other men who come and two married couples who couldn't be here. But that's usually all of us." He smiled. "Is there a reason for the question?"

"No, no. I'm curious, that's all. I want to know what kind of Bible Study you're leading for the people up here."

Luke shook his head. "We're not leading anything for the people on Table Mountain. There is no organization up here. We're all individuals who decided to heed Professor Orton's information. We're all doing our own thing. I'm sure if you walked around, especially where the motorized camps are, you'll find other Bible studies. You'll probably find as many churches as there are camps. Not to mention the ones who aren't affiliated."

"So you're not teaching people what to believe?"

Tav watched Luke's eyes. He kept his expression casual. "No. We're not preaching any special Word from the Lord. We don't have any inside information from Him about when an earthquake and flood will happen. We're a group of friends camping for the week. Or maybe two."

"But you have an idea when this earthquake will hit, right? And you warned people in Acorn."

Luke kept his smile. "We have Professor Orton's research. He believes there will be a major quake in the next two weeks. We decided we'd camp out in the event it happens." His tone hardened slightly. "We're not a cult. Never have been. Never will be."

Craig wasn't fazed. "I didn't mean to infer you were a cult. I only wondered what you were teaching and to whom."

Tav snuck a glance at Quinn. The mentor remained silent, letting Luke handle the opposition. And he handled it well. "The teachings are open to anyone who wants to listen. And anyone who doesn't is free to do their own thing. As I said, we're not an organized group. We're a bunch of families who want to camp together for a week or so. I'm thinking that's why you're here? Or is there another reason?"

Craig backed off. "No, no. I'm trying to get to know the neighbors up here. That's all."

Luke nodded. "Good. We're glad to have you. If you have any more questions, feel free." He looked at the cadre of others. "We were discussing any positive steps to follow the Lord in the hard places. Anyone care to share?"

Wendy raised her hand. "This whole week is a challenge to me." Tav watched Craig lean forward. *The better to hear you, my dear? Better to record you, I'll bet.*

Wendy continued. "I have two brothers who opted to stay in the valley. They're in their late teens. Legal to stay behind. That's what they chose. They all agreed Professor Orton makes a compelling case for the possibility of a major quake. They checked out the figures, agreed he was probably right…and still decided to stay back. Why? Because they don't want to look like fools if they're wrong."

The young woman looked down, then looked up again. She nailed Craig with a stern glance. "They're so afraid they'll be accused of being part of a cult they would rather risk dying. Who's the greater fool?" She dropped her gaze. "That's what I'm struggling with. My greatest challenge from the Lord. And I'm handling it the only way I can. I'm praying for them. And everyone else. And praying we're all wrong."

Tav added quietly, "I don't know anyone up here wants to be right. We all want to be wrong. We want nothing to happen. Any sane person would rather be made to look like a fool than see hundreds die so we could be right. That's the bottom line."

Luke decided now was the time to call it a night. He asked for prayer requests, then closed in prayer. The group wandered over to Micah's tent and the fire circle there.

Quinn muttered, "Should we break out the guitars and sing 'Kumbayah?'"

Grace shoved him lightly. "Stop it. I will say you showed great restraint tonight."

"Showed it. Didn't feel it."

"Yes, well, you're improving." She kissed her husband.

Ben gagged. Micah shook his head. "Not nice, Ben. They're married and have every right to kiss each other."

Ben walked over to stand in front of Quinn and Grace. "I am sor-ry. You have right to kiss." He looked sideways and added, "Not Tav and Jen." Having made one pronouncement, he went for broke. "Not Luke and Chay. On-ly Quinn and Grace."

Luke grabbed the boy. "I can kiss Chay all I want as long as she says it's okay." He slung the diminutive child over his shoulder. "So there." Holding him upside down, Luke walked over and kissed Chay on the cheek. He reversed the child, then kissed Ben on the cheek as well. "Kissing means you love someone. We can love people we're not married to."

Ben giggled and squirmed until Luke put him on the

ground. The boy nodded once. "Can love people not married to."

Tav nodded. "Right. Like Micah loves you. And you're not married. You weren't even part of his family, and he loved you. Wendy wasn't part of our family, but we found out she was, and we love her now, too."

Ben stared at Wendy. "Wen-dy part of your fam-ily."

"Right. And you're part of my family, too."

Ben had to see it coming. Had to. "I part of your family." The boy circled the fire pit. Pacing.

"So Wendy is part of your family."

Ben stared at the ground. After a full minute, he whispered, "Wen-dy part of fam-ily."

Tav reinforced it. "Part of your family. And my family. And I love her."

BB added, "I love her, too. She's a great friend." He grinned at her. "And throws a mean bowling ball."

Wendy laughed. "Occasionally, I even hit the pins."

Luke quipped, "In your own lane."

She glared at him. "Cute. Real cute." Luke gave her a snide smile.

Tav ignored the banter. "We all love Wendy, Ben. It's wrong to single a person out and say 'I don't like you' because you're jealous. It hurts your heart and makes it small. Jesus wants us to have big hearts that love everyone."

Ben kicked the dirt. "Je-sus loves Wen-dy."

"Yes."

The boy hung his head but said nothing more. Tav decided to let the matter drop. Micah signaled to him. *Thanks.*

No problem.

Luke rubbed his hands. "Whose turn is it to supply the marshmallows?"

Micah broke out the supplies. He looked at the remaining candy bars. "We may have to break into the main stash if we don't start rationing."

Quinn spoke. "The main stash stays in my tent. There will be no breaking in while I'm here."

Tav looked up and saw Craig still hanging on the outskirts of the tents. Still trying for a scoop, hmm? *Good catch, Quinn. That's why you're the mentor, and we're still the students.*

Micah laughed. "I'll take that as a challenge to get you away from the tent more often."

Quinn threatened, "No one touches my chocolate. No one."

Grace patted his arm. "Your chocolates will stay safe with us. These children all know better." She circled her finger in the air to include the whole of the Knights.

Tav suggested, "Just for the fun of it, Rolling Thunder in five."

No one objected. Each member who participated rehearsed their "set piece" of literature they would sign. It was a way to talk to one another in sign language and still confuse anyone wanting to "listen." Tav had invented it when the Knights were in junior high school, and there were only four of them. Now their numbers had swollen to nine (Ben didn't count yet), they could have three and four people "talking" while the others provided cover. Everyone would start with a poem or song the others knew by heart. A stanza or two would be sufficient. All signed at once, nine different poems in motion. Then, designated "talkers" would drop into actual conversation while the others continued to "chant." To an onlooker, it became unorganized chaos. To the Knights, they exchanged information no one could see. It was hard, it was intense, and it was confusing. But it got the job done.

As the group sat in their circle, each recited the name of their piece. "The Night Before Christmas." "Silent Night." "Battle Hymn of the Republic." "Green Eggs and Ham." "The Raven." And so on around the fire.

Everyone ran through their stanzas once. Tav called,

"One, five, eight." Quinn, Luke, and Wendy would talk first. Others would join in as they called numbers.

Tav watched as he signed. Luke wanted Quinn's assurance he'd handled Craig correctly. Quinn and Wendy wanted to compare notes about Craig and if they'd seen him before and with what organization. After several minutes of conversation, Quinn called, "Seven, four." Jen jumped in the fray to be filled in on whatever Quinn wanted to say to Micah. She would pass it on to Chay and Tav. Grace would talk with BB and Tav. No one would be left out. Everyone would be included and updated. And no one outside the group would be the wiser.

Quinn and Micah discussed Micah not speaking about the "main stash" again. His fault. Won't happen again. Tav went back to signing "The Battle Hymn of the Republic." Pay attention to your own chorus. Focus.

The thunder continued for twenty minutes until BB called, "Break. My hands are tired." By prior agreement, the Knights took a five-minute halt.

When time elapsed, Tav asked, "Anyone still out of the loop?"

No one raised a hand. Tav nodded. "Good session, people. Let's roast those marshmallows before Ben eats them all."

Ben grinned through sticky teeth. Mialma licked his fingers.

The ground shuddered.

* * *

WEDNESDAY

Micah heard Wendy's voice outside the tent. "We've got an issue."

He exited his makeshift home. "What's up?" The afternoon remained cool, and the heat in the tent had yet to become unbearable. The scents of unwashed socks, however, were another story.

"County Sheriff is canvassing the area, looking for who's in charge. Telling people they can't be here." Wendy scowled and folded her arms across her chest.

"That's not good. Where is Quinn?"

"He went with Professor Orton and a number of the others to look at the dam."

Micah sighed. He supposed Tav would be among the others. Which would leave the gracious dialogue to himself. Unless he wanted to dump it on Wendy. No, not yet. She was still new in her faith. And the corralling of her tongue. He nodded toward the hill. "Let's get this over with."

Micah ordered Mialma to stay. He, with Wendy, accompanied by BB and Addison, walked to the top of the hill where the County Sheriff had last been seen. The man stood a commanding six-foot-five and could easily be spotted. Micah prayed as he walked. *Your words, Lord. Tell me what to say. Guard my temper and my tongue. Through Your Spirit, Lord. Amen.*

He approached the sheriff and stuck out his hand. "Welcome, sir. Can I help you?" Two deputies stood at either side of the officer.

"Yes, you can clear all these people out of the area. Parties over twenty-five are not allowed without a special permit." The sheriff glared.

Micah nodded. "So we found out. But we're not a group of twenty-five. None of us have more than twelve, and that's the limit we're allowed in this camping area."

The sheriff gazed around. "Who's in charge of this gathering?"

"No one, sir. We're individual families who decided to spend two weeks or so in the hills camping. We're not one organized group." Micah kept his tone even. Reasonable.

"Don't tell me what you are. I know you all came up together to escape a supposed disaster that's coming. Which makes you a group of more than twelve. And that means you all need to clear out of here and go home."

Micah breathed. "We are individual families who looked at Professor Orton's data and decided—"

"—the world would end, and you wanted to escape to high ground. I know who you are and what you're trying to do. You can go play 'end times' somewhere else. But not on the crest of the town." The sheriff's eyes narrowed to small slits.

Micah maintained his composure. "It may look that way, Sheriff, but we aren't playing end-time games. We're on public property designated for family camping. We are families enjoying our privileges as set out by the town of Acorn."

"And those privileges have been rescinded. So you can all move along and play someplace else." He waved his hands.

"Rescinded by who? When?" Micah cocked his head. This was news to him.

"You'll have to come back into town to find out, won't you? And that's not a thing you people want to do. So just pack up and move out."

A crowd of campers gathered to overhear the conversation. And they weren't happy campers. Ugly muttering started. Micah tried again. "I'll be happy to come into town to read whatever motion may have been made in lawful assembly to remove the camping designation of these public lands. But since the town council hasn't met in four months, I know no such motion exists."

"The mayor put it through as an emergency request."

"Except he has no authority to unilaterally approve such a motion. Only the town council can vote on such a matter." He should know.

The sheriff's eyes narrowed. "Are you a lawyer?"

"No, sir, just a law-abiding town council member." *Gotcha.*

"I suggest you get a lawyer because I'm about to run you in for obstructing an officer in the discharge of his duties."

Quinn's voice rang out. "I suggest you think again. This man isn't obstructing anything. He's questioning the legality of an unlawful order you're trying to enforce."

The sheriff turned to face Quinn. "Oh, so you're the lawyer."

Quinn met the man's glare with an even gaze. "No. Better." He reached into his wallet, pulled out a card, and handed it to the sheriff.

The officer stepped back a foot. He eyed Quinn hard, then nodded. "I see. In that case, I stand corrected. Everyone can go on about their business."

While there were many surprised and confused countenances, none of the Knights were caught off guard. They'd seen Quinn pull this "card" too many times.

Micah grinned internally. *Psychic paper. Shows the man what he expects to see.* It wasn't, of course, but the idea was fun to imagine.

Quinn lowered the threat level and became almost cheerful. "Curious to know what the mayor has against families camping?"

The sheriff shrugged. "I heard he's trying to swing more business for the local area. Bringing in a new manufacturing plant. Looks bad if half the town is perched on a hill waiting for the apocalypse."

Quinn said drily, "I'd think he would sell it as the population enjoying the local amenities. Give the newcomers something to look forward to."

The sheriff shook his head. "I'll suggest it to him." He looked away, then studied Quinn. "Professor Orton sure about his facts?" The change in the man's demeanor struck Micah as odd.

Quinn nodded. "I wouldn't be here if he weren't. Neither would any of these other families. We may be the laughingstock of the county when it's over. But we'll be alive."

The sheriff ducked his head and turned to go. Quinn called, "Sheriff." The man looked back. "You're welcome to come up for dinner any evening. Bring the family."

The sheriff stared long at Quinn, then nodded. "Maybe we'll do that. Thanks." He motioned for his two deputies, and the three climbed into the squad car and left.

Micah shook his head. "Thanks, Quinn. I wasn't getting anywhere."

Quinn put a hand on Micah's shoulder. "No worries, son. Politicians. You gotta love them. Because no one else does."

* * *

FRIDAY

"You need to see this." Luke forced his phone into Micah's hand. The younger man's face appeared drawn and dark.

Micah took the device from Luke. He scanned the news report about five house fires the night before. All happened simultaneously; all were empty. Seems the families were camping in the hills. Firemen battled the blazes from late evening until the early morning hours. The nature and causes of the fires were reported as "suspicious."

Micah's hand tremored as he handed the phone back to Luke. "That's bad. How many more do you think will be hit before this is over?"

Luke shook his head. "I wish I knew, Mick." He paused. "You want to move any of your stuff to our place? Since we live in the apartment on campus, I'm guessing we'll be safe."

"Hedging my bets?" Micah scowled.

Luke ducked his head to one side. "We're praying nothing happens. Being prepared isn't a bad thing."

"Thanks. I'll consider it. I'm not sure what I would move."

"Can't move all the furniture, sorry. But anything Ben considers 'precious' you didn't bring."

Micah thought long and hard. "Yeah. A quick trip in…maybe his bed."

"We can disassemble it and store it for you. Anything

else?"

"BB's electronics. Those can be replaced, though." What mattered enough to risk lives? Ben's comfort?

It wasn't about comfort with Ben, though. More about stability. Order. Peace. Life, even. Ben's bed would be a touchstone if vandals targeted Micah's house.

Micah nodded. "Ben's room. Everything else can be replaced." He expected to replace items if the quake hit. But not if it didn't. That he could be wrong and still lose everything was a new thought. He stared at his brother in arms. What else? What else? What else was worth going back? He dropped his gaze to the ground, then met Luke's eyes. "Ben's bed. That's it." Luke extended his fist. Micah tapped it. "Thanks."

"No problem."

Tav marched over to join Micah and Luke. "Did you see the news?"

"About the five houses? Yeah. We were discussing making a quick trip into town to move Ben's bed to our place." Luke filled his brother in on the plan.

"Sounds good. Prudent. Nothing against prudence." Tav grinned. A forced grin, but he tried.

"I'll ask BB if he wants to move anything." Micah doubted it. When the group came to the mountains, they brought everything they thought could be valuable or irreplaceable. A minimal list. Micah still wondered if they thought everything could be replaced or if they were coming back.

Tav gazed around the campsite. "When do you want to do this?"

Micah shook his head. "I don't. I don't want to do it at all. Let me find BB." Ben was with friends. One advantage of the "vacation." Ben had friends to meet with. Social interaction mattered to the boy's development.

Micah tracked down BB and called him away from his "people." "Listen, the Knights are headed into town. We're going to move Ben's bed to Tav and Luke's place. Do you want to come? Is there anything you want moved? Think irreplaceable."

BB's eyes flicked to the side, then back to Micah's. "Naw." He grinned. "I was craving a new sound mixer anyhow."

Micah shoved his son. "Cold, man. Think again. Anything?"

"No. I'm good." BB held his dad's eyes. "Are you sure this is a good idea? Just for Ben's bed?"

"You didn't see the news, did you?"

"No." BB's eyes narrowed.

"Five houses were torched. All of them are people up here. If we get targeted, and the quake doesn't happen, I'd like Ben to have a level of stability when we return. If we return."

BB shook his head in disgust. "I hate playing both ends against the middle. We're trying to cover all the possibilities. Something's going to fall through the cracks." He shrugged. "Sorry."

"I get it." Micah sighed. "We can only do what we can and leave the rest to the Lord."

"Right. You prayed about this, didn't you?" BB eyed his dad.

"I thought about it. I'll pray about it." He grinned. "Wisest of sons, how did you end up with me as a dad?"

"Lucky, I guess." BB cracked a smile.

Micah hugged him then went to find his younger son. He was at the playground with Linda and Craig. Their daughter, Emily, had school with Ben. Micah saw him on the twirler. He yelled, "Ben! Come here a moment." Mialma barked and jumped and did zoomies.

Ben jumped off the still-moving equipment. Micah cringed but didn't rebuke the boy. He'd done the same thing at Ben's age. The joys of flight.

Ben ran up. "Dad! I am not rea-dy to leave yet."

"I know. Tav, Luke, and I are going to town for an errand. We will be back in two hours. Do you want to come with us or stay here?"

Ben's answer shot back. "Stay here."

"You'll have to stay with an adult while I'm gone. I'll ask Linda. If she can't, maybe Quinn can."

Ben nodded once. "Yes. Lin-da. Or Quinn."

Not Wendy. I know, son. I know. Still the same jealousy. He doesn't speak it outright, but it's still there. "Let me ask Linda."

Linda agreed to Ben staying with her. And understood the need. Her family lived in a condo, so she didn't feel the urge to move anything. But Micah asked, anyhow. Mialma would remain with Ben. She flopped on her belly near the children and promptly went to sleep.

Arrangements made, Micah hunted up Quinn to let him know what they were doing. All for one and one for all…

Quinn agreed. "Wise thinking. Consider it as covering all the bases. We don't want the quake. But it will be good to have something to return to if it doesn't happen." He put a hand on Micah's shoulder. "But don't tarry. Orton's calculations are precise. But not infallible."

"Right. We'll be fast."

Micah gathered Tav and Luke, and they headed back to town. Their route took them past the first of the burned homes.

Nothing remained. The entire structure had burned to the ground. Tav whistled low. "What kind of accelerant does that kind of damage?"

Luke snarled. "Depends on how fast the fire department responds. Maybe the mayor has them on the slow track."

Micah disagreed. "No. I don't buy it. Maybe a house sitting by itself. But in a neighborhood this close together? You'd risk a total conflagration. They had to be out here as soon as possible."

Luke pointed with his chin. "There's the family. Maybe we can get answers."

They pulled the car over, away from the "Keep Out" tape, and walked to the rubble. Mr. and Mrs. Gentry stood in the debris, gazing around. Micah saw the pain in their eyes. He extended his hand. "I'm sorry."

Mr. Gentry met Micah's look. "Thanks. We can rebuild." He shrugged. "We were wanting to downsize anyhow." Mrs. Gentry scowled at him.

Luke asked the all-important, "Were you covered?"

"Yes. Fortunately." The man scoffed. "I'm prepared to lose everything with the earthquake and flood. Being burned out is nothing I ever thought about."

"Not before the event." Mrs. Gentry's tone carried bitterness. "We always had the chance we could come back if nothing happened. But now…" She stared at Micah. "Now I hope it does happen." She growled. "So wrong."

Micah put his hand on her arm. "I understand the feelings. Believe me."

Tav asked, "Is there anything we can help you with? Anything you need?"

Mrs. Gentry sneered, "The heads of the arsonists on a platter."

Mr. Gentry put his arm around his wife's shoulders. "No. Nothing. We'll be back in the hills before nightfall. Thanks for checking in on us."

The Knights moved on. They drove past two more burned-out shells. The fire marshal parked at the third house. Micah wanted to stop and ask questions but decided against it. Nothing they could do anyhow. And knowing it had been arson would be little consolation. They already suspected it. Expected it. What would confirmation do?

Tav asked, "Why this neighborhood? Why these neighbors?"

Micah shook his head. "I don't know. How did the arsonists know this family was up at the campgrounds?"

"Were the sheriff and the deputies taking names?"

"Not that I saw. Doesn't mean they weren't."

"Someone knew." Tav drove around the block.

Micah suggested, "Maybe the campers tried to convince the neighbors to come, too. Maybe they told people they were leaving and why."

"I think this is more organized than random. This looks targeted." Tav continued his theory. "Think about the locations. One down on the south side. Two were more affluent neighborhoods. There's nothing to connect the families. No church I know told all their people to leave. While it's possible they were all part of one organization, I doubt it."

His friend made uncomfortable sense. Very uncomfortable. Micah prayed the remainder of the way to his house.

They arrived shortly. Tav and Luke set about tearing down the bed while Micah scoured the house for anything he deemed irreplaceable. At least in Ben's life. He found the boy's sketch pad and pencils in his office. Maybe he should bring those. At the very least, the pencils. Ben had particular feelings about drawing tools. They had to feel right. The graphite had to come off the point smoothly. And the line had to be the exact width. Yeah, he'd take the pencils. And if the pencils, then the pads, too. The paper had a feel. He'd take it all. Micah had already stripped the walls and rooms of photos that couldn't be replaced. Photos of Jeremiah. Photos of relatives long—or not so long—dead. Not just sentimental stuff. Irreplaceable memories. Those were safe in the hills. The truly irreplaceable were the people he loved. And they were all safe. Except Dad. He sighed.

With rope from Luke's car, they tied the mattress to the top of the vehicle and shuttled to the Vaughn brothers' apartment. A quick trip up the steps, deposit the furniture, and head back out of town. Two small tremblors chased them down the road. The tremors were becoming more frequent, if not more intense. The earth definitely moved under their feet. And not in a good way.

They drove past an empty lot on the outskirts of town. Micah studied it and determined it hadn't been empty long. He pulled over. Luke stared at him. "That's been burned. There's rubble there."

The three got out and walked to the wreckage. As in town, this place had been burned to the ground. Charred earth. That's all. Luke kicked a blackened brick. It fell apart at his feet.

The sound of a car engine drew their attention to the road. A battered truck pulled up behind their car and stopped. A large man climbed from his truck and lumbered up to the Knights. His face twisted with disgust. He shouted, "Come to gloat? Not happy with destroying my life, you gotta come see the wreckage? Well, take a good long look."

Tav stepped forward. "We had nothing to do with your place burning, sir. We're not here to gloat. We saw the lot and wondered what happened here."

"Yeah?" Suspicion ran deep. "No one comes out this way without a reason."

Tav continued with the lead. "We're on the way to the campgrounds. Were you up there, too?"

The man roared, "Orton's crazies! You're worse! You're the cause of all this. Fifteen years I've been building this place. Fifteen. Nights after work. One brick at a time. My own hands. And now, because of you, it's rubble."

Tav kept his tone level. "I'm sorry for your loss, sir." He didn't ask about insurance. Micah guessed anyone building a house for fifteen years probably didn't have insurance.

The man picked up a fallen tree limb and swung it at Tav. "Crazies! I should have never listened! Wait 'til they come for you, too!"

He missed hitting Tav by inches. Rather than fight, the three Knights yielded the field and raced back to the car. The man launched his missile and crashed it into the rear window as they drove away. The glass shattered but held. Only when they were out of range and out of sight did Tav stop the vehicle. The three men exited the car and examined the damage.

Micah suggested, "Some duct tape, and it'll hold for the trip."

Luke threw in, "Or we knock it out and call it a convertible."

"And get wet when it rains? I don't think so."

"By the time it rains, this will be over. Either you'll have it fixed, or fixing it will be the last thing on your list of worries." Micah raised his eyebrows.

Tav huffed but nodded. "Yeah, I guess." He opened the trunk cautiously, pulled out a roll of grey tape, and the men taped the window into place. No, Tav couldn't see out of it clearly, but that's what side mirrors were for.

They resumed their trip to the hills. Back at camp, they told the rest of the Knights about what had transpired.

Quinn frowned. "Orton's crazies, huh? I wonder what else we're being called."

Grace's voice stayed quiet. "I don't want to know. I can think of a few titles myself." She smiled at the group. "Let's stick with Christ-followers. I know we're each one of those."

Wendy sniffed. "Right. We're cultees. Waiting out the apocalypse."

Tav shrugged. "It may as well be for those who remain behind. If the quake happens."

Luke stared off into the distance. "What responsibility do we have if we're wrong?"

Quinn's voice became firm. "We're responsible for ourselves. We didn't force anyone to come up here. We didn't bribe anyone. We didn't threaten. We presented facts as we knew them, and people made their own decisions. We didn't light the fires in town." He faced Luke. "I understand the man's frustration and anger. But it's misplaced. The arsonists are the ones responsible. I hope they get caught."

"Hear, hear." General consent marked the group.

Tav gazed at the ground, then to Quinn. "You think we should post a guard?"

Quinn nodded. "It wouldn't hurt. Just among us and just in the lower camp." He smiled a straight-lipped smile. "Let the motorized campers make their own decisions." He gave Grace a mock glare. "I know, dear. But we have enough ground to cover with the tent campers. Especially with just the ten of us on duty."

"You're not going to ask anyone else?"

"And look organized? I don't think so. We'll do this ourselves. And keep it quiet."

She nodded. "Fine. I hear you. And I'll get a pad to write down the schedule." She looked at Tav. "Will Addison help?"

"He'll stand guard like the rest of us." Tav's tone was determined. Settled. Micah wondered if Addison would be as sure.

Grace wrote out the schedule. Three-hour shifts and only around the tent campsites. Tell anyone who asked you were restless and wanted to walk it off. Right.

Tav pointed out a position above the site that gave an overview of the area. The guard could start from there, canvas the area, then return at regular intervals.

Everyone agreed. Micah, Tav, and Addison drew the first night. Nine to twelve. Twelve to three. Three to six. After that, people were up and moving on their own.

The first problem came with Addison, as Micah suspected. The youngest Vaughn proved less than enthusiastic about going on watch. "This wasn't my idea. You brought me up here. Now, you want to put me to work pretending I'm some kind of soldier?"

Tav frowned at his brother. "You're a Knight of the Octagon. We're not pretending. We're not playing. You heard about the houses being torched in town."

Addison shook his head. "What about it?"

"Those were our people. People up here. What if the arsonists aren't satisfied with burning down houses? What if they come here?"

Addison paused. He stared at the trees. "What am I supposed to do? Stop them by myself?" Sarcasm laced through his voice. Addison held up his battered arm. "Motorcycle took most of that, remember? And my leg. What do I do if trouble does come? I'm useless."

"You're not useless. The arm still works. So does the leg. You didn't lose all the use of either of them. Trouble comes, you raise an alarm. Yell fire. Do anything but let innocent people die."

Addison turned back to his brother. "You really think those fires were set deliberately?" The set of his jaw said he felt otherwise.

"I am one hundred percent convinced."

The youngest Vaughn growled. "Fine. I'll take a watch. Tonight. Nine to midnight."

That had been Micah's shift. He stepped forward. "Good. Tav at midnight. I'll take the last shift."

Tav eyed Micah. Micah nodded slightly. Once. Once was enough. Tav tapped his brother's fist. "Thanks. I knew we could count on you."

Addison shook his head. "You take this Knight stuff too seriously. I thought you stopped that as a kid." He glared at his brother.

Tav pointed to a stump. "Let me remind you what this 'Knight stuff' is about. It's a way of living. It's being dedicated to the Lord and living as He would have us live day by day. Hour by hour. Moment by moment. We don't play at it. We breathe it. You accepted Him as Lord and Savior. Like it or not, that makes you a Knight, too. Jesus doesn't have halfway followers. You're all in, or you're not His."

Addison scowled. "And that's why everyone calls you a cult."

Tav stared at his brother a long moment. "Yes. That's why they call us a cult. Because we live for Jesus."

Addison nodded. "Okay, big brother. I'll take watch tonight like a good Knight." His eyes narrowed. "But I'm not buying into the whole 'live like Jesus' idea. Not if you get to tell me what it looks like. I'm not following a list of rules about what I can and can't do. Not from you, not from Him, not from anyone." He crossed his arms over his chest.

Tav nodded. "Agreed. Because Jesus didn't make a list of rules. He gave us one command: love each other the way He loved us. Those are our marching orders. That's what we're trying to do." Tav held his brother's eyes.

Addison stared at Tav side-eyed. After a moment, he said, "I see. Okay. In love"—he stressed the word—"I'll take the shift tonight. Who do I report to?"

"No one. You watch, you raise the alarm if anything happens, and you wake me up at midnight. That's all."

"I'll see you at midnight." Addison stood and dusted the dirt off his pants. Then, his hands. He spun on his heel and walked away back to his friends. Tav sighed.

Micah suggested, "We could leave him out of the rotation. With nine, we're still only on every third night."

"I want him involved. I want him to maintain discipline." He sighed. "I know almost losing his arm and leg has been hard for him."

Luke interrupted the conversation. "Look." He pointed to the road.

A caravan of cars moved down the mountain, headed back to town. Micah stared hard, trying to assess if this was a permanent return to the city or a temporary one like he'd made. Maybe moving furniture to a storage unit wasn't a bad idea. He hoped it was the only reason and not a large group abandoning the safety of the hills.

Quinn marched over to watch the cars leaving. He

pointed out, "Most of those leaving are couples or singles, not whole families. I'm betting this is a move to save belongings. In case the quake doesn't happen."

"You have anything you want to move? We can go down."

Quinn shook his head. "No. If an arsonist wants to take out our stuff, let him. We'll worry about it after."

Grace wore a grim smile. She nodded but added, "And they can worry about retribution."

The ground rumbled. Sharply. Tents swayed. Micah had to balance as if on a surfboard. When the tremblor rolled away, he went in search of Ben.

Ben sat with Linda and Amy at their tent. He looked up at Micah as he arrived. "Dad. That felt like a big one."

"Yeah, I know, buddy." Micah looked at Linda. "Thanks for watching over him. I'll return the favor when you need it."

Linda smiled. "Not a problem. Ben is fine."

Ben climbed to his feet and joined his dad. "Did you move the bed?" Mialma trotted along beside father and son.

"Yes, we did." Micah put his arm around Ben's shoulders as they returned to their campsite.

"Where is it?" Ben looked up, curious.

"We moved it to Luke and Tav's apartment." He didn't explain about the fires nor about feeling safer in a crowd. "I brought up your pencils and drawing pad. I thought you might want them."

Ben nodded his once nod. "I could not find them when we left." He skipped a step. Then hopped. Then marched.

"They were in my office." Micah didn't try to match Ben's cadence. He walked. "On the floor beside the desk."

"I put them there. I for-got." Ben hung his head.

"We all forget. We were packing important stuff, and the pencils were missed. But they're here with us now."

"I can draw the peo-ple here." Joy returned.

"I think that would be wonderful." Micah smiled. "It

will give you real work to do besides playing on the playground.”

“I like play-ing.”

“I'm glad you do.” Micah put his arm on Ben's shoulder and directed him to the campsite. BB waited with a small fire going. The teen asked, “Who's cooking dinner tonight?” He poked the fire.

“Thought we'd go see what Quinn and Grace are cooking.” Micah released Ben.

“No, you won't.” Quinn's voice came from behind the tent. “It's Wendy and Jen's turn to supply a meal. We were on the way to inform them. I'm looking forward to a good meal.”

Quinn and Grace made their appearance from around the tent. Ben's face became solemn. Quinn ignored the boy's lack of enthusiasm. “Wendy is such a good cook. She can make bacon and beans taste like steak.”

BB laughed. “You been in the hills too long, my brother.”

Quinn shrugged and put his arm around Ben. “We haven't seen Wendy in two days. She's been helping her mom take care of a baby in the motorized camp.”

“Sick?”

“Sick of being cooped up, probably. The mama has a thing about dirt.”

Micah lifted his head. “Ah hah. Sorry for her misfortune.” Mialma plopped near the fire. Near enough for warmth, far enough to avoid sparks.

“Right. Mrs. Smothers is trying to convince the mother a little dirt won't hurt, and the baby will do just fine. She's also giving her best advice about colic. The baby's mom asked Wendy and her mom to spend the night to see what the baby is like.”

Micah frowned. “If Wendy has been working and not sleeping, maybe we should cook instead.”

Quinn shook his head. “You failed to hear me. I'm

looking forward to a meal. If you cook, I will endure a meal." He scowled at Micah.

Micah sneered. "I'm not that bad."

Ben nodded once. "Dad cooks good. At home."

Grace's eyes twinkled. "I'm sure he does. But we're not at home. We're out in the wild." She patted Micah's arm. "And he doesn't have his full complement of supplies. We'll help Wendy cook."

Micah sighed. "I hear you."

MONDAY

Three days later. Addison had watch duty again. He resentfully walked the perimeter of the tent campsites. Then, he returned to his perch on the stump to overlook the whole area. "Stupid way to lose sleep. Stupid games. No one is going to come up here. We shouldn't even be here. I'd be in town if I didn't need Tav and Luke's support."

At a bar. Drunk. Again.

Addison snorted. "Fine. Sober is better. I understand them. They want to live on the straight and narrow. I do, too. Except their narrow is too narrow."

What were they missing?

"Parties."

Luke had a party the week before they came up here. Tav had study parties all the time.

"Yeah, but it wasn't a real party."

Why?

"No alcohol."

Getting drunk makes it a party?

"Well…no."

What?

"It's not the same. Sober parties are dull. No one has any fun."

Lots of laughter at Luke's party. Tav got thrown into the pool. Dragged two friends with him. Looked like they were having fun.

"Yeah, well, maybe. There weren't any girls there."

You can only have fun when there are girls present?
"No. Yes. I don't know."

Addison growled at his inner conscience. "Having girls there makes it different."

Chay, Jen, and Wendy have been at the parties.
"They're spoken for. They don't count."
You need single women. How many?
"Shut up. Just shut up."

Addison gazed at the road, then froze. In the moonlight, he saw four…five cars approach the campsite. All had their lights off. They stopped out of earshot of the camp. Doors opened, but no lights came on. Figures in dark clothing emptied from the vehicles. The figures gathered together as a mass and started up the hill. Not up the road, up the hill. Whoever they were, they didn't belong here.

Make an alarm. Call fire. Do something. Don't sit there in silence.

"I'm not a soldier. I never wanted to play this game. Let the others worry about it." Addison sulked on the stump. He would watch. If the intruders actually did anything, he'd yell. He would.

The shadowy forms approached the first tent. Addison had barely enough light to make out their actions. One silhouette slashed the guy lines to the tent. A second swung a solid object—a bat?—at the lumps under the canvas. There came the sound of flesh being pounded. A moan followed.

"Fire! Fire! Enemies in the camp! Everyone up!"

Wendy's voice roused the camp. The mass of intruders separated and attacked the campers who struggled from their sleep. The first figures out the tent door were met with bats and clubs. Addison watched Wendy trip one of the attackers from behind, then kick it. It stayed down. She went after another shape hacking at a second tent. A dark figure turned and swung an axe at Wendy's middle. She side-stepped it and slammed into the intruder. Other bodies struggled from tents not already under assault.

Addison lost track of Wendy in the scrum. *Run! This isn't your fight. Go!*

That's my sister. These are my people. I can't leave them. They didn't leave me. They wouldn't leave me.

Addison slipped off the stump and yelled, "Fire! Fire! Enemies in the camp!" He rushed at the mob and clubbed the first figure he saw in the back.

From the corner of his eye, he saw Micah and BB clash with the intruders. Micah had a tree branch; BB had a camp shovel. Both swung and clubbed and fought the invaders. Tav and Luke stumbled from their tent. Both grabbed anything they could and battled the mob. Grace fought with a walking stick, using it as a cudgel. Quinn used his fists. Others seized whatever they had at hand for survival. He lost all sense other than the need for survival.

* * *

Up the hill, a propane tank exploded. The motor campers joined the war. Shouts and screams and yells and groans filled the night. Dogs barked, and cats yowled. The ambush and element of surprise may have given the attackers the early edge, but they were outnumbered. After half an hour's pitched battle, the campers prevailed. The intruders fled, leaving destruction—and two companions— in their wake.

Roll call went out for first responders. They identified three physicians, two nurses, and five EMTs among the camp population. Wounds were dressed and damages assessed. 911 calls went out to the sheriff's office. The two invaders had their wounds bandaged. One had a broken leg. The other had been knocked unconscious. His concussion would need attention long after the fight ended. No one knew who hit him, though.

Sheriff Knott arrived and took over the interrogations. Seems the rowdies had been paid to come up and disrupt the camp.

"By who?"

"I don't know." The man with the broken leg refused to give up any information.

His addled partner, however, was far more helpful. "You remember, Ralph. Manson said the mayor wanted these people gone. Manson said it would be easy. Like shooting fish in a barrel. Just cut the strings and pound anything that moved."

The brain-wounded man smiled. "And that's what we did. We had fun." He lost his smile. "Until they started hitting back. No one said they would hit back." He looked at the sheriff. "Is it fair they did that?"

Sheriff Knott shook his head and motioned to one of his deputies. "Make sure he gets to the hospital first. Soon. And make sure someone takes down everything he says."

Ralph swore at the poor man. "Shut up, Darryl. Don't say another word."

"Why, Ralph? Aren't I supposed to say the mayor paid Manson, and Manson paid us?"

Ralph shook his head and sighed. He looked at the paramedic. "Can you give me drugs for the pain?"

The medic smiled. "For your leg? Sure."

Sheriff Knott apologized to Quinn. "I'm sorry, Mr. Magary. I never dreamed anyone would stoop to this. How many of your people are hurt?"

"They're not my people, but of the campers, I think there are two possible skull fractures. Too many bruises and sprains to count. Broken ribs. Three broken arms. Busted knuckles and cuts. Several people in the motor camp were burned, one of them seriously. We'll survive."

Knott shook his head. "I'll make sure this gets taken care of. No one wants this."

Quinn's face darkened. "Someone did. And they got it. But they didn't accomplish us leaving. No one is going to go back to town after this."

"Can't say I blame you." He looked at the ground, then looked back at Quinn. "I'll be bringing my people up tomorrow. All this ground shaking…it's time. I'm not leaving my family in danger. It'll be unofficial, though."

Quinn shook the other man's hand. "You'll be welcome. Official or not." Quinn walked the man back to his car and watched him leave.

Grace took her husband's arm. "What now?"

"Now we deal with the internal problem."

"What would that be?" Grace stopped walking and studied Quinn.

He said only, "Call them together. You get the women. I'll roust the men."

The Knights gathered. With the exception of Ben. He would ask after the boy when they were finished discussing their little "problem."

All the knights had suffered in the battle. Micah held his ribs. Luke leaned to one side, holding his ankle off the ground. Tav had a cut on his forehead. BB cradled his arm. Addison, Jen, Chay, and Wendy all sported bruises visible in the darkness. Quinn glared at the ground, then met each with an icy stare. "Who had guard duty?"

No one spoke. Wendy volunteered, "Me. I traded with Addison. My fault. I didn't call the alarm soon enough. I was out of position."

Quinn glared hard at her. "I see."

Tav asked the inevitable question. "Why?"

Quinn interrupted. "Doesn't matter. We need to shift to damage control. Help rebuild what we can." He gazed around. "Are all our people accounted for? Wendy, your mom and brothers? Mick, Ben?"

Wendy nodded. "Mom and my two are fine. They weren't assaulted."

Micah added, "Ben is with the Pope family."

"Go to him. Stay with him. That's your job." Micah left, taking Mialma with him. Quinn noted the man limp away.

Quinn motioned with his head. "The rest of you, go be

the hands and feet of Christ. Let's get this camp resettled."

Grace waited until the others were gone to mutter, "It wasn't Wendy."

Quinn grunted. "I know. I'll let them work it out." He moved to repair what remained of his tent.

* * *

Addison caught up with Wendy. He pulled her arm until she faced him. "Why would you cover for me?"

"Because you're my brother." Wendy turned back to go.

Addison caught her again. "That's not an answer."

Wendy scowled. "That's the reason." She pulled her arm away. Addison adjusted his pace to hers. She slowed hers to match his limp.

Addison snarled, "You don't have to cover for me. No one has to cover for me. I can handle my own responsibilities."

"Why didn't you?"

Addison scowled. "I don't have to answer to you, either."

"No. You have to answer to the people who got clubbed while they were sleeping in their tents. Don't talk to me about handling a responsibility."

Wendy marched ahead. Addison caught her arm again and stopped her. "I didn't ask to be included in your Knight games."

Wendy jerked her arm away. "You think protecting innocent people is a game? You think we're up here playing soldier for the fun of it?"

She stared him down. Addison considered his words. "I don't think you're playing. But I'm not part of this. I'm only here because Tav feels guilty about—"

"Stop right there." Wendy's tone tore into him. "Tav doesn't feel guilty about anything regarding you. You made the choice to ride out on the motorcycle." She faced him. "You were warned and went anyhow because you 'knew

Mom better' than Tav, Luke, and Micah. You suffered for your arrogance. You're still suffering for it." She glared at him. "I covered for you because I know Quinn."

"What's he going to do?"

"Nothing. He wanted to know who was on duty to correct the hole in the defenses. That's all. He's not our commanding officer. He's not a drill sergeant. He's our friend and mentor." She stared hard at him. Wendy spaced her words. "We are not a cult. There is no hierarchy. Only a group of us trying to survive what may be a cataclysm. Or the aftermath if there isn't one." She turned away and walked toward the center of the destroyed tents.

A frantic cry stopped them both cold. "Wendy! Addison! Help!"

Micah. Wendy and Addison raced back to where Micah and the others were. Breathless, Addison demanded, "What's wrong?"

"Ben's missing. He was with the Popes. They said he went in shock, not speaking or moving. Then, suddenly, he dashed out away from them and took off. They lost him in the darkness. We need to find him."

Wendy snatched a flashlight and took off, yelling, "Ben! Ben!"

Micah ordered, "Stay with her. No one should be out alone. Make sure you can find your way back here. Don't get lost." He shoved Addison in the direction Wendy went.

Addison swore under his breath but commandeered a light and followed his sister. He hobbled to catch her. "Wendy! Wait. You can't go off half-cocked." He breathed hard as she stopped to wait for him. "Listen, I'm not a Knight, but I know the things Tav taught us. It's no good getting lost when you're trying to find someone else. The Knights don't trade lives." *I did that.*

"This isn't any life. This is Ben."

"I understand. But what good does it do to find him if you're lost, too?" He carved a mark into the nearest tree.

"We have to leave a trail." He waited for her to understand, agree, and comply. Her belligerent nod told him all he needed to know.

They walked and called and called and walked. Wendy's flip-flops added percussion to their cries. After a few more calls, Wendy stopped. "You call. He doesn't like me. He'll come out to you. He won't if he thinks it's me."

Addison's eyes narrowed. "A lost child would be happy for anyone to find them."

"You don't know Ben."

Addison wasn't going to argue. He yelled, "Ben! Ben! Come in, buddy!"

They walked for an hour, took a break, and walked another hour. Nothing. No sound of a human child. The birds, the animals moving in the brush, the wind in the branches overhead. But no Ben.

Addison called a stop. "I need to rest."

Wendy started to move on but paused. She glared at the ground, then looked up at her brother. "Do we need to go back?"

"Not yet. I hurt, but I can push another hour." He rubbed his leg. *We'll push, right? Another hour?*

"And three hours back?" His sister's voice carried sarcasm.

"He's a kid. He's lost. I can push." *You'll see I can do this.*

"I'll find you a stick to lean on." Wendy started off into the shrubs.

Addison snarled, "You know how I feel about canes."

Wendy snapped, "But you don't know how I feel about Ben. It doesn't matter if I have to carry you. Finding Ben matters, not your ego. You got it? You can lean on a stick, or you can lean on me. But we're going that hour you say you got in you."

A resounding crack rent the hills. The ground heaved and rolled. Wendy and Addison tumbled from the rocks. A ridge of earth split from the ground, creating a rift where level ground had been. Rolling waves toppled a tree and uprooted bushes near them. The land shrieked and groaned. Addison caught Wendy's hand and held on, falling, rising, and falling again. They fought desperately to avoid being crushed under rocks or foliage. The motion stopped, but the carnage continued. Boulders continued to bounce from higher elevations to lower, remaking the lay of the land as they bounced along. Addison shielded Wendy as best he could from the debris. Both took several small rocks to the back and midsection, ducking enough to save their heads from direct contact. Only after the dust settled did they sit up and survey the area.

Wendy pointed in the direction they'd come. Her flashlight illuminated fallen trees and twisted shrubs. "You think we'll be able to find our marks?"

Addison shook his head. "I have no idea." He studied his sister's face. "What do we do? Start back? Wait until daylight? Push on looking for Ben?"

Wendy hesitated. Her shoulders sagged, and Addison could see her spirit was broken. "We need to wait until it's daylight. If he's hiding, we might find him. But if he's hurt, we could miss him in the dark. We can't risk going back unless we can see the marks clearly. They could have shifted. Daylight is around five. We've got a couple hours. We'll rest."

Addison pulled a flint firestarter from his pocket. "Maybe a fire will draw him in." Addison didn't mention it might pull in other creatures as well. A few they didn't want to see. Like the marauders. But the warmth would be worth the risk.

Wendy set about retrieving as much dead wood as she could find, then lit it. She had a small but brilliant fire burning in no time. The heat eased a portion of the aching of Addison's muscles. Not pushing ahead did the same. Real rest would be good.

Wendy sat cross-legged in front of the fire and closed her eyes. She prayed, "God, please. Bring Ben back to us. I can't stand to think of Micah without Ben. I know You have Your will. What You do is always perfect and right and good. But if there is room in eternity, if You can see Your way clear, please bring Ben back. I trust You, Lord. Thank You for keeping Addison and me safe. Protect the others, Father. In the Name of Jesus Christ, my Lord and Savior, amen."

Addison waited. When Wendy finished, he knew he should say something. Anything. It would be his chance to demonstrate the slightest bit of faith. Gratitude for being alive, even.

But nothing came. He added, "Amen." That was it. That was all he had. It wasn't enough. It wasn't even right. But it was all he had. God could figure the rest out. If He cared. But he had one thing he needed to know. And since they were going to be sitting, now would be the time. He rubbed his knee. "You said I didn't know how you feel about Ben. I know you care about him. You even love him. What don't I know?"

Wendy stared at the ground. Finally, she lifted her eyes and gazed at Addison. "Ben is the center of Micah's heart. He loves the boy like nothing else. If anything happens to Ben, Micah's heart will be broken. He'll be less than whole the rest of his life. Oh, the Lord will fill the emptiness and will dry the tears. But nothing and no one can fill the loss. I don't think I'm woman enough to stand with him through all that. I'd try. But I don't know if I'm the one he would need to help him through it. He'll need someone far closer to the Lord than I can ever imagine being."

Addison stared at her dumbfounded. "Do you love the man or not?"

Tears reflected in the firelight. "Of course, I do."

"Does he love you?"

"He says he does." She wiped her nose on her sleeve.

"Do you believe him?" Addison moved his toes away from the fire. He could smell his shoes melting.

Wendy nodded slowly. "Yes." She barely whispered it.

"You'll work it out. The two of you. Yeah, there would be a hole. But you want to make it bigger by taking off? 'I'm not saint enough, so good luck?' Is that it? Do you realize how stupid you sound?"

Wendy stared at the fire. After a few moments, she looked up. "That wasn't what I meant. But looking back on it, I'm not sure what I meant. Except losing Ben will hurt him. Deeply."

"You don't think losing you would?"

Wendy waved him off. "I don't know what I'm thinking. Except we need to get Ben back."

"That's the first intelligent thing you've said in a while." He shifted over and gave her a hug. "I'll take the watch."

"No, I will. I need to think. And get my head together." She smiled at him. "You sleep. Spell me when you wake up. I love you, Addison."

"Love you, Wendy."

Addison stretched out beside the fire, put his arms over his eyes, and went to sleep.

* * *

Wendy took the first watch. She sat and hummed to herself and poked the fire with a stick. Where was Ben? Was he alive? Hurt? Had he run as much from her as from shock? Did she cause this?

Micah always said Ben could handle himself better in the woods than anyone short of BB. But that had been when they first came to civilization. Could Ben handle himself still? Would he be able to find his way back to the camp? Would he come back if he knew Wendy looked for him?

She glanced at her feet. Flip-flops were never meant for traipsing through the woods. She had them on because she had been going to the porta-potty. Until Micah called, and she'd taken off. At least she slept in her sweats. She'd stay warm.

Maybe too warm for tomorrow. But let tomorrow deal with itself. She would spend the remainder of her shift praying. For Ben. For the campers who'd been hurt. For the marauders. Yes, even for them. She was learning, Lord. She was.

Two hours later, Addison woke up. He rubbed his face, then rubbed his leg. He sat up. "I'll spell you. You rest."

But rest wouldn't come, and she ran out of names to lift before the Lord. The ground continued to rumble and shift. Finally, she sat up and tossed a rock into the fire. After a moment, she asked, "Do you think that might have been the 'big one?' Or just another precursor?"

Addison frowned. "I never thought there'd be a big one. I can't say if it was *the* big one or not. I guess it will depend on what happened to the dam." He tossed a rock as well. "It should make Quinn happy, anyhow."

Wendy turned her focus to her brother. "Why do you think anyone would be happy for an earthquake? No one here I know of wanted to be right. That's been the hardest part. None of us wanted to believe it would happen. We all wanted to be wrong. You think we wanted to see people's lives upended? People dying?"

"That's not what I meant. I meant he would be happy…" Addison trailed off.

Wendy hoped he rethought his statement. Quinn would not be happy. Quinn would never be the type to enjoy being right at another person's expense. Maybe for one of the Knights, and the stakes weren't high. But beyond…

Addison shifted subjects. "What do we do now? How will we know when the big one does hit?"

"Did you bring your phone?" Wendy realized they had a lifeline.

"I did." Addison pulled it from his pocket to show her.

"I left mine. I was on the way to the porta-potty when

I saw the bad guys coming. You should be able to find a report about it." *And we should be able to find our way home.*

"If we had a signal up here, I could." Addison slipped the phone back into his pocket.

Wendy eyed him. "Who's your carrier?"

"Way-band."

Wendy frowned. "I have them, and I had service at the camp." She wondered at his choice. Tav and Luke used a different service. One that gave them credit for multiple lines. Addison's use of a separate carrier said he wanted his own plan. His own independence. Freedom from his brothers.

Addison frowned. "I don't have any now. All I've got is empty bars."

"What about the satellite phone? That should have a signal." Hope. She had hope.

Addison cleared his throat. "Maybe. If I bought one."

"Which you didn't." Wendy's tone reflected disgust. So much for hope.

Addison started to defend himself, then stopped. "Yeah. I didn't. Didn't think it would be necessary."

Wendy stressed her words carefully. "The next time Quinn strongly recommends we buy equipment, buy the equipment." *Idiot! Why, Lord? Why?*

Because he's Addison.

Fine.

"Yes, ma'am. Yes, ma'am." Addison tossed a rock into the fire. "I'd do a lot of things differently if I could." He glared at the blazing logs. "Starting with not riding that cursed bike."

Wendy paused, hearing the desperation in her brother's voice. She softened her voice. "You won't move on if you don't let it go, Addison."

His tone came back bitter. "You were quick to bring it up."

Wendy nodded. "I did, and I was wrong. I shouldn't

have thrown the accident at you. I'm sorry."

Addison shrugged to the side. "I deserved it. I wanted to blame Tav."

"He's the easy target. But the fault didn't lie with him. Or you. The blame falls squarely on your mom." *Her. I'm working on forgiving, Lord. I really am. You know how much I'm working.*

"She's your mom, too, you know," Addison stated the obvious.

A detail Wendy refused to acknowledge. "The fact she abandoned me as an infant and tried to kill me when we met disqualifies her from that title." She had moved past the bitterness. Honest. She had. Wendy continued, "Your mom created the problems leading to your accident. Tav hurts for you and wants to help, but he doesn't feel guilty. You're his brother. He loves you." Wendy waited for Addison to respond.

Footsteps in the darkness interrupted them. Wendy and Addison turned sharply to see who the newcomer would be.

A man stepped into the light. He wore disheveled camouflage pants and shirt. Both were torn and grubby. In the firelight, Wendy couldn't make out definitive features. She did detect stubble on the man's face. Like he'd been out in the woods a while. And the woods hadn't been kind. She stood, as did Addison. She directed, "No lead. Equals."

Addison made the first move. "Welcome to our fire. Come on in."

The man hesitated. "How many of you are there?" He tried to peer into the dark around the fire.

Addison countered, "How many do we need?" Wendy's eyes narrowed, and she reached for a sturdy wooden stick. Just in case.

The man held up his hands. "No, no. Not like that. It's only me, my brother, and my boy. We got hit by the quake. The boy's kinda in shock. Won't say much. You know how it is."

Addison nodded. "We do. Is anyone hurt?" Wendy did not drop the stick.

"No, no. The boy's quiet, that's all. Come on in, Roger."

Wendy watched as Roger and a diminutive figure stepped out of the shadows. Roger had a hold on the smaller figure's arm. Wendy's breath seized as the light caught the youth's face.

Ben.

Wendy startled forward, then covered it with a fit of coughing. The man's hold on Ben troubled her. Better to find out what was going on before attacking anyone.

Roger led Ben to a spot near the fire and made him sit. He sat directly beside him, careful to keep one hand on the boy's arm. Tightly. Securely. Ben would go nowhere.

The first man introduced himself. "I'm Gil. Roger's my brother. The boy is…Pete. He's my son."

Addison said nothing but sat, as did Wendy. He settled, then asked, "What are you doing here?"

"Looking to see who survived. The quake took our cabin."

Addison nodded. "Yeah, we were out here, and it nearly took us. Biggest I've ever felt."

Gil picked up a stick and poked the fire. "What are two young people like you doing out in these woods? Especially with no gear?"

Addison shrugged. "Living off the land. Survival. Three weeks in the wild, and last team wins."

Wendy nodded. "Right." Knight's rules said only the lead should talk. But as equals, Wendy thought the sooner these men knew she could talk, the better. "We started out two weeks ago. Never expected an earthquake."

"So, you're not part of those crazies camping in the hills on Table Mountain?"

Addison feigned surprise. "Crazies?" Even his eyes widened.

Gil's voice hardened. "It was in all the news. Bunch of crazy people sold everything, put their money together, and went up in the hills on Table Mountain to wait for a disaster."

Wendy snorted. "Maybe they weren't so crazy after all. Wonder what kind of damage this quake did to the town?"

Gil laughed. "Yeah, maybe they weren't. But you're not part of them?"

Addison shook his head. "No. We're out here surviving, that's all." He stared at Roger.

"Which way you headed?" Roger joined the conversation.

Addison shrugged. "We figured we'd spend a day or so here. Good place to make camp. Plenty of firewood, and the hollow makes for protection from the wind and rain."

Gil's eyes narrowed. "I see. Well, we won't be bothering you, then." He stood up. "Let's go, Roger."

Addison jumped. "Why leave so soon? You could wait until daylight, at least. Where are you going, anyhow?"

Gil's eyes glistened in the firelight. "Looking for others who survived. Gotta be some of 'em in these hills."

Wendy asked, "Like the crazies?"

Gil snapped around to stare at her. "Yeah, girl. Like the crazies. Maybe they got what we need, seeing as how we're not as handy as you at living off the land."

"Trea-sure." Ben's voice broke into the conversation. "They have trea-sure."

Wendy stared at the boy. "Treasure? What kind of treasure?" She made her voice as soft as she could. And leaned forward to hear him better.

Gil shook his head. "Don't mind him. He's off his head. First words he's said since the quake. I think he hit his head too many times." He glared at his brother. "Comfort him so he don't keep talking crazy."

Roger clasped Ben tighter, putting an arm around the boy's waist. "Come on, Pete."

He dipped his head. "See you around, maybe."

Addison held up his hand. "Why not wait until daylight? At least you could see where you're going. Might get you there faster. And you wouldn't miss them in the dark."

Gil shook his head. "Pete here knows the way. He's been up to Table Mountain before. He knows how to get there."

Addison challenged, "But the landscape has changed. Things aren't where they were before. You'll miss the landmarks. You'd do better to wait." He stirred the fire to give it more life. Sparks flew into the air and skittered along the ground.

A crow knocked. A mate cawed back. Nervous tweets filled what should have been silence. Even the animals were on edge.

Gil and Roger exchanged glances. Ben muttered, "Things change."

Gil nodded once. "Maybe we better." The men settled back around the fire. Ben still sat closely guarded by Roger.

Wendy measured the silence, then asked, "What do you know about those crazies?"

Gil shrugged. "Just what I told you. I heard they sold everything and went into the hills by Table Mountain."

Wendy shook her head. "Sold out but took the money with them? That doesn't make a lot of sense. If you think the world is ending, what good will money do?"

"I didn't say they thought the world was ending. Just some sort of calamity would happen, and they wanted to be away from it."

"And your boy thinks there's treasure?"

"I told you, he's off his rocker. Got hit in the head. He doesn't know anything about treasure." Gil's voice hardened.

Wendy backed off. "Yeah, well, I suppose there are different treasures. In a famine, food would be a treasure. Blankets, tents, and clothing can be a type of treasure if you're homeless. I'd hope that's the kind of treasure the crazies would have."

Roger's eyes fell to slits. "What do you know about the crazies?"

Wendy shrugged. "Only if I thought there were going to be a catastrophe, like a major earthquake, I'd want to go where it would be safe. And take supplies to help other people if it did happen. Maybe I'd be considered crazy for going. But maybe God would use me to save others. I'd like to think that's what the crazies were planning."

Gil accused, "You are one of them."

Wendy nodded. "Yep. And that's what we did. We didn't bring cash into the hills. We brought food, equipment, and supplies to share with anyone who needed it. Even you two." She motioned with her head. "You can let the boy go. And his name is Ben. He doesn't talk much. He meant what he said about treasure, though. All the food and supplies are treasure for those who need it."

Gil smiled a crocodile smile. "I don't think so, missy. The boy said treasure. Even a kid knows the difference between camping supplies and treasure."

"Except Ben has a different value system. What's important to him isn't the same as you."

"We'll see. We'll all go together. And your boy will show us where the treasure is. We'll decide what is and isn't important."

Addison directed his attention to Ben. "Are you okay, buddy?"

Ben nodded. "I am o-kay." He looked at Roger. "I hug my mom?"

Wendy's heart slammed in her chest. Did he mean it? Or was he trying to give her a message?

Gil did a double take. "She's your mom?"

Ben nodded. "Oops."

Wendy shook her head. "Never oops, Ben. Never an oops."

Gil snarled. "You didn't mention him being your son. What game are you playing?"

"No games. You come up here holding my son, claiming he's your child. I want to know what's going on before he gets hurt." She stared him down. "And don't give me a lie about you'd never hurt him."

The crocodile smile returned. "Since you're so close, I'm sure you won't pull any tricks so long as we have your son." He looked at Addison. "You the dad?"

"Uncle."

"Nice little family affair, huh?" His smile belied the sentiment.

Ben repeated his question. "I hug mom?"

"Sure, kid. Hug your mom."

Ben stood, walked over, and hugged Wendy. He whispered, "He has knife. Throws it well."

"I hear you."

Ben returned to sit beside Roger.

* * *

TUESDAY

Daylight slipped above the ridge. Not enough to navigate, but enough to see the terrain. And the damage to it. The ground shuddered. Dirt and rocks shifted again, still looking for equilibrium. Wendy closed her eyes and prayed, *God, help us. Let that have been the big one. No more, please. But in Your will. Always in Your will.*

The group of five began walking. Addison had trouble picking up the markers at first. Many of the trees were down. But between the stumps and the bushes, he could determine a direction. As the day wore on, he had a harder time. It took all of them searching to find the slashes in the trees and agree they were man-made and not victims of the tree's own demise. Twice, the five had to stop and crawl over crevices in the land. The first was daunting. The second, they had to find a way around. The search took an hour or more before the group finally found a means down and back up again. Then, they had to make their way back to the starting point, check their heading, and finally get back on track. The day waned when they reached a third crevice.

Addison's shoulders slumped. He called out, "That's it. We're done. At least for now. I need a break."

Gil swore at him. "You'll push on until…" He stopped as he looked into a canyon. He glanced up at Addison, and his eyes opened wide. "That wasn't there before. I been all over these parts, and I've never seen a canyon here."

Addison sank to the ground. "It wasn't there when we

came through last night, either. Nothing is the same."

Wendy stared into the abyss. Not wide, but deep. Very deep. She joined Addison on the ground. "What do you think?"

"I think we're done. We'll have to spend the rest of the day going either uphill or down and hope we can find a passage of sorts." He admitted, "I'm done, Wendy. Done for today. I can't keep pushing."

Wendy nodded. "I hear you." She stared at Gil. "My brother has a bum leg. He can't keep marching. We're going to have to stop for the night."

Gil commanded, "I'll say when we're stopping."

Wendy pointed to the crevasse. "Fine. You tell me how we're going to get across, and I'll be happy to keep walking with you. But my brother is done. We'll leave him here to rest."

"Let me see the leg."

Addison huffed. "Sure." He pulled his pant leg up, revealing a mass of surgical scars. The muscles were smaller than usual and had been stretched to make a connection with the bones. Scar tissue grew in rock hard protrusions at the ankle.

Roger gagged. Gil waved his hand. "Cover it up. I believe you."

Addison started to reply, but Wendy nudged him with her foot. He lowered his pant leg without comment. Wendy dipped her head to Gil. "So we can leave him here, and the rest of us go on. Or leave both him and Ben here, and I'll take you."

Gil shook his head. "I'm not an idiot like your son. You'd try to pull an escape, and I'd have to kill you."

Wendy huffed. "Which would make me the idiot, wouldn't it?"

Ben glared at Gil. "I am not an i-di-ot." He nodded once to Wendy. "I am learn-ing."

"Yes, you are, Ben. And you're learning well. I'm

proud of you." Her voice choked. "Your dad will be very proud of you for staying alive."

Ben hung his head. "But not run-ning a-way." Tears filled the boy's eyes.

Wendy scowled at Roger. "A moment, please?" Roger released the boy. Wendy hugged Ben and soothed him. "Right now, we need to survive."

"Dad will find us." His face filled with hope even as moisture cascaded down his cheeks.

Wendy nodded. "Yes, he will." She looked up at Roger and repeated her offer. "I'll take you. Let the boy and his uncle stay here. They can wait until someone comes looking for them."

"Who would that be?"

Wendy lifted her head. "The crazies. Because we don't leave anyone behind." *If they're still alive and can come.*

"Yeah? How many will come out?"

Wendy thought fast. "Maybe fifty." *Maybe five. Maybe they're all dead.*

Roger snorted. "I heard there wasn't but fifty of you to start with. You mean they'd all come out? And leave the treasure unattended?"

Wendy nodded. "That should tell you what we think of the treasure, shouldn't it?"

"That's your word." Roger leered and poked Wendy in the chest with the tip of the knife.

Wendy maintained her composure. "That's my word." She pointed to the crevice. "You tell me, how are we going to get around this?"

Gil studied the opening and finally pointed. "Up. We go up." He stared hard at Addison, then at Ben. "Brother stays here. Boy comes with us."

"He'll slow you down. Hard as it will be for adults to cross, it'll be much harder for him. Leave him here."

Gil chewed his cheek. "I'll have more control of you if I bring him."

Wendy hissed, "You'll have no control if anything happens to him." She moderated her tone. "Right now, you got me thinking about how to get back to the main camp and the cache of supplies." She mocked him. "The treasure." She straightened up. "If he comes, I'll be thinking about protecting him and not watching where we're going. Your choice."

Roger pitched a rock down the crevasse. "Let 'em stay behind. We don't need them. All we need is her."

Addison took Wendy by the arm. "You want to think twice about this?"

"I already have. Three and four times. I'll be fine. They won't hurt me. They want treasure. Can't get it if they kill me."

Addison dropped his voice. "They don't have to kill you to hurt you."

Wendy nodded. "I know. I'm trusting the Lord on this. I get the sense I'll be fine."

Addison shook his head. "I don't."

"Work on it. God will take care of me. One way or another." She glanced over her shoulder at Gil. "Do we have a deal?"

Gil scowled. "Yeah. Let's get moving."

Wendy put both hands on Ben's shoulders. "Take care of Addison and yourself. I won't be able to live with myself if anything happens to you. Be safe."

Ben cocked his head. "Dad be sad?"

"Your dad would be very sad. I don't want to see him sad, so you take care of you."

Ben cocked his head the other direction. "He be sad if you gone?"

Wendy grew solemn. "I suppose he would be. But we can talk about this when we get back to camp."

Ben stared at the ground. He waited, then looked up at Wendy. "We not make Dad sad."

Wendy hugged Ben. "Right." Her gut twisted. *Lord,*

make this real and true. But only as You want it.

She walked away with Gil and Roger without looking back. Too afraid she'd cry.

Wendy and the men hiked up the hill for two hours before they found a stretch of the crevice narrow enough to risk jumping across. It was cross here, or give it up. Light dimmed in the sky. The sun slipped below the hills but still cast enough radiance to see. Upended trees and boulders littered the forefront. Across the canyon, more debris lay strewn about. The devastation had been far-reaching. The quake had to be the big one. It had to be.

Gil looked at the distance from side to side and grumbled. "I don't like it. I can't jump that."

Roger studied the expanse as well. "I don't like it, either." He looked up and down the visible length of the canyon. "But there's nothing else. We could walk for miles and not find anything closer. We have to cross here or risk going so far out of the way we never find the camp."

Gil shook his head. "I'd rather go back than try to cross here. No treasure is worth this. 'Specially if it isn't even real treasure."

Roger snarled at him. "The boy said it was. That's good enough for me."

"The boy could have been wrong, too. She said he doesn't always make sense. I've seen kids like him. They don't think like we do."

Wendy held her tongue. She could defend Ben's mental processes or let the men think what they wanted. If it benefited her at the moment, she'd let them believe their own thoughts.

Roger looked up and down the length again. "We can do this. We can make it across."

Gil pointed, "You go first."

"Woman goes first. If she can make it, so can we."

Wendy glared at Roger. "You think so?"

"Yeah." He gloated. "Little thing like you can get

across, I certainly can. Jump it. Do it. Now."

Wendy drew in a deep breath. She measured the distance, estimated how long a run-up she'd need, and paced it off. She knelt down and prayed aloud, "Lord, if You want me on the other side, You'll have to give me wings to fly. Help me make it across, Lord." She tucked her flip-flops into her sweats. She'd run faster and land more securely in bare feet. She hoped.

Roger humphed. "I don't need God's help. I can do this on my own."

Wendy stood. She eyed the distance, eyed the distance, eyed…took off running. She closed her eyes as she launched into the air, reached forward, and tumbled onto the far side. She rolled to her feet, jumped up, and yelled, "Thank You!" She threw her fist into the air and danced in joy.

Roger paced off several feet further, took two attempts at a run-up, and finally jumped. He, too, made it across.

Gil watched, walked up, looked down the canyon, then smiled at his brother. "See ya." He turned and walked back the way they had come.

Roger shouted at him, "Gil! Get over here! You coward! Get over here!"

Gil continued to walk away, unconcerned with the vitriol and curses Roger threw at him. Only when Roger started throwing actual rocks did the man on the far side of the crevice duck and run away.

Roger glared at Wendy. "Don't you get any ideas of running off. I know I can catch you."

Wendy shrugged. "Why would I run? We're going the same direction. We both want to get to my camp. I want to find my friends and prove to you there's no treasure. Only food and supplies. The sooner we get there, the better." She put her shower sandals on and marched ahead.

They walked south until they ran out of light. They continued to walk by flashlight until they guessed they'd walked about even with where they'd started. Wendy could just make out the flicker of Addison's fire. She hoped he and Ben stayed warm. And no more varmints came to bother them.

Roger and Wendy spent the night in darkness. There was enough moon to illuminate their figures. No chance of disappearing unless she caught Roger sleeping. And precious little chance of that happening. No trust, no sleep. Even when Roger snored, Wendy wasn't convinced the man truly slumbered. She would take no risks.

Morning came early, with light hours before the sun. Wendy and Roger rose and began their trek east. If her calculations were correct, she should reach the campsite at Table Mountain by noon. She knew she and Addison only walked two hours out to find Ben. Given the changes in the landscape, she and Roger should still see signs of life by lunchtime. Sooner if a search party had come out looking for them.

Trees she and Addison marked were down and twisted. She had to search to find a slash. On lower bushes, they had tied limbs together. When the whole bush had upended and woven into another, locating a specific stem became impossible. Wendy closed her eyes and prayed. "Lord, show us the way to go. You directed Your people in the desert. You can direct my feet in this wilderness. Please."

Roger laughed. "You think God is going to help you? I don't need God to tell me which way to go. I know which way I'm going." He pointed. "Table Mountain is north of here. That's the direction we need to be going."

Wendy scowled at him. "You go north. I know we came west when we left the camp, and we need to go east to get back." She pointed toward the sunrise. "And that's east."

Roger pointed the knife at her. "Like you would know. I lived all my life in these parts. I know north. And I say we need to go north." He caught hold of her arm and pulled. "And you're coming with me."

Wendy started to pull her arm back when the sound of

a big cat yowled in the hills. Wendy jerked upright. "What was that?"

"Mountain lion. They hunt in these hills. He won't bother you."

A second call yowled. Wendy relaxed in Roger's grasp. "Fine. Go the way you want. I won't stop you."

Roger jerked his head. "I know you won't. You'll do what I say. You'll take me to the treasure. Then we'll see what happens."

"Yes, we will." Wendy followed the path Roger led. After half an hour, a twisted tree trunk bore a definitive arrow carved in its broken side. Wendy pointed. "There. That's one of the signs we left."

"You sure?"

Wendy nodded. "Yeah. We came this way. I know it." She touched the tree with her foot.

"North, I told you. See? You aren't as smart as you think you are." Roger glowed. Triumph colored his eyes.

No, I'm not. But I have smart people on my side.

The marks continued to show up at regular intervals. Roger didn't find it strange the patterns appeared in the gashes of trees fallen because of the earthquake. Wendy did, but she'd take it up with the one making the marks later. Nothing like obvious. But that was the point, right? The indicators were too precise and too clean. Roger should have noticed. But the man remained laser-focused on his treasure.

The big cat's occasional growl reassured Wendy she wasn't alone. There would be an end to this little hunt. The sooner it came, the sooner she would like it. She felt tired, hungry, dirty, thirsty, and scratched…and concerned about her brother and Ben. Had anyone found them? Maybe she should ask.

Wendy made a point of having to search for the next sign, though she spotted it straightway. She poked through the brush, pushed it aside, and finally stood in defeat. "I can't find the blasted thing. I'm as lost as Ben and Addison. You think anyone found them?"

The cat gave a long, low purr. A satisfied purr. A contented purr. Wendy whispered, "Thank you." She leaned back into the brush and called, "There it is. I found it."

Roger examined the mark. His eyes narrowed. "Pretty easy to see."

"You find them. I'm tired." Wendy sat down. "Keep following the arrows, and you'll get there. They'll lead you right to the treasure. Have at it."

Roger pulled his knife. "You think I'm stupid? An idiot could follow this trail. No one would make it this easy to find a cache of gold coins."

Wendy's head jerked up. "Gold coins?" Weary as she was, she could still be startled. "Who said anything about gold coins?"

"Fine, it's not coins. It's bars. Troy ounces. I don't care. I know you exchanged all your money for gold before you came up here. Cults always do. They bury it to come back to after the disaster is over. Don't tell me this is the way to the stash."

He held the knife against her neck. Wendy remained still. Except for the shaking in her insides. And her hands. And her voice. "I've told you all along there is no treasure except food. Don't you think bankers would get suspicious about money being exchanged for gold? The Feds would be all over those transactions."

"I don't care about the Feds. I care about gold. You have it. I want it. Take me there, now."

Roger jerked Wendy to her feet. He placed the knife in her back and pushed. "Go. Now. Before I kill you and find it myself."

Quinn's calm, authoritative voice spoke from directly behind them. "Drop the knife."

Tav stepped into the clearing. "Drop the knife."

Micah moved in from the opposite side. "Drop the knife."

Luke and BB strode in from alternate angles. Men and women surrounded Roger with nothing visible in their hands.

Roger waved his knife at Wendy. "I'll kill her."

Quinn continued in his quiet tone. "We'll sacrifice one for the good of the many. And you'll die with nothing."

Roger darted glances at the crowd around him. Wendy saw more faces joining the circle. All stern and determined. All held hands at their sides, palms hidden. Roger blanched. "You'd let her die?"

"Drop the knife." The command came from all sides at once. Wendy felt the chill of death in the voices. Roger spun around, trying to catch someone's eyes. But all eyes were vacant, staring at him but not seeing him. Robotic. As one, they all intoned, "Drop the knife."

Wendy straightened. She looked at Quinn, standing dead still. Her voice became monotone. She droned, "Drop the knife."

Roger jumped back from her, his eyes wide with terror. He stared at Quinn. "How are you doing that? How are you controlling them?"

The group took a step closer. "Drop the knife." Hands that had been at their sides moved to the centerline, the back of their hands still visible. All as one. The knuckles came together. Touched. "Drop the knife."

Roger stepped toward Quinn, knife out. The circle chanted, "Drop the knife. Drop the knife." Took a step in.

Roger screamed and threw the knife on the ground. He bullrushed Quinn, who stepped aside and let the man go. Wendy watched Roger hightail it back the way they had come, scrabbling past rocks and shrubs, never looking behind him.

Quinn leaned in and picked up the weapon. He smiled at his "robots." "He dropped the knife."

The gang relaxed in one breath and began laughing. Luke doubled over in merriment. Micah hugged Wendy, his face covered in tears from glee. Everyone sighed and leaned against the rocks and trees. People thumped Quinn heartily on the back as the campers returned to their own areas. Wendy let Micah lead her to Quinn and Grace. Wendy shook her head. "How in the world did you think of a stunt so bizarre? You almost freaked me out!"

Quinn smiled at her. "Ah, but you caught right on. I think that proved the final straw for your captor. If I could control you…it was too much for him."

"Who came up with this idea?" Wendy stayed in amused shock. BB raised his hand. "You? How?"

The teen shrugged. "People keep insisting we're a cult. I figured it might work if we really acted like it." He beamed in pride.

Wendy sank down on a stump. "Addison and Ben?"

"We've got people with SAT phones who've backtracked your path. They found them this morning and are working on getting them across the new divide. They should be here in the next hour."

Grace put her arm around Wendy. "But now it's time for you to get something to eat, drink, and finally rest. I can guess you've had none of the above since yesterday."

Wendy nodded. "I won't fight you on it. But let me know when Ben gets here. I want to talk to him."

"I'll be sure to wake you."

* * *

WEDNESDAY

Micah sat with Ben in their tent. Ben looked rested. As rested as anyone, what with the ground still rumbling and shuddering. The whole camp stayed on edge. Most of the tents had to be reassembled. Two of the motor homes had capsized. The seven occupants were offered accommodations elsewhere. Other smaller vehicles had to be releveled or repositioned. Overall, only minor damage showed for all the quake had thrown at them. And still, the question remained: had that been the big one?

Professor Orton staunchly insisted the "big one" hadn't happened yet. It would be unmistakable. Everything up to now was a foretaste, a warning of what would inevitably happen. Stay ready.

Reports came in from town. There were widespread power outages, houses off their foundations, and trees down. Ten people died, and another fifty were missing. Two were killed when a tree fell on their car. One perished from carbon monoxide poisoning when his gas line broke. The rest were victims of collapsed roofs and houses. Primarily in the older, poorer side of town, where houses had been constructed before the earthquake protocols had gone in place. Most of the missing were from the south side. The dam held steady. Cracks were minor, so the report stated. A dozen more families moved to the hills and joined the campers. Most had lost homes, and many were fearful of what might be.

Micah kicked his heels. What more could they do to be

ready? *God? Have we done enough?*

Wendy called. "Can I come in?"

Micah called, "We'll come out." He and Ben rose to sit in a more visible location. Even with all the uncertainty of the situation, Knights still did not compromise morals. Mialma followed them out the door and took a seat near the grassy outskirts of the tent.

Around Micah, the camp moved and resettled. Children brought sleeping bags and one-eyed teddy bears to new places for sleep. Adults carried well-used blankets and worn-out pillows, also relocating from damaged campers and ruined tents. In the background, children climbed and called excitedly from newly downed trees. Different playthings after two weeks in the hills. Joy!

Not so for parents still aware of the rumbling deep beneath their feet. Crows and starlings continued restless flight. An owl flapped aimlessly in the sky. Searching for a new home? Its woo-woo differed from the doves. All the earth remained unsettled.

Wendy pulled up a sling chair. She smiled at Micah. "I told Ben we'd have a talk when we got back to camp. May I have a word with him?"

Micah turned to Ben. "You want to talk to Wendy?"

Ben gave a single head nod. "Wen-dy, I talk. You stay."

Micah glanced from Ben to Wendy. "Is that okay with you?" He, too, took a sling chair as a seat. Mialma stretched out at Ben's feet, then went belly up.

"If Ben wants it that way, it's fine."

Ben stood. He put his hands behind his back and stared at the ground. "Dad lost Ben. Dad was sad. Wen-dy was sad. Dad lost Wen-dy. Dad was sad." He looked at Wendy's face. "I am sad." He held out his hand and took Micah's. He took Wendy's and put it in Micah's. Finally, he grasped both adults' hands. "Dad has Ben. Dad has Wen-dy. Dad is hap-py. Wen-dy is hap-py. Ben is hap-py." Mialma woofed.

Wendy stared at Ben. "You're happy I'm with your Dad?"

"We not make Dad sad. We all to-ge-ther. All of us." Ben stopped and grew a sly smile. "You not kiss. Not yet."

Wendy grinned. "But I can kiss you?" She bent over and planted a warm kiss on the boy's cheek. Ben put his hand to his cheek and held it there. After a moment, he leaned over and kissed Wendy's cheek. "I kiss Wen-dy. Wen-dy kiss BB." He paused, then pronounced, "Wen-dy and Dad kiss on cheek." He shook his head. "Not like Luke and Chay."

Micah laughed. "I hear you, buddy." He leaned over and kissed Wendy on the cheek warmly. He whispered, "For now."

She returned the caress. "For now."

Tav approached from the grassy field. He grabbed a metal bucket, turned it over, and sat down. "Nice to see the family united." He motioned to Ben sitting with Wendy. "Does this mean you're good with my sister again?"

Ben nodded. "I am good with Wen-dy. But she cannot kiss Dad. Only on cheek."

Tav laughed and rubbed Ben's head. "You're too much, buddy. I love you." Mialma came over for the requisite scratch behind the ears. Once received, she went and laid at her master's feet.

"I love you, Tav." He hopped on one foot, then the other, then jumped with both feet. Mialma barked at her charge, trying to get in the middle of Ben's play.

Tav smiled at the two and got down to business. "We're wondering about going into town to help where we can." He tapped the bucket with his fingers, drumming lightly.

Micah asked the obvious, "Who is 'we'?"

"The Vaughn brothers, the Windloes, and a handful of others." He leaned forward. Micah wondered who Tav meant to convince. "We always intended to be up here to assist the townspeople when the quake hit. Be prepared to bring aid. Well, the quake hit, and we need to be busy helping our neighbors."

Micah nodded. "Sounds right. If we're sure the 'big one' really did hit, and we're not still in the waiting period."

Tav sat back. "We could sit up here and second guess the question for the rest of our lives. Do we have any assurance it hasn't?"

Micah shrugged. "Do we have any assurance it has?"

"I say yes. Look around at the damage done just up here. Look at the images of what it's done in town. People down there need our help." Tav's expression drew into one of total commitment. "I'm going."

"I think you should. Are you planning on taking the supplies?"

Tav's darkened. "That's the problem. Not all those supplies are ours. We all bought into them. It has to be a unanimous decision. Or at least..." He thought, then continued, "It has to be unanimous. We may be a contentious bunch, but we need to stick to first principles."

Micah stuck his fist out. "Thank you." The two men tapped knuckles. "When do you want to call the meeting?"

"Now. I need to locate Quinn and Grace. I think they're up helping the motor campers get leveled. I don't want to pull them away from anything critical. But I want to get into town before dark."

"What do you want me to do?"

"Can you help me find Quinn?"

Wendy cleared her throat. "Do the women get to help, or are we supposed to keep the home fires burning like good women do?"

Tav held up both hands. "I never meant to sound like you weren't invited. I thought more of your mom."

Wendy gave him the stink eye. "Sure you did."

Micah grinned. "Let's table the discussion and see about finding the rest of the knights. We can argue later about who meant what." Wendy glared at Tav, then smiled.

Rounding up the knights took an extended amount of time. Afterward, they employed Rolling Thunder to discuss the supplies and their distribution.

With twenty-two hands moving (Ben moved his so as not to feel left out,) no outsider would possibly determine what the group said. And the discussion looked animated.

Quinn stated his opinion. *Not time to bring out cache. No knowing if big one happened. Might be more in need down the line. Wait.*

Tav disagreed. *Town needs help now. Tomorrow can deal with itself. God can provide for later. People in town suffering now. Distribute.*

Micah jumped into the dialogue. *What word from Professor Orton about big one?*

Says still to come. Quinn caught Tav's eyes and held them.

Luke strove to be a peacemaker. *Has he verified figures with new data? Current quakes?*

He doesn't see necessity.

Eyebrows raised around the circle, and all focused on Quinn. Quinn ducked his head. *Looks bad, agreed. Still have faith in him.*

Maybe not his figures? Micah directed his comment to Quinn.

Quinn shrugged.

Micah leaned forward. *Suggest he go to the laboratory. Check out damage. Send persons to accompany him. He check figures while there.*

Luke asked, *What of other areas? Other towns nearby?*

Wendy had the answer. *SAT phone info says Elkins, Chestmont hit hard. Casualties, deaths there as well. Acorn epicenter.*

If knew how deep could tell more what to expect. Micah added the obvious.

Which fueled Quinn's frustration. *Got it. Got it. We need data. I will talk to Orton. Again.*

Jen entered the fray. *What if send out scout team to assess actual need? Contact Red Cross or disaster management team. Will know if supplies needed now, or are coming from other sources, and ours can serve the camp.*

Addison leaned forward. His signing moved slower, but he worked at it. *Maybe if we bring in small load supplies, authorities will know we are serious and not looking for places to loot.*

Agreed. Agreed with talking to Red Cross. Micah felt as if they had a solid plan and should go on and vote on it.

But Grace had an objection. *Red Cross will want all supplies. Are they the best source of information?*

Who else? Tav kicked a pebble into the fire.

Sheriff's Department. Search and Rescue. A joint command. Not just Red Cross. Grace held her head high.

Quinn supported his wife. But modified her demand. *Scout team can locate any joint command and ask them.*

Addison added a question to his suggestion. *Will scout team be working recovery as well as evaluating? Can spend time searching for family, friends?*

Dad. Micah signed immediately.

Wendy added, *Brothers.*

Kenmore. BB's concern.

Quinn added, *And look at houses they can reach. But no one enters without certification house is safe. Will not lose family here.* He glared around the circle, holding each person's eyes. Micah knew behind the glare, Quinn experienced deep pain. The man never spoke of his family, except as the Knights. Any other pain stayed locked away.

The lively discussion went on for nearly forty minutes before calling for a break. Five minutes passed, then they went at it again. In the end, Tav, Luke, Addison, and BB would go into town with a single load of food and first aid supplies. They would contact the powers that be and see what help might be needed. They would also run by each residence and see what condition they were in. Figure out what repairs might be required. Then, they would report back, and more discussion could take place.

It was mid-morning when Micah and Mialma went with the four designated scouts to load the SUV. The wind had kicked up, and the air stayed cool. They tried to prevent as many prying eyes and questioning bodies as they could. With repairs still going on in the camp, it wasn't hard to move the vehicle. A great many motorized conveyances were shifting around, looking for more level ground on which to camp. One more car wouldn't be noticed.

But as the men left, Micah saw unwanted interest in what they were doing. As he and Mialma walked back to camp, Jonas Martin stopped him. "Saw you up at the caves with your friends. They drove off with a carload of stuff. What's going on?"

Micah prayed to the Lord, then said to Jonas, "Tav is moving boxes of his personal items from the caves back to town. He's gotten more afraid of water damage from the cave than earthquake damage in town."

Jonas' widened, then narrowed. "Really? Does he now?"

Micah pointed to his tent. "I've got to go check in on Ben. The brothers will be back later this afternoon. You can ask him."

"I'll do it." Jonas left, but the scowl on his face said Micah's answer did not satisfy him.

Micah frowned. So, it wasn't the smoothest answer he could give. Let Jonas chew on it and ask later if he really wanted to. Micah would report to Quinn…

Report to Quinn? Weren't they supposed to be independent families?

Yes, but the Knights were the Knights. They operated as a unit.

And Quinn was the head?

No. He was the mentor…the oldest member, and thus to be respected.

But consulted on every decision?

One for all and all for one. Yes, consulted. Micah ignored the nag in his head and climbed down the path from the caves in search of Quinn. He sent Mialma back to the tent to be with Ben. Having completed her walk with her master, she jaunted back down the path toward home.

Micah found the older man in heated discussion with Professor Orton. Both men's voices were intense. Orton had one finger in Quinn's face and shook it at him. Rather than appear to listen, Micah caught his mentor's attention and signed *Back later.*

Quinn responded back. *Do that.* His rigid posture spoke volumes.

Hmm. Quinn had something to talk about. Micah went to his tent and found Ben sitting with Wendy. She sat on the ground drawing stick figures in the dirt, and Ben filled them out into real beings. Mialma had gone paws up beside Wendy, waiting for a belly rub. Micah examined the earth. "What are you two up to?" He looked at the drawings and grinned. "Ah, good job, Ben. Are you teaching Wendy how to sketch?"

Ben shook his head once. "No. She says she hope-less. I a-gree."

Wendy laughed and held up her soil-colored hand. "I am. Never could get the hang of art. I hated coloring as a kid. I always picked the wrong shades."

Micah pulled up a director's chair and joined them. "I hear you."

Ben cocked his head. "Can you draw, Dad?"

"With a straightedge and protractor. Freehand, not so much."

"I will teach you." Ben went back to his art.

Micah smiled. "I'd like that, Ben."

Wendy asked, "The boys get off okay?"

"Yeah. Jonas saw them take off. He's asking questions. I told him Tav moved boxes of his stuff back to the house.

Afraid of water damage from the cave."

Wendy's eyes widened. "You think there's a problem?"

"I felt uneasy with his questions. Maybe it could have been the way he asked them. I wanted to talk to Quinn, but he was in conversation with Professor Orton. He said I should come back later."

Wendy motioned with her head. "He's coming to see you."

Micah looked up to see Quinn stalking across the campground. His back locked ramrod stiff, his fists closed at his side. He joined the trio, taking time to admire Ben's drawings. "You always amaze me, Ben. I wish I had half your talent." He looked at the figures Wendy drew and chuckled. "I wish my intern had a quarter of your talent."

Wendy sneered at Quinn. "Thanks, boss. I'll remember that."

Micah waited until Quinn pulled up a seat, then asked, "What did Professor Orton have to say?"

Mialma snuffled over to Quinn and forced her nose under his hand. Quinn scratched her ears, then frowned. "Nothing good. I asked him about double-checking his figures with the new data. He insists there's no need. Even with all the quakes we've had and continue to have, he insists there's still a 'big one' to come that will destroy the dam.

"No one certain of their calculations should be afraid to replicate them with new information. Smacks of arrogance."

Micah grimaced. "That's not good. People here are convinced the worst is over. They want to go home—or to what's left of home."

Quinn gave a straight-lipped smile. "I hear you. And I'm not far behind them." He stretched his shoulders. "Any word from the scouts?"

"Not yet."

The mentor nodded. "What did you want to talk to me

about?"

"Jonas Martin saw the guys leaving with the supplies. I told him they were Tav's, and he worried about moisture damage from the cave. I'm not sure he believes me."

Quinn chuckled. "I wouldn't believe you, either. That was a pretty lame excuse."

"Short notice." Micah scuffed his heel. "You think there's going to be a problem with the campers about the storehouse?"

"What kind of problem?"

"Thinking they should share in what we bought and brought. Since we're all here, you know. One for all and all for one." Micah ground the base of his heel into the ground.

"Except that's for the twelve of us, not the entire camp. And we bought those supplies. Specifically to supply those in need." Quinn took a stick and drew lines in the dirt.

Ben's eyes narrowed. "I can-not make an-y-thing from straight lines. You give me some- thing to go on."

Quinn chuckled. "These lines aren't meant to represent anything but my frustration, Ben. You can make them into a growling monster if you like."

Micah continued. "Jonas will think the need is greatest here. He's close to out of food. He only brought food for one week. He's subsisting on the goodwill of his neighbors."

Quinn shook his head. "And why is that my problem?"

"Because our Christian witness says to feed the hungry."

"And he who does not work should not eat. Let him chew on that Scripture."

Micah dipped his head to the side. "You don't see this as an issue?"

Quinn huffed. "You're going to make it one, I can tell." He sat back. "Okay, we call a round table. Discuss it like Knights do. If the vote is to feed the locals, we'll do it, and the town survivors get the leftovers, if there are any."

Wendy threw in her two cents worth. "Or we vote to

supply the town like we originally planned, and the locals fend for themselves. At least they are all able-bodied."

Micah raised his index finger. "Or we wait for the scouts to come back and see what is happening—truly happening—in town and make our decision."

Quinn held up both hands, palms up. "Can't have a round table with people missing. We'll wait."

About then, Jonas Miller walked up with five men from the tent camp. They all looked resolute about a matter. Micah guessed he knew what. He dipped his head. "Jonas."

"Micah. Mr. Magary. We want to talk to you about the supplies you're hoarding."

Quinn's eyes widened. "Hoarding?"

"You're keeping supplies hidden from the camp."

Micah and Wendy motioned to Quinn. The older man took the lead. "Whose supplies are they?"

Eyes blazing, he demanded, "They rightfully belong to the camp."

"By what right? Who purchased them?"

Jonas' eyes narrowed. "Doesn't matter. They're here."

Quinn shook his head. "It very much matters. If the supplies were purchased on behalf of the camp, with the camp's input and monies, yes, the food would belong to the camp. But that isn't the case, is it? No one here organized any such purchases." Micah could hear the smoothness in Quinn's tone but noticed the man's shoulders straighten.

A man stepped out from hiding behind Jonas and complained, "Well, someone did."

Quinn shook his head again. "No, no they didn't. Individuals in our Bible study decided to purchase additional food and supplies to help the townspeople if the big quake happened. Twelve of us. We went together and stored up equipment to help out in the event of a catastrophe. Like the one that happened down below."

A taller, lankier, but scruffier man demanded, "You're hoarding. We want our share."

Who are you to call another person scruffy? Have you looked in a mirror lately?

"Did you contribute to the purchase?" Quinn continued his rational tone.

The lanky man glowered. "You know I didn't. No one told any of us what you were doing."

Quinn stretched. "Gentlemen, we have not stolen from you. We didn't take your supplies or food. Each of you has exactly what you brought up. All of you came because you thought Professor Orton had good data to warn of a quake. You came up prepared to wait it out. If you didn't plan enough for the length of stay, I suggest you head into town and purchase or start scouting for what you need. At least you're able to, because most of the folks in town are in a much worse position. But we owe you nothing at this point."

Jonas stepped forward. "You haven't heard the last of this." He spun on his heel and departed, followed by his posse. Mialma gave a soft, short growl. Voicing an opinion, no doubt.

Quinn scowled at Micah. "Watch yourself. Don't go out of camp alone." He pointed at Wendy. "That goes double for you." He rose and started off, then stopped. "Maybe we ought to maintain a presence in the Knights' camp. Keep one of our people here at all times. Just because."

Micah glared at the backs of the retiring men. "I think that's a good idea. I'll take first watch until the guys get back."

Wendy scratched out her last stick figure of what could be a horse. Or a long-legged dog. Hard to tell. "I've got to get back and spell Jen on Mom duty. And fill her in on what's going on."

Micah laid his hand on her arm. "I know you and Jen are feeling isolated. Only one of you can be away at a time. It makes it hard to feel connected."

Ben cocked his head to the side. "Why can on-ly one be a-way at a time? A-way from who?"

Wendy dusted off her hands and wiped them on her jeans. "Mom is the same as you in many ways, Ben. Micah doesn't like leaving you by yourself for very long. He's afraid something will happen to you. Jen and I are afraid if we leave Mom alone, something might happen to her."

"You are a-fraid she get hurt do-ing what she should not?" Ben stopped his drawing and gave his full attention to Wendy.

"Yes."

"Or she will run a-way if she gets frigh-tened?" He hung his head below level.

"Yes. That she might run away." Wendy's lips formed a sad smile. "Mom can't always think clearly. So we feel as if one of us should be with her."

"What a-bout your bro-thers? Can they stay with her?"

Wendy cleared her throat. "My brothers are still too young to be very good caregivers for Mom."

Ben cocked his head to the other side. "They are the same as BB. He is a good care-giv-er."

"BB is an excellent caregiver. And I would trust him to stay with Mom. But my brothers aren't as responsible as BB is. So Jen and I stay with Mom."

Ben lowered his head. "I would stay with Mom. I like Mom."

Wendy smiled. "And she likes you. I appreciate your offer, Ben. When you're older, you can stay with her." She stood. "For now, I'll go." She risked a quick kiss to Micah's cheek and kissed Ben on top of the head but pointed at Quinn. He waved her off. Wendy disappeared back to her own tent.

Micah eyed Quinn. "You're thinking we can move back to town?"

"I'm thinking I'd like to move back. I haven't convinced myself yet." He drew another line in the dirt. "Grace is ready. I'd feel better about it if Professor Orton would verify his numbers."

A rolling tremblor bowled over camp. Like ocean waves that undulate and disappear, they pulsed through the hills. Trees leaning from the first quake gave up their hold on the earth. They didn't crash as much as gently collapse to the ground. Stones rolled downhill in slow motion. Dirt cascaded in the rocks' wake. Cries of dismay came from the upper camps. Children cried. Dogs howled. Ben came to his feet.

Micah held Ben. When the motion stopped, Ben looked up at his dad. "That felt fun. Like a rol-ler coas-ter." He sighed. "Do you think ground will e-ver stop mo-ving?"

Micah hugged his son. "It will, Ben. A few more days, and we'll forget all about this."

Ben hung his head. His voice quivered. "I will not for-get. I will re-mem-ber I ran a-way. I hurt you. I hurt Wendy. I will not for-get."

Micah laid his cheek on top of Ben's. "It's okay, bud. I forgive you. That means it's all okay. When Jesus forgives us, He doesn't bring it back to remind us how bad we were. He chooses not to remember what we did. We need to forgive the way Jesus does."

Ben blinked several times. "I can for-give me?"

"Yes. Absolutely. It doesn't mean you're free to do the same things over and over. We're supposed to learn from our mistakes and not repeat them."

Ben gave his singular nod of agreement.

Quinn stood. "I'll go check and see if everyone is okay." He huffed. "In our camp." He sighed. "And I'll check on the rest of the heathens."

Quinn walked off. Ben finished a sketch of a ferocious monster. He pointed to it. "This is Quinn's mad." He hesitated. "I wish I draw a thing eat the mon-ster."

Micah patted the boy's shoulder. "I wish you could too, Ben. Let's go sit at the fire circle."

They moved to the center of the Knights' circle of tents. He could survey the area better. Watch for enemies, real or imagined.

They waited several hours for Tav and the others to get back. When the SUV pulled in, the guys got out looking dirty, dusty, and dragged through the mud. Addison had a bandage on his left hand that hadn't been there before. His limp was noticeably worse. BB followed in the last of the four. He had a deep bruise on his head and a wrap around his right wrist. Micah rose to greet them. "What happened to you four?"

Tav sank to the ground, as did his brothers. "Search and rescue. We've been digging through rubble and remains of houses."

"Did you find anyone?"

Luke volunteered, "Five live people. One dead. Three dogs made it out to be reunited with their owners."

Micah kept his tone soft. "Sounds like a tough day."

Tav stretched, groaned, caught a rib, and nodded. "It was. Tomorrow won't be much better." He held Micah's eyes. "There's a lot of work to be done. People are hurting."

Micah directed his attention to BB. "Did you find your friends?"

"Yeah." The tired boy ducked his head. "They're alive. Lost everything, but are alive."

"Jen and Wendy's family?"

"We weren't able to locate them. Word is they're in a shelter across town." BB sank into a camp chair and sagged.

Micah hesitated. "Dad?" He held his breath.

Tav shook his head. "Nothing. No word. Didn't even find his car. His place has been demolished." Tav put a hand on Micah's shoulder and squeezed it.

Micah took the blow silently. He would process the information later. Right now, his friends needed aid and comfort. "Hit the showers. Come back and get some rest. We're going to have an all-call meeting tonight."

Addison groaned. "I don't have the energy for Rolling Thunder. Much less the brainpower to follow it." He threw a rock into the fire.

Micah agreed. "Understood. We'll do this one live and let the chips fall where they may."

Tav nodded. "Thanks." He pulled himself to a standing position and limped toward the showers, followed by Luke, Addison, and BB.

Ben offered, "They look ve-ry ti-red."

"They were digging through rubble all day. Trying to find people who were trapped and needed help."

Ben cocked his head. "I said I would not come. Would I be un-der rub-ble, too?"

"You might have been. That's why I wouldn't let you stay behind."

Ben stood and hugged his dad. "I love you, Dad."

"I love you too, buddy." They stood together for a long time.

Forty-five minutes later, the scouts had showered, eaten a meal, and were relaxing around the fire pit. Quinn torched some logs and broke out the marshmallows and chocolate. Sparks flew and floated into the night. Stars overhead shone as ice. Any contentment proved short-lived. "This meeting is called to order."

Tav asked, "Who's got the agenda?"

"The question before the group is—do we go back to town, or do we continue to hang up here another week?"

Luke sniped, "And another and another and another." The fire crackled and popped. Luke stuffed a marshmallow in his mouth.

Tav waved him off. "We get the picture."

Micah leaned into the circle. "Quinn spoke with Professor Orton. No movement from him to change his opinion."

Wendy added, "But the ground moved here. Did you feel it in town?"

Addison nodded. "Brought down the house we were about to enter. Fortunately, we were pretty sure no one was in it." He held up his wounded hand. "We still checked."

Quinn frowned. "The fact we're still having tremors gives Orton credibility."

"Except they could be aftershocks and might go on for days." Grace grimaced. She flamed a marshmallow and let it drop into the fire rather than eat it.

Micah handed her another pillow of goodness. "Right. No one knows if we're done or not."

Tav dipped his head to the side. "But we know there are people in need. Not just of food, but of hands to rescue."

"I don't see how we are the Lord's hands and feet if we sit out this crisis because we think a bigger one will come. The need is now. Tomorrow can take care of itself." Luke's eyes flashed as he stared around the ring.

Quinn nodded once. "Agreed. What about the people up here who want our food and supplies?"

Tav's head jerked up. "What?"

Micah tossed a woodchip into the pit. "Yeah. Jonas saw you leave, and he's demanding the goods be distributed here. He says we owe the camp."

Tav's eyes burned. "Owe them? We bought the cache with our own money. We don't—"

Micah waved him down. "—owe him anything. I agree. And we told him as much. He disagreed. I think we're not done with his disagreement."

Quinn laid his hands on his knees. The fire silhouetted his face. "Where is the need greatest?" He turned to Tav. "What relief does the town have?"

"The Red Cross is there. They're mobilizing what and who they can. But they depend on people to give. The government is sending aid, but it's slow to come. Towns around here were affected as much as ours. So, I would say the town needs help above all."

"And people here who are out of food? What do we owe them?" Quinn's gaze cast the question around the circle.

Voices went silent. The night creaked and snapped and

chirruped and howled. Grace suggested, "We could share with our current supplies…the stuff we have for our own survival. But the supplies we stored are for the town. We pledged that."

BB spoke. "But we pledged it to each other, and we can change our pledge. If we all agreed."

Micah asked his son, "Is that what you want to do?"

"No. I'm just saying we *could* not we *should*."

Jen held up her hand. "Can we do both? Resupply people here and give the rest to the ones in town?"

"Or make it a condition of getting food that they have to go into town and help with the rescue." Addison took a chocolate bar and snapped it in two. He demolished the corner of one half.

"Except we'd be forcing people to go into a dangerous situation so they can get food for their families. That's not fair." Chay frowned at Addison. She made little circles in the dirt with her foot, then brushed them out.

Quinn asked, "So what scenarios do we have?"

Micah enumerated, "All the food for the town. All the food for here. Part of the food for here, part of it for town. Part of it for here, but they have to be willing to work for it. Any others?"

No one corrected his summation.

Quinn gazed around at the Knights. "Any more discussion?"

Jen cleared her throat. "Maybe I should have brought this up earlier, but I just thought of it. The parable of the ten maidens with the lamp oil. Five were wise and brought oil. Five were foolish. The wise didn't share with the foolish in case there wasn't enough for all of them. Jesus commended the wise. He didn't say they should have shared with the ones who didn't bring enough."

Faces turned to Micah. Tav asked, "Preacher?"

Micah gritted his teeth, prayed, then said, "There are plenty of scriptures to say we should share with others who have nothing. If we don't, how can we say the Love of God lives in us? Jesus wanted to make a point about being prepared when the Lord would return. That we should always be ready. The parable wasn't about who stored enough food and who didn't. It would be a stretch to say it fits this situation."

Jen continued her questioning. "But what about this situation? We bought food for people who need it. What's the difference between where they are? If they're here, they need help. If they're in town, they need help. What would keep people here from going to town to get part of what we give the Red Cross?"

Luke disagreed. "It's the idea people in town went through a tremendous loss. They don't have anything. Giving them food we stored makes that better."

Chay spoke. "We've got people here who came with nothing except the clothes they have on. Because they haven't experienced the tragedy of what went on in town, does that mean they deserve less? Many here have lost everything as well."

BB asked, "Are we penalizing people here for leaving town? For coming prepared to help but not bringing 'enough?' Who knew what 'enough' looked like?" The young man's eyes narrowed.

Micah held up both hands. "I think we're missing the point. We've got food to share. We shouldn't be talking about who needs it most. We need to discuss who gets it. And how to deliver it."

He gazed around the circle and caught as many eyes as would meet his. After a few moments of silence, Micah repeated Quinn's question. "Any other discussion?" He took care not to emphasize the word other. No dissing Jen. She had a legitimate question. And he was glad she'd asked.

Tav studied the group, then volunteered, "Not until we vote." A breeze rustled through the bushes. Tav spun around to see if it meant they were being watched. No sign of intruders. He turned back to Quinn.

Quinn dipped his head. Once. Micah directed. "Thumbs up, thumbs down." Eleven fists went into the center. Micah stated. "All food for town." Three thumbs went up.

"All food for here." No one.

"Part for here, part for town." Five went up.

"Work for it." Two thumbs went up. Addison and Ben. Micah didn't ask his youngest why he would vote for the plan. No one would be forced to give a reason unless the vote had tied.

Micah held up eight fingers. "We split it."

Luke asked, "How? Fifty-fifty? Eighty-twenty? Ninety-ten?" Micah sensed frustration in his friend's voice. He felt the same, but they had to be in agreement.

"Maybe we should find out who is staying and who is going back to town." Grace urged, "That could decide for us."

Micah smiled at her. "Good idea. Shall we go out and canvass the area tonight? Or wait until tomorrow?" Not that he wanted to go out bothering people. But it would be good to know who and how many were staying.

Tav tossed his stick into the fire. "I want to be in town early to be as much use as I can." A branch snapped. His head spun a second time. Still nothing.

Quinn stood. "Let's go ask our neighbors who is staying and who is going."

"And who needs what food," Grace added.

Quinn acquiesced to his wife. "Right. And who needs what food." He directed traffic. "Grace and I'll hit the high road. Who wants to come with us to Motor City?"

Addison raised his hand. "I've got friends up there. More than down in the tents."

Tav, Luke, and Chay headed for the north end of Tent City. Micah looked at BB. "Your choice."

"I'll go with Addison. I know some of the folks there.

I've been helping them get resettled."

Leaving Wendy and Jen. Ben would go with Micah.

Except Ben moved over to stand by Wendy and Jen. He looked at them and said, "I will come with you. Dad can stay with your mom."

Micah's eyebrows shot up. "Oh, I can, can I? Do I have a say in this?" He grinned so Wendy knew he would stay. Jen and Wendy needed away time. "Maybe she won't want me to stay with her."

Ben already had his answer. "You can say you su-per-vis-ing bro-thers. They need su-per-vis-ion."

Wendy laughed. "They do. Okay, Jen, if you're down with it, Micah will stay with Mom, and we'll canvass the south side. See you all later."

Jen crossed the area behind the fire pit. "I'll tell Mom we're leaving. She can come sit at the fire with Mick and roast marshmallows. She does love a delicately toasted marshmallow."

"I'll do my best. I'm more of a flaming torch kind of guy. But we'll have a good time."

The group split up. Wendy walked Micah to her tent and told her mom what the discussion had been. Mrs. Smothers seemed happy to have company. The boys, not so much. But Wendy refused to be gainsaid. Micah would stay. Mialma approved.

* * *

The Knights reconvened sometime later to compare notes. Tav started off the tally. "I found five families who have run out of food. When we told them what we were discussing, they chose to forgo getting anything. They said they would rather depend on neighbors as they've been doing than take food out of the mouths of people in the town."

Applause greeted the display of altruism. Addison voiced the reaction for the group. "Wow. I wish others had expressed the same opinion." He continued, "Of the ten families I saw, eight were still good on food, and two were out. The two wanted to share in our cache."

Jen reported, "The people we talked to were ready to share our cache until they heard it would come at the expense of the townspeople. Then they agreed to combine resources as much as possible, maybe take a few necessary items, and get by with a little help from their friends."

Quinn shared what he and Grace had learned. "Same with the crowd we spoke to. People here, for the most part, are grateful to be alive and have their immediate families accounted for. They all have extendeds in town and want those people to get supplies as needed."

Tav's face fell dark. "I spoke with Jonas and his ilk. They all want to be restocked from the cache." He scowled. "Well restocked. Like, better than they had it before."

BB's eyes narrowed. "Yeah, the ones I spoke to weren't as self-seeking, but they did want to get free food." He scuffed the dirt with this foot.

Micah sat with Mrs. Smothers and her sons. The younger boys had nothing to offer. Mrs. Smothers suggested snidely, "Let them eat cake. People in town need those supplies."

Wendy ducked her head. Jen giggled but agreed. "Not far off from Mom's opinion."

Quinn gazed around the group. "I'm not going to be the one to make suggestions for a solution, so no one can say I'm leading this cult."

Tav suggested, "Rolling Thunder?"

BB groaned. Addison seconded the opinion. Micah asked, "Do we need to?"

"I'd feel better about it." Tav cocked his head over his shoulder very, very slightly.

Micah understood the hesitation. Didn't like it, but understood it. He hadn't heard anything, but maybe Tav had. It made sense.

Wendy explained the ruse to her mom, who knew ASL

from working with disabled foster children. She signed *I'll stay quiet and listen.*

Once the thunder got rolling, Tav stated Ninety-ten split. 90% to town. 10% leave here.

Micah signed, *Everything here goes in pile. Each family chooses one item. Goes around circle. When gone, gone.*

Tav stroked his chin. *Great idea.*

Quinn agreed. *Excellent. Love it.*

Micah smiled at Mrs. Smothers. *Her idea. Best one going.*

Tav called the vote. "Hands in." Eleven hands went in.

Micah motioned to Mrs. Smothers. "You can vote, too." No one would suggest otherwise. It was, after all, her idea.

Tav intoned, "All in favor of the split?" Twelve thumbs went up. "Second vote. All in favor of the distribution plan put forth by Mrs. Smothers." He smiled at the woman. "And, yes, you get to vote on your idea." Twelve thumbs went up. "Moved and carried."

Micah spoke before anyone else could. "I move we wait until the morning to divide the cache. Then we can tell the camp about our decisions."

Tav jumped in. "No discussion. Carried. Let's get some sleep."

BB dropped his voice low. "We want a guard on the cache?"

Addison held up his hand. "I'll take first watch. Spell me in two hours." He threw another log on the fire and settled in to watch.

* * *

THURSDAY

Micah moved silently around the rocks and shrubs outside the range of the caves where the supply cache lay. The night-vision goggles he'd borrowed from Quinn gave the luster of midday to objects around him. *I need to get a pair of these. Especially as BB and Ben get older. Catch 'em sneaking in after curfew. Not that my sons would ever break curfew. Not them. They're good boys.* Uh-huh. And there was a bridge in Arizona he could buy, too.

Across the clearing, he saw four men trying to sneak their way to the cache. What else would they be doing? No one hunted. No one trapped. And there were no fishing streams in this direction. No, they had to be after the supplies. Jonas led them, followed by the scruffy man from the day before. Two others Micah recognized but didn't know followed single file through the brush. They cracked and snapped and popped their way along the trail. *Not exactly stealthy, are you boys?* There would be little danger of them actually locating the cave, much less the supplies. But Micah had to decide what to do about it. Confront? Misdirect? Lead them on a wild goose chase in the opposite direction?

He lifted the goggles slowly, letting his eyes adjust to the darkness and not lose sight of the men. He crept behind them for several minutes. He tossed a rock off to the side. One of the men whirled to look. "What was that?" he hissed.

Jonas waved him off. "Nothing, Glenn. Animals

moving. Tree branches falling. Forget it."

Five feet later, Micah snapped a tree branch. Glenn's head snapped as well. "Did you hear that? Something is following us."

Jonas snarled. "Knock it off, coward. You afraid of Bigfoot? It's nothing."

Micah's eye sparkled. Bigfoot? *I'll give you Bigfoot.* He'd watched enough documentaries. He picked up a sturdy branch, moved away and ahead of the group, then knocked three times hard on a tree trunk. The reverberations sounded across the forest.

Glenn wasn't the only one who jumped. Micah made sure to race across the trail and knock from the other side. Glenn froze. The entire group followed suit. Micah dropped his goggles into place. If he could, he wanted to see the fear in Glenn's eyes. But even with the goggles, he couldn't see the man's eyes.

Glenn proclaimed, "I'm going back." Another man didn't bother to declare it. He simply turned and headed back the way he came.

Jonas cursed both men. Micah filtered the actual words into a more acceptable phrasing. And moved further into the woods. He grinned evilly. *Thank you, BB, for teaching me all the animal calls. Even the ones that don't exist.* Micah faced away from the group and let out a Yeti howl to wake the dead. He spun and yowled in the opposite direction. Two Bigfoots in communication. That should rattle even Jonas.

And it did. Jonas' remaining partner headed back to camp. Jonas swore and cursed and called down imprecations to no avail. He was alone. And alone with no courage of his own. He kicked a bush and followed his fleeing companions.

Micah smiled. Ah, life can be fun. Brain over brawn. *Thank You, Lord.*

* * *

Wendy relieved Micah at dawn. Micah returned to camp the long way around. He could survey for early risers.

And see if Jonas made it back to safety. He passed by the man's tent but didn't see anyone stirring. Just as well. The morning breeze brought a reminder the porta-potties needed to be emptied. If the company could still make house calls. Big ask. But worth having the crew going to town check.

Micah picked a spot in the clearing away from his tent. He didn't want to go in and wake Ben or BB. He'd wait until the Knights' camp began to stir. Birds twittered and cheeped. Crows cawed and knocked. The rustle of the leaves and twigs made for sweet communion with his Father. All of creation sang His glory.

From nowhere, Jonas stomped into the clearing, a baseball bat in his hands. He spoke not a word but swung the weapon hard and fast, smashing Micah's bicep. Micah grabbed his arm and curled in pain. Jonas swung again, this time at Micah's middle. The bat connected with Micah's ribs. Micah screamed, "JONAS!"

Jonas cursed and swore. "You did this! You think you're better than all of us. Going to give us your leftovers, right? Take control of all of this camp. Dangle food in front of us and make us obey you! Well, not in my lifetime."

There were a great many expletives and obscenities and profanities, but it was the gist of what the raging man meant. Micah closed his eyes in agony, doubled over in tortured pain. He raised his arms to protect his head. Jonas continued to seethe with every stroke of the bat.

A whir. Another whir. Thumps. Jonas screamed. A dog's roar. Micah opened his eyes in time to see BB throwing stone missiles at Micah's attacker. Mialma tore at Jonas' pant leg. Tav and Luke tackled the man from both sides. Tav went high. Luke went low. Jonas lay flattened on the dirt. Micah closed his eyes and let the darkness take him.

* * *

Tav knelt beside Micah's crumpled figure. He gently checked his friend out, careful not to add to the injuries. He spun to yell at BB, "Get the doctor. He's in the Swiftrunner fifth wheel." Mialma nosed her master's unresponsive shape, whimpering.

BB took off at a dead run. Luke snatched a blanket from his tent and covered Micah with it. Tav's eyes burned with tears. "God! Don't take another one! We need him. Please, leave him with us." He dared Luke to say anything. "I'm not losing another friend."

Moisture poured down Luke's face. "I'm with you. I'm with you. Lord, please."

Quinn, Grace, Jen, Addison, and Chay all gathered around. Quinn grabbed Jonas by the arms and wrenched him to his feet. He yanked him along the path to the motor campers where Sheriff Knott stayed.

Grace brought a wet cloth and wiped Micah's face and neck. Jen closed her eyes and bowed her head. Addison kneeled beside his brothers. "What can I do? How do I help?"

Tav shook his head. "Pray. That's all we've got. Pray."

Addison sat back on his haunches and folded his hands.

Ben stepped out of his tent. Jen jumped to his side and directed him away from Micah. "Ben, Dad is hurt. But he's going to get good care when the doctor gets here. Let's stay over here out of the way."

Ben eyed Jen. "Dad is hurt? How?"

Jen caressed the boy's head. "A bad man hurt him. But God is going to take care of your dad."

Ben gave his singular nod. "Dad will be o-kay. Je-sus will make him bet-ter."

Tav saw Jen bite her lip as tears streaked her face. "That's right. Jesus will make him better." Jen raised her head and looked at Tav, pleading in her eyes. Tav nodded.

BB and Doctor Stevens raced down the path. They were accompanied by two nurses and one EMT. The doctor and the EMT both carried bags and packs. Medical supplies, Tav hoped. Mick would get the best care possible.

Tav stepped back as the medical personnel took over.

They worked swiftly and efficiently. Dr. Stevens ordered, "We need a stretcher." Tav, Luke, and Addison went to work to create one from blankets and tree limbs. With a quiet, "One, two, lift," they moved Mick to the stretcher and then to his tent. Micah came to and groaned. Stevens instructed, "He needs to stay quiet. I'm guessing he's got broken ribs along with the broken arm. I don't know about internal injuries. The hospital would be the best place for him." The doctor held Tav's gaze.

Tav shook his head. "We were there yesterday. They lost the annex and the mobile trailers. The building is still standing, but they're overrun with the wounded. Most aren't receiving timely treatment, if any." Tav added, "Word from the surrounding counties is much the same. Those hospitals that are still standing are taking in the sick and injured from the ones that collapsed. It's bad all over. And the roads are almost impassable. It'll take three hours to get him there, and who knows what the ride would do to him."

"Then he'll have to stay here and stay quiet." He laid a hand on Tav's arm and listed acute symptoms to be on the watch for. "I can give him something for pain. And I'll come by to check on him. If anything changes, come get me immediately."

Dr. Stevens squeezed Tav's shoulder and left the tent. Tav knelt beside Mick's cot. He whispered, "You do not have permission to leave, you hear me, Knight? Permission denied. You will come through this. And you will take up your post again." Moisture burned Tav's eyes and spilled over his face. He swiped at his cheeks angrily. "I can't lose you, too. I can't. Please, Mick. Fight. Stay away from the light. I know I should be praying for God's will, but I can't. I need you, Mick. I need your stability. You have to stay." Tav turned his head to Heaven. "Please, God, please. Leave him with us. You took Jeremiah. Leave Mick here. He's got too much work to do to leave. He's got Ben and BB. And me. Please?" Mialma licked his saltiness.

Jen and Ben walked into the tent. Tav didn't try to hide his weeping. Jen put her arms around him. Ben did as well. Jen laid her head on top of Tav's. Ben laid his on Tav's back. Tav sobbed. Jen didn't say anything. She held him.

Ben declared his understanding. "Dad is hurt. Dad will get well. Je-sus loves Dad. Je-sus loves us. Dad will get well."

Jen reached around and hugged Ben. "That's right, Ben. Your dad will get well." Tav noted she did not add, "One way or another." Now was not the time to be theological. Now was the time for faith, the substance of things hoped for, the evidence of things they couldn't see. Mick would get well. Period.

The entire cadre of Knights, along with Mrs. Smothers, gathered in the tent. Quinn spoke quietly. "We need to set up a roster. Set a watch in here."

Grace added, "We've got enough people to have two at a time. We can—"

Tav jumped in. "I'm staying. You can organize however you want. I'm not leaving."

Grace caressed Tav's neck. She gazed around the room. "Volunteers?"

Addison asked, "What about going into town?"

Tav shook his head. "Not 'til I know Mick is okay. I'm not leaving." He looked to his brother and said, "It's okay if you want to go. I understand. They need help, and there's nothing we can do here." His jaw quivered. "But I can't leave. I can't."

Luke squeezed his brother's shoulder. "We know, Tav. We know."

Tav pulled up a chair beside Mick's cot and sat down to wait. However long it took.

* * *

Luke motioned to the others and jerked his head toward the outside. Jen remained with Tav. The others all followed Luke back into the outdoors. Luke kept his voice low. "We

124

can split up. We need to pack the cars for town. And we need to distribute the food for here. Who wants to organize the circle for the campers?"

Grace declined. "I'll be more use in town. I'm accustomed to digging through rubble. I'm an archeologist, remember." She rubbed the back of her neck.

Wendy held up her hand. "I'll stay." She choked. "I want to be close to Mick, too." She tossed her head to throw off the tears.

Quinn numbered on his fingers. "Grace, myself, Luke, Chay, Addison, and BB." He looked at the Andres boy. "It will give you work to keep you busy and your mind off your dad." Quinn lowered his head for a moment, then held BB's eyes.

BB ducked his head.

Wendy spoke for her sister. "Jen, I, and our mom can organize the gifting here. I'll get my brothers to assist us. We'll manage fine."

Quinn caught Wendy's eyes. "Make sure you don't get overrun. Get help from the Windloes and the Munchinsens. They've got strong men. I don't anticipate a stampede, but I don't want you caught in one, either."

Wendy nodded. "Agreed." She glanced off up the hill to where the two families were situated.

Luke suggested, "While we load the cars, why don't you alert the camps to what will happen? Anyone who wants food can meet down at the playground in, say, an hour? And you'll have the pile of food for them to choose from. We won't deliver the extras until then." He stopped, then added, "Send the Kramers, Billings, the Walkens, and the Parsons to the cave. We'll need all the help we can to get the stuff to town."

Wendy headed to speak to the Windloes. Mrs. Smothers climbed to talk to the Munchinsens. Luke led the remaining troops to the cars and SUVs. One car, one van, and two SUVs drove cross-forest to the caves. It took the seven of them nearly an hour to load the vehicles top to trunk with the supplies for town. Only after the additional hands and feet arrived were they able to load up everything for Acorn and what remained for the camp. The Walkens, with their four-foot trailer, were privileged to carry the tenth portion to the playground.

* * *

Wendy roped off the area, leaving access for one vehicle. Campers who wanted additional food stood around the barriers, waiting to see what might be coming their way. There were astounded murmurs as the convoy passed and the trailer pulled in. Not all the words were complimentary, even if the sentiment was.

Wendy stood on a picnic table. "Any family who wants extra supplies can gather now. We have food." She addressed the Feltons with their littles. "And diapers and formula." Mrs. Felton sighed deeply. She lifted a hand in response.

Wendy smiled tight-lipped. "I want families to get in groups. No stragglers." She glanced around the playground. The morning dew moistened the merry-go-round and the slides. Too wet to play. No one's children should be complaining at this hour. Wendy waited until the families separated. She narrowed her focus to be sure each family stayed together. No hanging back and getting more than two cans per round. Considering Micah's condition and how he had suffered to protect the supplies, she would not allow anyone to cheat.

Once the families were organized, Wendy called again, "We explained this to you when we talked before, but we'll go over it again. You'll have a minute to grab two cans or items. The next family will have a minute, and so on. We'll go around as many times as we have food." She growled to herself but added, "And we'll make it come out even in the end." How would be another story, but she and her mom and sister would figure it out later. It shouldn't be an issue, but

Wendy felt sure it would be. Some people.

A man in blue overalls Wendy didn't know called, "Where'd all this food come from? How come there's so much? And you say it's leftover? Leftover from what?" He stared at the assortment of cases, then stared at Wendy. He had a sleepy look on his face, as if he'd only just gotten out of his sleeping bag.

Apparently, he hadn't gotten the message. A woman in a yellow jumper pulled his sleeve and spoke fiercely to him. At him was more like it. He nodded after several sentences. Wendy went back to surveying the crowd. "Is everyone ready?"

Variations on the theme of "yes" were called back. Wendy pointed to the family closest to the entrance and said, "Go. Get two items."

Wendy counted twenty-five families. She didn't bother trying to figure how much food they had. When they got down to individual cans, she'd start worrying about divvying up equally.

Twelve rounds in, a good number of the families dropped out. By mid-morning, the final items cleared the figurative shelves, and everyone went home. Figuratively. No one complained. If they did, they hid it well. Maybe they thought there would be more "leftovers" later. Foolish people.

Wendy wound up the rope, returned it to Quinn's well-stocked tent, and went back to sit with Tav and Jen. Micah slept. Dr. Stevens had been over at least once an hour to check Micah's blood pressure, pulse, and respirations. So far, he held his own. It was the least they could hope for. The best would be complete recovery. With no lingering effects.

Mom stuck her head in and whispered, "We're praying out here."

Wendy nodded, her expression tight-lipped. Mom came into the tent. She kept her tone soft. "It's going to get unbearably hot in here. Maybe you should move him outside until it cools off. You know what these tents can feel like."

Wendy turned to Tav. He glanced at Mom, then back at Micah. The air in the tent felt close. Another hour and it would be unbreathable. He nodded, then choked. "Can we get someone to help move him? And his bed?"

Mom disappeared, then reappeared with Wendy's brothers. With Tav at one end and the young men at the other, they were able to carry Micah's still form outside. Jen, Wendy, and Mom set up his bed under an elm tree with plenty of shade. Even with the sun's circuit, Micah would stay covered from the heat.

Tav and her brothers lowered Micah back onto his bed. Mialma took a place as near to his side as she could manage. Tav did the same on the other. Jen and Wendy pulled up chairs. The vigil continued.

* * *

THURSDAY

Acorn

The sheriff's department instructed the seven Knights the Red Cross would be the organization most able to distribute the supplies they brought. After dropping off the much-needed—and gratefully received—bounty, the group split up to search separate areas. Addison headed to the Vaughn apartment to see what remained. The building stood. A green checkmark meant everyone had been accounted for and the place deemed empty. Other than cracked windows, the outside looked fine. He slipped upstairs and opened the door.

Every shelf had been emptied and scattered on the floor. Cabinets were open, and their contents also in a pile. The refrigerator had landed on its face. No electricity. The brothers could rebuild, refresh, restore. Time to move to Quinn's house.

Addison had to dodge around broken streets and roads covered in debris to get across town to Quinn's home. The edifice looked in one piece until Addison noted the entire structure had slid off its foundation by three feet. A green X marked the place empty. Red Xs showed it unliveable. Quinn would have to rebuild from the ground up. Addison sighed in frustration. At least Quinn and Grace had taken everything they held most important. They had warning. How many others didn't?

Addison drove to the Smothers' house. Everyone had warning. The wise heeded it. Others didn't. Choices had been made. He grimaced. His had been made for him. Tav and Luke threatened to hogtie and drag his anatomy if he didn't go willingly. Which he didn't, but he did go. And now?

Now, he was grateful his brothers loved him enough not to leave him behind. The Knights' credo. Leave no one behind. They may have saved his life. Again.

He passed trees down on cars. Power lines fringed the streets where power poles had collapsed. House fronts lay crushed in front yards, exposing the remains of interiors jolted and jostled and buckled. Sirens keened from every direction. At a distance, but a background note to the otherwise silence. No birds. No dogs barking. No children calling to one another. No parents yelling for their offspring. Sirens and the sound of equipment moving the wreckage of people's lives. Would they ever get back to normal? Would there ever be a normal?

Addison called on the SAT phone to the shelter. He waited several minutes before hearing, "Shelter Five."

"I'm looking for my…brothers. Kevin and Peter Smothers. I heard yesterday they were there."

"Let me check."

Fifteen minutes went by. Addison refused to hang up. Time didn't matter. Connection did.

"I'm sorry. We don't have anyone here by those names and no record of them being here."

Addison eschewed the "Are you sure?" inquiry. These people were professionals. They would know. "Thank you."

"Try the other shelters."

"I will."

Addison disconnected the call and headed the car to Wendy's place. Maybe the young men thought like Addison had. *I don't need help. I can take care of myself.* Addison hoped they were right, for Wendy, Jen, and Mrs. Smothers' sake.

He drove out to the outskirts of town to the rural areas on the fringe of town. The houses were farther apart, but the damage just as severe. Hundred-year-old trees had toppled into houses that collapsed under their weight. Farmhouses caved in, their building codes grandfathered into the newer earthquake-resistant restrictions. Basements had been shoved above ground. Houses leaned cattywampus, ready to fall at any moment. Power, cable, and internet lines dangled impotently from broken poles.

Addison drove to the front of Wendy's house. No Xs. The place hadn't been searched. Not by a professional. Addison parked the car and jogged to the side door. It laid off its hinges, lying on the ground. Addison stepped over it and looked at the walls. They leaned precariously. The second floor had collapsed to the first. A fireplace held the rubble of the mantel. Timbers and studs and bricks covered the front of it. Glass lay shattered on the twisted floors.

Addison called, "Kevin! Peter!" He didn't expect an answer. But he called a second time, "Kevin! Peter!"

A muffled voice whispered, "Help."

Addison leaped into the room and began moving boards and rubble. He shoved as much detritus as he could away from the fireplace. He couldn't move the mantel, however. Its marble stones blocked the way. Addison yelled, "Are you in the fireplace? Both of you?"

Kevin coughed hard, then whispered, "Yes. We thought it would be safe." He coughed again. "We didn't think about the chimney collapsing in."

"How bad are you hurt?" Addison continued to move the wreckage. "How is Peter?"

"I don't know. He's under the bricks. He hasn't moved today."

Addison grabbed a timber and shifted it under the marble mantel. He tried to lift it.

Nothing. His second attempt returned the same results.

Fulcrum. You need a fulcrum. Geometry. That's why they teach it. So you can save a life.

He pulled the SAT phone from his pocket and dialed. "Luke! I'm at Wendy's. I found Kevin, but he's trapped. I need help."

"We'll be there."

Addison put the phone back and assured Kevin. "Help is coming, man. You hang on." He threw and tossed and slung anything non-useful out of his way. Finally, he found the wooden tree stump Wendy's father had carved years before his passing. Wendy always said it looked ugly as sin, but her mother refused to get rid of it. Now, the stump might rescue her sons' lives.

Addison rolled the stump as close to the mantel as he could. He wedged the timber under the face of the stone and pulled down on the lever with his full weight. It moved an inch. Addison yanked down on it again, hanging from the lever. The mantel groaned. Addison strained and pulled and jerked for all he was worth. The timber screeched, then snapped in two, dropping Addison to the floor. He moaned as he landed on his crippled arm. *Failure. I'm a failure.*

Not if you get up and try again.

Addison lay still for several moments, then climbed to his feet. He called, slightly out of breath, "I'll be back. I need a stronger lever." And wedges to shove under the mantel as he inched it up and off the two trapped men.

He was still tearing through the rubble when he heard vehicles pull into the driveway. He looked through the remains of the picture window, around the maple tree that had come through the glass. Two cars, an SUV, an EMT truck, and a heavy rescue vehicle all parked in the front. He dashed outside and yelled, "In here! Quick! I've got live victims."

Luke, BB, and Chay climbed out of the SUV. Addison didn't recognize the four men who spilled out of the car, nor did he care. They were warm bodies, and they could help.

They may have been volunteer firefighters from their garb. Five firefighters also rushed into the building. One of the men looked around and stated the obvious. "It's not safe in here."

Addison snorted. "All the more reason to get in and get these guys out of here."

"You're sure you've got someone alive in here?"

Addison yelled, "Kevin! Talk to me."

Silence. The fireman looked at Addison warily. Addison yelled into the fireplace. "Kevin! Don't give up on me now, man. Talk to me!"

After a moment, there came a cough and a, "I'm alive."

Luke ordered Chay back to the SUV. She went without argument. The rest of the rescue crew went to work and immediately sized up the situation. More fulcrums and more levers were employed. Addison shoved wedges into the space as the others lifted. However well-planned and efficient, it still took over an hour to raise the marble mantel. As soon as it cleared the hollow in the wall, Addison squeezed into the space and knelt. "Kevin. Come on, brother. We've got you now. Let's go. Take my hand."

Kevin coughed. "I can't. I don't have the strength."

Addison chided, "We've got enough strength for you. All you gotta do is reach up. Come on, Kev. You can do this. Think of your mom. She'll never get to say, 'I told you so' if you don't reach out."

Kevin chuckled, then coughed. Addison felt an arm brush his. He closed his hand around the arm and pulled. Kevin gasped and groaned and screamed…but Addison wouldn't stop nor let go. He grabbed Wendy's brother around the chest and strained. Half a minute later, the young man came free of his prison. Addison toppled over, and Kevin landed on top of him. The firemen immediately took over and began to check him out. Addison asked, "What about Peter? Anything?"

The Chief stared at Addison. "There's another person

in there?"

Kevin nodded. "My brother. He was under me. He was alive this morning. I can't swear for now." He coughed, then pleaded, "Get him out, please? Please? Don't leave him in there."

The Chief grimaced but ordered, "Let's move this thing further. We'll see if we can reach him." The house groaned. The Chief added, "Before the whole thing comes down on us." He pointed to Luke and the others. "You all, out. We'll take it from here."

Addison objected, "But you might need us."

"If we do, we'll yell. But it's getting too dangerous for civilians. Get out. Now."

Luke pulled Addison's arm. "We're wasting time arguing. We'll go out and wait and pray. That's the best we can do right now."

Addison growled but followed his brother and BB outside the house. The four volunteer rescue people stayed. Luke led Addison to the SUV, where they all leaned against its side. Chay hugged Addison, then hugged Luke with equal warmth. Addison bumped Luke on the arm. "Thanks for not leaving me in town when I wanted to stay."

"Thanks for not making us tie you and drag you." Luke stared at the house. "You think Peter is alive?"

"I don't know." He let out a long breath and stretched his back over the front fender. "What's left to check? Who is where?" A warm breeze added to the sense of relief from the labors inside.

"Quinn and Grace are downtown searching the offices. We checked out Micah's place. It's trashed. He'll have to rebuild."

"Same with Quinn and Grace. The house is off the foundations." Addison heard bricks being tossed. Not set. Tossed. Someone needed speed.

"Bad." Luke stared off at the wreck of a house. "We tried to search the place in case Mick's dad had sheltered there. No luck. We couldn't get in. We went all around it calling, but no answer. If he's there, he's buried deep. According to the Xs, it's been searched before."

It might be a long shot, but Addison asked, "Did they run the dogs over it?"

"I don't know. The authorities pronounced the house empty. That's all I can tell you."

Addison nodded. He stared at the ground. "Where do we go from here?" Furrows ran through the yard like giant moles had been busy fashioning a freeway.

"Search and rescue is still working the downtown area. We can join them, or we can canvass these homes here. But ours would be an unofficial exploration. They'll go back over it themselves."

"But we could maybe find people before the official searchers get here." Addison pointed to three houses beyond the tree line. Two remained standing. One had fallen in on itself.

"True." Luke turned to Chay. "Vote?"

"If it's a question of where resources would best be applied, I'd say downtown. But if it's humanitarian, I'd say here." Chay presented both sides.

Addison grimaced. "Which do you think is best?"

Chay circled her hand in the air. "Here."

Addison agreed. "Got my vote."

Luke eyed BB. "Brother?"

BB hesitated, then said, "Downtown. I've still got people unaccounted for."

Addison held up his hand. "Retract the vote. If it's personal, we go downtown."

BB shook his head. "No, we don't—" The young man lowered his head.

"Yes, we do." Luke put a hand on BB's arm. "We do. We'll go downtown." He looked over at Chay. "Right?"

She gave a straight-lined smile. "Absolutely."

Addison chuckled. "We made a decision and didn't

vote on it. We're making progress."

Luke shoved him. "There's only four of us."

Chay suggested, "Should we wait until we find out about Peter?"

Addison sucked in a long breath. What would BB think?

He didn't have to wait for an answer. BB jerked his head toward the house. "We don't leave until we get closure. We don't leave a man behind. Not until we have to."

They waited another hour as the professionals worked to free Peter. Or Peter's body. They rolled Kevin away in an ambulance and took him to the regional medical center. And still, the rescue crew worked.

Finally, the volunteer fire squad emerged from the house carrying a body between them. Body? Live or dead? Addison raced to find out. He caught up with the men as they lay the silent figure down. The man was crushed and bloody and pale. Addison caught the eyes of the leader. "Is he…?"

"Just barely. If he makes it through today, it will be a miracle."

Addison dropped to his knees. He leaned over and ordered fiercely, "You hang in there, brother. I'm not telling your mom anything but you're alive. Don't you make a liar out of me. Hear me?"

Another ambulance arrived and carried Peter away. The firemen painted a red X on the doors. The crew cleaned up and drove away.

Luke waited until the sirens faded. "We need to pray."

Addison volunteered. "I will." *And it's about time I did.* "God, thank You for sparing Peter and Kevin. Thank You they're alive, and we were able to find them. Please save them both. Keep them alive. Lord, I know we're supposed to only ask for Your will. But You said to bring our wants to You. So we are. Keep them alive, please. And heal them back to full health." He paused, then added, "I know You can. I know You could have healed me. But You didn't.

Please, heal them. Show me the reasons why, Lord. And if You don't…" He trailed off, then finished, "…give me faith to understand. We love You, Lord. In Jesus' Name, amen."

Luke squeezed his brother's good shoulder. "He cares, Addison. He'll honor that prayer for wisdom. Sooner or later." He looked up and said, "Everyone in the car. We're going downtown."

* * *

THURSDAY EVENING

Tav slept on BB's cot. Volunteers had carried Micah back into the tent. Wendy guessed Tav slept more from overwrought emotions than any physical exertion. Wendy sat with Micah, wiping his face with a wet towel.

His lips moved. "Thirsty."

Wendy leaned over and kissed his head. "The doctor hasn't said anything about you eating or drinking. Maybe a few drops won't hurt."

Since there were no ice cubes to suck on, Wendy moistened the corner of a towel and laid it on Mick's mouth. "Here. Suck on this."

He obeyed but immediately groaned, "More."

Wendy jumped from her chair and went into her brother's tent. She yanked two bottles of an electrolyte drink from his stash.

Tim yelped, "Hey! That's mine. You hate that stuff."

"It's for Mick. Maybe it'll help him."

Her brother nodded. "Great idea, Wenders. You need help?"

She didn't answer him, but he followed her as she ran back to Mick's side. She stuck the corner of the towel in the liquid, then gave it to Mick. "Go slow. Just a little."

She heard cars approaching the camp. Wendy motioned to her brother. "See who that is."

Tim complied. He looked out of the tent, then turned and said, "It's the others. Quinn and all of them."

Wendy let out a sigh. Safe. Her heart caught. Kevin and Peter? Had they found them? Were they alive? She breathed a prayer. "Lord, You know it all. Please. Better knowing than not. Whichever way it goes. In Your will."

Funny how she prayed "Your will" about her foster brothers, but "MY will" when it came to Micah. Wendy bowed her head. "I'm sorry. I love Mick. I want to spend my life with him. But if You have other plans, in Your perfect will, take him." Her throat caught. "But please, if there's a way, please leave him here with us."

Tav's voice behind her finished with, "Amen." He squeezed her shoulder. "I've been fighting with that, too. Every ounce of me wants to wrestle with God like Jacob did. I want Mick to live. But I have to give him up. I don't like it. It hurts. But I have to accept it if God says so. Because what other choice is there? He's God, or He isn't." He gave a tight-lipped smile. "End of story."

Quinn walked into the tent accompanied by Grace and the others who had gone to town. They gathered near the entrance, hanging back away from the injured man. Quinn asked for the group, "How is he? Any change?"

Wendy reported, "He drank a little water. I gave him a few drops of an electrolyte solution. He swallowed that, too." She shook her head. "But nothing else."

Grace raised her eyebrows. "If he's drinking, it's great news. We have to keep offering him liquids. And fantastic thought about using the electrolytes. It'll give him a boost on recovery. You did good, Wendy."

Jen and Mrs. Smothers came into the crowded tent. Wendy's mom asked, her voice trembling, "Any word on Kevin and Peter? Were they at the shelter?"

Quinn motioned to Addison. He took Mom's hand and kept his tone even. "We found them. They were trapped in the house inside the fireplace. Kevin is stable. Busted up, but he'll pull through. Peter..." He hesitated, then finished, "...is in critical condition. He was alive when they got him to the hospital. The last report we have is he's hanging in there."

Mom glanced at Jen. "I need a ride. I'm going."

Quinn held up his hand. "Mrs. Smothers…"

She glared at him. "I'll walk if I have to." The woman started toward the open tent flap.

Grace took her arm. "Think. The hospital is overcrowded as it is. They're flooded with patients who are as critical as your son. They need to be free to work and not have to trip over desperate loved ones. I understand wanting to be there. I do. And when the roads get open and the crowd thins out…"

Mom shook Grace off. "I won't leave him to die alone."

Chay tried. "Mrs. Smothers, I gave the doctor my SAT phone. He's been told if anything changes, he's to call us, no matter what time. He promised he would. I believe him."

Mom sagged. She wept, "My poor boys."

Addison gripped her shoulder. "I told them both they had to live long enough to hear you say, 'I told you so.' Kevin said he'd be happy to hear it. I'm sure Peter will as well."

Mom smiled at Addison. "You're a good young man, Addison. Thank you." She slipped back to the outer edges of the group.

Quinn brought Tav and the others up to date on what they'd found and done. His face darkened as he reported, "Nothing on Kurt Andres. We searched the downtown offices, searched his house, searched Micah's house. We found his car downtown, but no sign of him anywhere."

Tav glanced over at Micah, then asked quietly, "Any chance he left town with someone before the quake?"

"Not that anyone is saying. He's disappeared. Unless he's buried under rubble that hasn't been cleared yet. Right now, we can only list him as missing."

Tav ordered, "Go get a shower. Relax. Get some sleep.

We'll hit town again in the morning. I'll go with you if I can get Wendy to stay with Mick." He smiled. "I'll take the night shift."

Luke shook his head. "We'll all take turns. Regular watch." He eyed Wendy. "Except you. You've been with him all day. You get the night off."

Mom chuckled. "Your new brothers are sure pushy, aren't they?"

Tav corrected her. "We prefer protective."

"I prefer thin, too, but saying it doesn't make it so." She laughed. "You're good boys, all of you. I like how you take care of Wenders."

The town squad dispersed. BB grabbed a bundle of clean clothes. "I'll sleep out in the circle tonight. Less disruptive."

"I would agree." Wendy hugged the young man. "He's going to recover, BB. I know he will."

BB's eyes reflected pain and longing. "I hope so."

Ben stood beside his brother and declared, "Je-sus loves Dad. Je-sus will make Dad well. He will. He told me."

Wendy's throat caught. She swallowed hard. "When did He tell you?"

"I asked Him to make Dad bet-ter, and He said He would. Je-sus loves Dad. Je-sus loves me. Je-sus loves BB. Je-sus loves you. He will make Dad better."

Wendy chewed the inside of her lip. "I hope you're right, Ben."

BB whispered, "I don't know how to tell him it might not happen."

"You don't. You let God deal with it."

BB nodded. "Yeah. I hear you."

The young men disappeared out of the tent. Wendy hung her head. "You have to get better, Mick. You have to." Silent sobs wracked her body. "Please. Please."

* * *

The Knights split the watch two hours each. Tim and

Ury, Wendy's younger brothers, offered to watch as well but were excused. Micah wasn't as familiar with them, and if he woke up, the Knights didn't want him to be surprised or distressed. They excused Ben as well. They moved his bed out into the open next to BB's so he and BB could sleep undisturbed by the coming and going. Mialma crawled out from under Micah's bed to eat and relieve herself but crawled back as soon as she was done.

Sleeping in the open during the day provided Micah with fresh air. A wispy breeze swirled around the camp area. The smell of pine, the crackle of a fire, the low sound of voices murmuring in camps around the Knights created a soothing atmosphere. If Micah could hear it. He continued to breathe, slow and steady. Tav squeezed Micah's good shoulder. "That's your job, Knight. Your only assignment. Breathe and get better."

The remainder of the Knights gathered, sitting on slingback chairs, folding chairs, director's chairs. The better to be able to poke the fire. Ben sat on the ground to be closer to his drawing canvas. BB sat on a stump and leaned against a tree. "What are we looking for tomorrow? Any idea what area needs the most help?"

Tav eyed Quinn closely. Quinn nudged an errant log that wasn't burning quite right. "I'd say back downtown. That's where the largest concentration of people live. Or lived. There's still a lot missing in those blocks."

Mrs. Smothers asked, "Can we start to go home? Or back to town permanently?"

Chay kept her tone soft. "There's no place to live in town, Mrs. Smothers. Everything has been flattened. People there are living in tents like we are. Except they're scrounging for water and soap and basic living necessities."

A shrill cry lanced through the upper campgrounds, followed by raucous laughter. A body up there got hosed. Tav could hear the splashing of water. The trees shivered in the air, raining pine needles. Tav pitched a pinecone into the fire pit. "Maybe we invite them up here?"

Grace cleared her throat. "We did, remember? Before this all started. We invited the whole town. Look around. The ones here are the ones who believed and accepted the invite. It's a little late to come to the party now."

Quinn patted his wife's arm. "I hear you. My fear is people will decide now would be the time to come up here and will try to take over or push us out."

Luke cocked his head. "You really think they'd drive this far?"

"Maybe not. Not if there are supplies and help in town. But the longer it takes for FEMA to get here, the more desperate people may get. And then any distance wouldn't matter."

Addison leaned forward. "What do we do?"

Tav stretched. "Share what we have." He bent forward and stared at his brother. "The Lord gave us what we have. It's His. If anyone needs it, we share it. No one can take by force what's freely given. No one gets hurt. Like Mick."

Eleven faces turned to gaze at the prone man.

After a moment, Grace shrugged her head to the side. "You have a point. And you're right. I don't see it happening, but if it does, we'll give what we've got."

Addison scowled. "Our supplies aren't endless, either. Where do we get more?"

Quinn scratched his upper lip. "When the time comes, if there's nothing to be had in town, we send a team to Elkins. And then Chestmont. Then, wherever we can. But first, we pray about it. We've been doing a lot of 'doing' and not a lot of 'praying.' We need to get back to first principles."

Chay raised her hand in the air. "Hear, hear." She nudged the fire pit with a stick. "I vote we start now. Ring of prayer."

Ben chimed, "A-men." The trees nodded. The shrubs gave their assent, bowing in the breeze.

Quinn stood, went to his tent, and retrieved his Bible.

He read, "'Heaven declares the glory of God, and the universe shows His handiwork.' Look up, children, and remember Whose you are."

The crackling light of the fire wasn't enough to outshine the stars overhead. Tav looked up, deep into the vastness of Creation in all its wonder. The expanse dizzied him, so he felt he would fall off the face of the earth. And all this came from One Mind, One command: "Let there be light."

Tav whispered, "Who are we? Who am I You would even consider me? In Your majesty and Your splendor, in Your eternal grandeur, You stoop so low as to see us. Know us. Love us. How? Why? And how do we repay You for all You do?"

Jen raised a hand to the sky. "We sing Your greatness. We tell of Your mercy. We share Your grace."

Wendy whispered, "In Light and Life, You give us life. It comes from You, the giver of life."

Luke lifted both hands. "You are my all in all. My everything. Nothing exists without You."

Addison cleared his throat. "God, I'm not eloquent like my brothers and sisters. All I can say is I love You. And I'm trying." He hung his head.

Quinn laid his hand on Addison's shoulder. "God respects the honest prayer and the one who prays it. Never apologize for the simple prayer." He sniffed. "Shortest prayer in the world is 'help.' And He answers it every time."

The Knights went on around the circle praying and praising. When they were done, they said their goodnights and slipped into their tents. Tav sat alone by the fire, stirring the embers. He got up and walked to Micah's side. He tucked the blanket in close around his friend. He laid his hand on Micah's chest so he could feel the rise and fall. "We miss you, Preacher. Addison needs your influence. You're not nearly done working here. You know, right? You've got years and years of teaching yet to do. Don't even think of shirking your duty." His voice caught. "I miss you, Mick." He sat down and began his vigil.

* * *

145

FRIDAY

Quinn sat at the fire pit, watching the coffee bubble in the pot. He looked up as Professor Orton approached the circle. The man appeared haggard and drawn, his eyes dark and hollow. His clothes were rumpled, more than would be expected at a campground. He carried a sheaf of papers in his hand. Quinn stood. "Professor. What can I—"

"You must warn the town. The quake is coming today. I ran the numbers. Four times. It's today."

Quinn's eyes narrowed. "You mean there's another one coming? Bigger than the last one?"

"Yes!" The man shook the papers in Quinn's face. "I put in all the current data. And it's going to be today, and it's going to be massive. We have to get as many people to high ground as possible."

Tav and Luke exited their tent and joined Quinn. Both were dressed in sweats for sleeping but were sharp-eyed. Quinn guessed they'd heard Orton's pronouncement. Tav glanced at Quinn. "When do you want to leave?"

"After we assemble the troops. And see who stays with Mick."

"There's no time for that. We have to move now." Professor Orton threw his papers in the fire. "What good is the research if no one listens?"

Quinn caught the man by the shoulder. "We're listening, Professor. We're going. But we're not going out without a plan and an organization. Let us get prepared."

Orton calmed down a notch but continued to pace around the circle. He stopped long enough to look at Micah. He moved his pacing away from the injured man.

Quinn pulled the coffee off the fire. He raised the pot. Five cups appeared in front of him. No one objected to the strength of the brew for once. Tav, Luke, Addison, BB, and Grace all accepted coffee and swilled it down. Anything for inner strength. Jen and Chay passed. Wendy waved him off from her station beside Micah's bed.

Luke noted, "Most of the buildings have collapsed as it is. People are away from them. Shouldn't they be safe?"

Orton asked, "Do you know what liquefaction is?"

Blank looks met him. Grace said, "It's when the shaking is so violent the ground acts like a liquid and loses its solid nature."

"And sucks down everything standing on it. That's what's going to happen. People need to get away from town altogether. The further into the hills they can get, the better it will be."

Quinn drew in a deep breath. "Tav, Jen, you take the south end. Addison, BB, you go east. Luke, Chay, west. Grace, you and I will take the center of town. We'll give them two hours. Then everyone gets back up here. Is that clear?"

No one argued. People went back to their tents to get dressed. It would be a long morning.

Half an hour later, the group climbed into three cars and left for town. Wendy and her mom stayed with Mick. Quinn prayed before they parted ways. And continued to pray as he drove. *Lord, watch over my family. They're all I have. You know what these men and women mean to me. Protect them. Yes, if You take them, they will be laying down their lives for others. And no better way could there be for them to go. But if You will, please let them continue here to be the men and women You designed them to be. Amen.*

He reached the center of town. Search and rescue

teams were starting their labors in the half-standing buildings. Amid the bricks piled on the road, the upturned cars, the overturned buses, people still combed through the debris, looking for life. Or a body. Anything that might remain of the hundreds of people still missing. It would be a grim task.

Quinn approached the nearest worker. He prayed, desperately looking for words to convince a man to give up hope. There were none. He looked over at Grace and Ben and shook his head, his eyes pleading. What could he say?

Grace stepped up. She tapped the man in front of her. "Sir, there's another quake coming. Soon. We need to clear this place." Ben stood close by her side.

The ground shuddered. The rescuer shook her off. "Let it come. My brother is missing. I'm going to find him if it's the last thing I do."

Grace shook her head. She turned to another man. "There's a larger quake coming. Everyone needs to get away from the buildings here."

The man held Grace's eyes. "I can't stop. I can't."

Grace began tossing bricks from the pile the man searched. "Let me help you and get you out of here sooner."

Quinn joined his wife at the man's side. The three of them made quick work of moving the pile of rubble to reveal the street and nothing more. No life. No bodies. Just the street.

The man sagged. "I knew he would be here. He always parks here."

Quinn suggested, "Maybe the slot had been filled, and he parked somewhere else and survived."

Hope colored the man's eyes. He straightened his back and looked at the flattened ruin that had been downtown. "You think?"

"Maybe. I found a lot of my co-workers got out of the building before it collapsed. They made it. Maybe your brother did, too."

The weary man shook Quinn's hand. He turned to Grace. "Another quake? How could there be anything bigger? Look at this place."

Grace kept her tone soft. "There's still the dam. Please go to the hills. Get as far away from here as you can."

He stared at her intently. "You're from the cult, aren't you?"

Grace sighed. "We're not a cult. But yes, I'm from the hills. We rode it out there. No buildings to fall on us. We're still safer than here. Please go join the ones there."

"If you're convinced there's another one coming, why are you here?" A brick fell from the remains of the bank and landed on the street. Another one plunked beside it. The façade continued to fall, piece by piece.

"To try and talk you into going to safety." Grace dusted off her gloves on her pants.

"You left safety to talk me into going? That's nuts." The man shook his head side to side slowly.

Grace smiled a straight-lipped smile. "Christ-followers."

The man turned to Quinn. "You with her?"

"Yeah."

"I'll think about it." The man moved to another pile of bricks and began tossing them aside.

Quinn and Grace, walked up the street. Ten people and an hour later, and still no takers. The rumbles of the ground grew stronger. Quinn pulled out his SAT phone and called the other Knights. "Abort. Unless you've got converts. We need to get out of here. Head back to camp. That's an order."

Tav reported in. "We're with you."

Luke followed. "Headed back."

Addison answered, "One more house, and we're done."

"Make it fast. Get out."

"Heard."

Quinn disconnected the call. He turned his crew toward

home. "We tried. It's all we could do."

Beneath them, the ground shuddered.

* * *

"One last stop. I gotta get Kenmore. I'll drag him if I have to." BB pleaded with Addison. "Please, man."

Addison nodded. "I hear you. But it's the last one. This is getting ragged, BB."

The ground convulsed. Addison drove the SUV as fast as he could to the address BB gave him. They pulled up to the flattened structure. Kenmore and his family were busy tossing pieces of shattered lumber away from the base of the house. They were trying to force a way into the interior. Struts held the front of the edifice. BB scrambled out of the car and yelled, "Everyone! Clear out. You gotta go. This isn't over."

Kenmore raised his head at BB's cry. "Hey, BB! I thought you were up in the hills with the weird bunch."

"I am. But I had to come down to try to talk you all into coming up." He spread his hands wide. "Look around you. It's gone. It's all gone. And what isn't is about to be." The ground growled. "Feel it? The next one will be the big one. And it's coming. Soon. Now. You gotta take your family and get out of here. Head to the hills away from town. We'll take you. I swear it, man. You gotta get out of here."

Kenmore stared at BB. He gazed around at the destruction he could see. His eyes widened. "Bigger than this?"

"That's what the man said. Big enough to break the dam. You gotta come, please." BB turned to Kenmore's father. "Mr. Nance, please. I'm begging you. Take the family and head for Camp Philo. If I'm wrong, you haven't lost anything but a day sifting through rubbish. But if I'm right, you've saved your family. Please. One day."

Mr. Nance shook his head. "No. I got things I need to find. Important things. I need help." He looked at Kenmore. "You need to stay here. Not go running off with some nutcase."

Kenmore shouted, "Nutcase? He was right! We had a quake."

"And now it's done."

BB motioned to the ground. "Does this feel like it's done? There's more coming. Please, come away now."

Mr. Nance's eyes hardened. "I said no." He glared at Kenmore. "If you loved me, you'd stay here."

Mrs. Nance touched her husband's arm. "Just for one day? What's so important we gotta stay and find?"

"Doesn't matter. I say we stay, we stay."

Kenmore shouted, "It matters to me!"

All the while, the rumbling underfoot grew stronger.

Mr. Nance shouted, "My lockbox! Got all my medals in it. I'm not leaving my medals."

Mrs. Nance laughed, bordering on hysterics. "Your medals? Those matter more to you than your family? You old fool! I'll buy you new medals!"

Mr. Nance picked through the broken lumber that had been a staircase. "Wouldn't be the same. It wouldn't. Those were awarded to me. Anyone can buy a medal." He turned to his wife and repeated, "If you loved me, you'd stay."

"Stay and die over a box of trinkets? That's crazy!"

"Is that all they mean to you? What am I?"

She stepped into his chest. "Those medals don't make you the man I love. If you loved us, you'd come away and see us to safety. I'm not willing to lose my life over a thing that...can be replaced."

Addison thought for a moment she might say, "A thing that means nothing," but wisely changed her mind. But would the appeal matter?

Mrs. Nance kissed him. "Please, husband. Please. Think of us. Come with us."

"You not staying?" He stepped back from her to look her in the face.

A timber vibrated off the wall. A bookshelf collapsed.

Addison seethed, "BB…we gotta go, man."

BB caught Kenmore's arm. "Come on, Kenmore. Come with us. Mrs. Nance, please."

She made one last entreaty. "Please, Jamal. Come with us."

He snorted. "If I don't mean enough to you to stay, then go. Go run away to the hills. You'll be back tomorrow. We'll see who's right."

Kenmore, Mrs. Nance, and BB all climbed back into the SUV. Addison floored the accelerator, and the vehicle leaped forward. Half a mile down the road, the street buckled in front of them. Addison swerved, dodged, and kept driving. He glanced in the rearview mirror, and the street undulated like an ocean wave. He gritted his teeth and seethed, "Hang on."

Mrs. Nance gripped the front seat and started to turn. Kenmore caught her arm. "Don't look back, Mama. Don't look back. He made his choice."

The woman's face hardened, and she looked straight ahead. Tears flowed down her cheeks.

The path to safety dipped and swayed and juddered. Trees crashed down beside the road. Addison stared in horror as a stately oak disappeared in front of him. The morning's warning echoed. *Liquefaction. The ground acts like a liquid…swallows everything.* The young man prayed, "God! Help!" And kept driving.

He approached the crest of a hill when water splashed against the tires. To his left, he could see a mountain of mud and debris riding on a wave, crashing downhill. They were on the fringe of the torrent, far enough removed to see it but not get caught in it.

BB sagged in his seat. "The dam. It must have burst. Oh, Lord, have mercy."

In the back seat, Mrs. Nance rocked back and forth, repeating, "Oh, God. Oh, God. Oh, God."

Addison pulled ahead of the destruction and stopped.

He watched as much of the town disappeared under billions of gallons of water. Life drained from him, leaving only emptiness. Gone. His home. His family? Had Tav and Luke made it out? Quinn and Grace? Were they safe? Why was he alive?

His eyes refused to focus. Twice now, he'd been spared. For what? The first time, he hadn't exactly been grateful, given his arm and leg would never be fully functional. Today, though, he was whole. And alive. How many others weren't? Why him?

He prayed, Whatever You want, Lord. Whatever You ask. I'm Yours. I've said it before, but I never fully meant it. Now, I mean it all. I'm Yours. Anything You ask. Anything at all. I'll live like Your Son. Teach me what it looks like, and I'll do it. In Jesus' Name. Thank You. Amen.

He came to himself, started the car again, and drove the rest of the way to camp.

* * *

Tav and Luke met up near the outskirts of town, by the city civic center. Tav pulled up beside his brother and pointed. "I've got one more stop."

"For who?"

"My conscience." Tav looked over at Jen and advised, "Ride back with Luke and Chay."

"I'm not leaving you."

"This is a wild goose chase, but I gotta try. Go."

From his SUV, Luke demanded, "What conscience? Absolved! Forgiven! Come on, Tav. Now is not the time." He slapped the steering wheel.

Tav grimaced. "There won't be another time. Gotta be now."

"Fine. Stop arguing." He slid out of the car and instructed, "Jen, Chay, you go back. We'll—"

"No, you will not!" Chay shot back. "If you're going to be stupid, we're all going."

Tav's face burned. "It's not stupid for me, but it would

be for you three. I've got to find the mayor and give him one last chance at repentance."

Luke was aghast. "You really think he'll listen?"

"No, but I hate him enough to have to make an attempt."

Luke crawled back into his car. "Let's go. We're wasting time arguing."

Tav eyed his brother. The resolute cut of his jaw said there would be no further debate. Tav pointed the car toward town hall. They had to detour four times to get around the block, but they finally pulled up where the city employees worked to clear the destruction. Yes, heavy equipment would be needed, but for now, they needed to save what could be saved. Files. Books. Notebooks. Anything that hadn't been buried.

Mayor Lutz directed his employees on what to save and what to ignore. Tav noted his hands were clean, unlike the rest of the work crew. Tav shook his head. This would be harder than he thought. *Lord, forgive me. Give me the strength to reach out. And please, let them listen.*

He picked his way through the rubble and approached the man. Mayor Lutz looked up from his commanding and shouted, "Where have you been? We've been working all morning."

Tav noted a few dirty looks at the "we" comment. He didn't respond in kind. "Mayor Lutz, I want to warn you and your crew there's another quake coming."

Lutz scoffed, "Oh, another bunch of lunatics. Like we don't have enough in the hills?"

Tav bit back what he wanted to say. He kept calm. "The lunatics are batting a thousand with their predictions. These tremors you're feeling? They aren't aftershocks. They're precursors." He raised his voice. "Everyone here needs to head for higher ground. Go to the hills."

Lutz laughed harshly. "Right. Run to the hills! Everyone's safe in the hills."

Tav snapped, "They were until you sent your goons to try to run us out." Heads turned to stare at the mayor. Work stopped. People dropped the bricks they were clearing.

Lutz eyed Tav, and his eyes burned. "You have no proof—"

"We have an admission." More workers stopped. They dusted off their hands and moved closer to hear the exchange between the Mayor and Tav.

"Your admission is hearsay. Not admissible in court."

"I'm not worried about a court of law." He turned to the employees. "Yeah, we're lunatics. But we're safe. The next one coming will bring down everything. The dam is going to be breached. Feel the ground? It's setting up a resonance that will make it act like liquid. It's going to swallow all this and more. Get your families and get out of here."

Two…three…four people turned and walked away from the worksite. Mayor Lutz screamed, "Get back here, or you're fired."

One fleeing employee shouted back, "Better than being dead!"

Luke muttered, "We gotta go, Tav."

"I feel it." Tav eyed the mayor again. "I hated you for what you did to the people up in the hills. But I'm giving you fair warning. Leave now and save your life."

Lutz laughed, cold as death. "I'll decide when to leave."

Tav turned. "We're done here." He made one last call of "Go!" before piling into his car and heading for camp.

Luke gunned the SUV and screeched out. Tav followed. No one looked back. Ahead, the road dipped and rose. The ground vibrated and pitched and shuddered. They were cutting it close.

Too close. Tav's car bogged down as the pavement gave way beneath him. Luke swerved to a stop as Tav's car pitched onto its side. The passenger window shattered. Tav rolled his side down. There would be no opening the door. He crawled out of the opening, then reached back to haul Jen out after him. Jen shimmied through the window, blood pouring from her head. Luke kept the SUV idling while Jen and Tav clamored in. Tav ripped his shirt and held it over Jen's head.

Luke growled, "I hope it was worth it." He looked back over the seats to glare at his brother.

Tav applied pressure to Jen's wound. "If we saved a life." Luke grunted. Tav ordered, "Drive. We'll fight when we're in camp."

They dodged around falling debris, trees, and buildings that hadn't come down the first time. The SUV veered right, then left, then right again. Luke panted hard as they made their way higher and higher into the hills. The shuddering of the ground added to the pounding in Tav's gut. *Hurry hurry. You killed all four of you. Stupid move.*

A tree slid down the hill beside them. Craggy boulders followed the trees. The rocks crashed into the stump as it caught along the ground, went airborne, and smashed into the road in front of the SUV. Luke swerved, swerved back, swerved again, but couldn't avoid the landslide. The car rolled up on two wheels, spun, caught the edge of the rocks, and capsized. The engine died.

So did all sound.

* * *

FRIDAY EVENING

Addison pulled into camp. Mrs. Nance and Kenmore climbed out of the vehicle, shaken and exhausted. Mrs. Nance wept openly. Kenmore held his mother but tapped knuckles with BB and Addison. He whispered, "Thanks. You saved our lives."

BB nodded. "Glad to."

Addison jerked his head in assent, then went to find Tav. He didn't see the car or the SUV when he pulled past the tents.

Quinn hustled out to meet him, followed by a pale Grace. Her face was tense. She reached him first. "Did you see them? Tav and Jen? Did you pass them?"

Addison's stomach dropped. He drew in a deep breath. "No. But they would have gone a different direction. Ask Luke."

Quinn's voice shook in time to his hands. "He's not back, either. We thought you might have seen them on the road."

Addison turned to his car. Quinn grabbed his arm. "It's too late in the day, Addison. It'll be dark in two hours. You'll miss them coming up the hill."

Addison started to shake Quinn off, but the older man maintained a firm grip on his arm. He repeated firmly, "It's too late in the day, Addison. We can't find them in the dark."

The younger man stared hard at Quinn but finally backed down. Quinn was right. Tav and Luke were survivors. They would be fine. They would. His brothers both reported leaving town before Addison. And Addison made one last stop. Maybe they had, too. Maybe they went a different direction. Came up a different hill. They would be fine. They would be.

Wendy and Mrs. Smothers came out from their tent. BB introduced Mrs. Smothers to Mrs. Nance. Mrs. Smothers asked, "Is your husband coming?"

Mrs. Nance choked back, "My husband is a fool. He stayed behind."

Mrs. Smothers seemed to wilt. She looked at Wendy, her eyes wide. Wendy said softly, "Mom, it's okay. She's upset."

Kenmore patted Mrs. Smothers' arm. "She'll be better tomorrow." They followed BB as he led them into the Andres' tent.

Grace tipped her head to the side. "More refugees?"

Addison nodded. "Yeah. Mr. Nance insisted on staying behind to find his medals." He kicked a metal bucket and sent it flying across the campsite. "Medals!" He breathed hard, collecting himself.

Quinn asked, "You feel better now?" The man raised his eyebrows.

Addison lowered his head. "No. Now my toe hurts."

Quinn put an arm around Addison's shoulders. "I understand. We should get a fire going. If your brothers wander in tonight, we want to have the home fires burning."

Addison looked sideways at Quinn, then pulled his SAT phone from his pocket. "Stupid. Why didn't I call them before?"

Quinn offered, "Angst?"

Addison scowled at him but signaled for Tav. No answer. He called Luke. No answer. Jen. Chay. No one answered.

Quinn intercepted the feeling of dread. "Just means they're not answering. Don't read more into it than you have to. We have hope, Addison. Maybe all we have, but we have it."

Wendy's head snapped over to eye Addison. "Who did you call?"

Addison saw fear in Wendy's face. He cast his eyes to her mom, then back to Wendy. Her eyes widened doe-wide. She drew in a deep breath and let it out with a tiny, "oh." She bit down on her lip, then looked at her mom. "Will you help Ben fix dinner for us all? I'll sit with Micah."

Mrs. Smothers smiled. "Of course, Wenders. I'm sure Micah will wake up soon. He's been sleeping a long time."

Wendy walked over to stand beside Addison. "You were calling our brothers. And they didn't answer, did they?"

Addison looked to the side, then held Wendy's eyes. "Yeah. I don't know what happened to them."

Wendy covered her mouth with her hand, then turned her back to Addison. Her shoulders sobbed though she made no sound. She walked away from the circle. Grace came over to comfort her, but Wendy shook her head. Grace dropped her shoulders and walked back to stand beside Quinn. The two moved off to return to their own tent.

Wendy moved to sit beside Micah, her eyes closed. Tears poured down her cheeks and bounced off the collar of her shirt.

Addison knelt beside her. He put his arms around her and held her. Wendy sobbed. "I can't lose Jen, too. I can't. Micah…now Jen? Tav and Luke? Chay? What's happening? What are we doing wrong?" Sobs tore through her.

Addison assured her, "Nothing. This isn't punishment, Wendy. You know. I know. This is God loving us. Yeah, it doesn't feel like it, and it doesn't look like it, but it is."

He stroked her hair. "Don't give up on Him, Wendy. Don't. Mick won't. Tav and Luke…" He choked. "…my brothers won't. We can't."

A hoarse voice croaked, "Are…you…trying…to

steal…my woman?"

Wendy and Addison both jerked to look at Micah. His eyes were open, if not entirely focused. Addison whirled from facing Wendy to facing Micah. "Mick! You're alive!"

Micah closed his eyes. "If you say so. I hurt everywhere." His tone was barely above a whisper.

Wendy bent down and kissed him. "Mick. Oh, Mick. I thought I'd lost you."

"That explains the hug?"

Addison squeezed Micah's good shoulder. "Don't make jokes, man. Or go ahead. We'll take your stupid jokes since it means you're alive."

"Did you doubt?" Micah opened his eyes but didn't move.

Addison noticed. "Move your hand, Mick. Wiggle your fingers. Your toes. Something."

Micah whispered, "I can't. I know they're there, but they won't move."

Addison shouted, "Quinn! Get the doctor!"

Quinn and Grace raced from their tent. Addison grabbed the man as he approached. "Mick's awake, but he can't feel anything."

Micah strained. "I can feel. I can't control anything. Nothing wants to move."

Quinn dashed away from the campsite and ran up the hill, yelling, "Doctor Stevens!"

Grace took Micah's hand and squeezed it. "Can you feel that?"

"I can feel it. I know you're squeezing my hand. But I can't move my fingers."

Wendy carefully lay her head on Micah's chest. With the exception of Mrs. Nance and Kenmore, the others came out of the tents to see what the yelling was about. Wendy sat up so BB could reach his dad. BB took one look at Mick's face and beamed. "Dad! You're awake! You're alive!"

Micah closed his eyes. "Why does everyone keep

saying that? Was there any doubt?"

BB's voice caught. "Yeah, man. There was a lot of doubt. You've been mostly out for days. We weren't sure you were coming back." He brushed the tears back from his face.

"Oh." Micah's voice came back small. He opened his eyes. "Well, I guess I need to be grateful. Who do I owe for saving my life?"

Addison nodded. "God. It's all Him. Nothing any of us could do besides pray. Not even Dr. Stevens. Just let you sleep it off."

Micah smiled. "Nice hearing that coming from you, little brother." He moved his eyes, cleared his throat. "Where are the rest of the miscreants?"

Silence. Micah's eyes widened. "Tav? Luke?" Panic colored his eyes.

Wendy sniffed. "With Jen and Chay. But we don't know where. They went into town—"

Grace cut her off. "—and haven't come back yet. They'll show up soon."

Micah blinked. "This not moving stuff is the pits."

Ben came over to the cot. He climbed onto the bed before anyone could stop him. "Dad. You are a-wake. I knew you would be. Je-sus told me you would get bet-ter."

Mick mouthed to BB, "Put my arm around him." BB complied. Micah said, "Thanks for believing, buddy. Now I have to work on getting all well."

Quinn and Dr. Stevens jogged into the circle. Dr. Stevens pulled up the blanket from Micah's feet and ran his thumb up the bottom, from heel to toe. Micah's foot curled into the thumb as a proper foot should. He picked up Micah's hand and said, "Squeeze my fingers."

Micah shook his head. "Can't."

"Try. You need to re-establish the neuro pathways from the brain to the muscles."

"Would love to. How?"

Dr. Stevens kneaded Micah's arm from shoulder to fingertip. He looked at the others. "I need one of you to volunteer to massage Mick's muscles. Three times a day. More often would be better. And I'm not talking a gentle massage. I'm talking work them hard. The harder, the better."

Micah stared at Dr. Stevens. "I got beat up once. Now you want them to do it again?"

"They won't beat you up."

"This bunch will. And gladly."

The group hooted at him. Micah's eyes shone. Addison chuckled. "Mick's back."

The smile left. "Not yet. But I will be." He closed his eyes and breathed deep.

Quinn shook Dr. Stevens' hand. "Thanks, Doctor. I appreciate you coming to take care of our circus of clowns."

Stevens ducked his head. "Always happy to help the living." He looked up the hill. "And those who want to go on living." His eyes narrowed, and he scowled.

Addison pulled up short. "What do you mean?" He tucked the blanket back around Mick's feet.

"Reports are the town flooded. Some up here think there's nothing to live for. Families lost people. Others lost things. I'm having a hard time having proper empathy for the latter." The man marched back up the hill to his fifth wheel and the motor campers.

Addison explained to Micah, "Kenmore's dad stayed behind. He wanted to locate his medals. They meant more to him than life. More than his family's lives."

Tears filled Micah's eyes and ran into his ears. He blinked and choked, "A little help, here."

Wendy wiped the moisture from his face. He sighed. "People. The pinnacle of God's creation on Earth and the dumbest creature to draw breath."

He looked at Wendy. "Tell Mrs. Nance I'm sorry. She can have our tent. Since I seem to be resting in the open air these days."

BB nodded. "Already gave it to them. We'll rough it out here."

Addison offered, "You can sleep in our tent. We have room." *Especially until Tav and Luke come back. And they will come back. Right, Lord? Please?*

BB tapped Ben on the back. "Do you want to sleep out here with Dad or sleep in the tent with Addison?"

Ben cocked his head. "Does he snore?" He gave his dad a sly look.

Addison grinned. "Not that I've been told."

"I will sleep with Ad-di-son. Dad snores." He hesitated, then added, "Mi-al-ma snores more."

Micah laughed, then coughed, then gasped for air. The group froze, waiting. After a moment, Micah regained his breath. "I see where your loyalties are. That's okay, Ben. I'd probably sleep with Addison, too."

* * *

Tav crawled out of the upside-down SUV. Blood clouded his vision. He raked his arm over his eyes and turned back to the vehicle. He grabbed the first body part he could reach and pulled. Jen groaned. "Come on, lady," he urged. "You can do it." Tav pulled the arm and felt it follow him. After a few moments, Jen tumbled out onto the ground beside him. She moaned and lay still.

Tav didn't try to assess her injuries. Luke and Chay remained motionless in the interior of the crushed SUV. Tav shimmied in through the window and caught hold of his brother. He dragged the still figure as far as he could. The steering wheel blocked his progress. Tav backed out, straightened Luke out, and pulled again. His brother made no sound. Tav yanked and heaved and hauled and finally wrenched Luke free from the wreck. Tav rolled Luke on his side near Jen. Now, there was only Chay.

Tav wiped the fluid out of his eyes once again and went back into the jumbled mass of glass and metal. Chay lay crushed against the passenger side door, curled in a ball. Her shoulders were slippery with blood. For the third time, Tav pulled and dragged a lifeless figure from the ruins of what had been Luke's SUV. And their ride home. Time to think about that later. He extracted the last body, then collapsed beside them. His own injuries began to make themselves known. Adrenalin and the Lord had kept him from realizing their magnitude. Now, they demanded attention.

His left shoulder felt dislocated. Blood continued to seep into his eyes from a head wound. The perpetually bad knee had been wrenched. All in all, he would live.

But what of his brother? Tav crawled beside Luke and checked for breathing. He lay his hand on Luke's chest to feel for a pulse. A strong heartbeat pumped. He checked his brother's limbs for breaks. Nothing he could feel. He ran his hand over Luke's head and discovered a solid lump on the side. That explained the lack of consciousness. Hopefully, it would be temporary. Not like Mick.

Was Mick still alive? Had Addison made it back? What about Quinn?

Chay jerked and hissed. Tav wove next to her and asked, "Can you hear me? What hurts?" He checked her arms and legs.

She groaned. "Besides everything? My hip." Chay dropped one bloodied hand to her side.

"Broken?" Tav's worst fear. If one of them couldn't walk, how would they get back to camp?"

"I don't know." She seethed the words.

Tav crawled over to Jen. "How are you doing?"

Jen inched to a sitting position. "I'm alive. We'll go with that." She touched his head. "You're bleeding."

"Yeah. Wait here."

If the hatch on the SUV had broken open, maybe he could reach the First Aid kit. He dived back through the wreckage and fished around until he felt the case. Tav pulled it out and rolled back to Jen's side.

Jen took the kit and bandaged Tav's head. She worked on Chay's injuries as well. Tav turned to his brother and tried to rouse him. "Come on, Luke. Wake up, bro. We can't stay here. We've gotta…"

The impossibility of the situation overwhelmed any other thought. Where could they go? Injured as they all were, there would be no walking out. Not tonight. And walk where? Better to shelter in place than risk getting lost in the darkness.

Tav hung his head. "I need you, Luke. I can't do this alone. I can't leave you here like this. I won't leave you. I'm sorry, man. I did this. If I hadn't—"

"Oh shut up." Luke's voice was strained but beyond welcome. "Stuff it, Taylor."

Tav grinned. "One time. Just this once, I forgive you." He laid his hand on Luke's shoulder. "Where's it hurt most?"

"My chest, probably from the seatbelt and airbag. I think I broke my wrist. Not sure about anything else until I try to stand up."

"Don't. We're not going anywhere tonight. We'll camp here and see what tomorrow brings." Tav helped Luke scoot to lean against the shell of the SUV. Jen and Chay joined them.

Luke reached into his pocket. "I still have my flint. Maybe we can start a fire."

Tav thought hard. "I've got a better idea." He crawled to the back of the SUV and dug out the road flares. He ignited one. The blaze flared bright red and gave enough light to see the immediate area. Debris from trees and rocks surrounded them. Tav scavenged enough dry dead wood to start an actual fire for warmth. Thrusting the flare into the middle of the woodpile ignited the flames. A cheery fire for a dreary situation. Ah, well. You do what you can.

Tav scooted back against the SUV as well. After a few moments, he asked, "Anyone feel like talking?"

No one answered. Tav tried again. "Come on. We need

to stay awake. It's the only way we'll know who's alive. Someone has to tell the first story. Who's it going to be?"

Luke groaned. "No ghost stories."

"Faith stories. Chay, Jen and I don't know yours. You want to share?" He remembered the Magary Chase. "When we first met you, you said you wanted nothing to do with the Lord. Didn't want to hear about Him, even."

Chay cleared her throat. "Yeah, I was…um…pretty determined not to follow Mom's example." She settled back against the pile of metal, winced, then said, "Mom was a single mother. I never knew my father. Oh, I knew what people said about him, but that's all. No part in our lives. It made Mom bitter, which made me bitter. Bitter at her. I blamed her for my dad not being around. After all, who wouldn't love me, right? Had to be her fault.

"Until I actually met him and realized he didn't want to be in my life. Wanted nothing to do with me or her. He had a family of his own. Having me around would mess up his fairy-tale life with the other woman. Deacon in the church. Sang in the choir. Doing the whole God-thing."

Chay's tone turned acid. "Suddenly, I'm unloved and unloveable. Mom didn't help. She had her own world of pain. Which she pacified with alcohol. Me? I turned it all inside. Except for the God-thing. I hated Him. He stole my dad from me. What kind of loving God does that? I didn't want anything to do with him."

Chay pulled her feet up to her bottom. Tav heard the sudden inhale of breath, and then she continued, "I moved out when I turned eighteen. Mom went back to school and finished her degree in archeology. We checked in with each other but lived separate lives. Out of nowhere, she changes. Suddenly, she's 'found God.' Like He was lost or something? I didn't know. But I saw a difference in her. Different than my dad, for sure. And she carried it in everything she did. We even spent time together. Went on mother-daughter vacations. She didn't push her religion on me. She respected my 'no talking about God' requirements. But she didn't have to talk about Him. She lived and breathed Him. Even when she was wrong. She had changed completely.

"Then we went on the Magary Chase." Chay shook her head. "I still don't know why I let her talk me into the thing. But I did. Four days in the mountains. Right." She smirked at Luke and Tav. "You know that part."

Luke chuckled. "Oh, yes. You were a ray of sunshine." His voice reflected pain, however.

"Me at my best. But then, you guys. And you're just like my mom. God in everything. Even in Jeremiah's murder." She stopped. Chay looked off into the fire. "I wish I'd gotten to know him better. He was a good man."

Tav's throat closed up. He cleared it and managed a, "Yes, yes, he was."

"Then we go back to civilization and win all the money, and Quinn gifts us even more, and you still never change. Death didn't change you. Wealth didn't change you. Life didn't change you. I had to admit what you knew seemed real in you. And I wanted it. I wanted Him. I talked with Mom. She introduced me to the One Who could forgive all my sin, all my mess, all my rebellion. Cost Him everything…even death on a cross.

"But, when He rose again, He carried it all away. He loved me. He wanted me. And I wanted Him. I asked Him to come in, and I've been living as close to His feet as I can."

A warm, contented silence followed Chay's confession. After a few moments, Jen cleared her throat. "My story isn't dramatic. I went to church. I heard about Jesus. I did all the 'right things' and said all the right words. But I didn't know Him. I knew *about* Him but didn't *know* Him. I never understood how Wendy could grow up with me, do the same activities, and attend the same church but come to a totally different conclusion. For her, God was a myth, a non-entity.

"I met Tav, and I saw what Christianity means: living like Jesus did. Following Him. Giving up my own self and taking on Him." She admitted, "Blew my self-image right out the window. I knew I needed to give it all up and submit to Him in everything. Ask His forgiveness, accept His Spirit, and live for Him. Big ask. Bigger reward. Having Him with me? There's nothing that matters more."

Chay stretched and groaned. "Ouch. That hurts."

Luke leaned over to check on her. "What hurts?"

"Everything, okay? My shoulder. My head. My neck. My hip. I'm fine. I'll be fine when we get back to camp, and I can lie in my hammock bed."

The ground rumbled and pitched around them. All four people shrank back against the wreckage of the SUV as if it could protect them from the quaking.

Maybe not the quaking, but rocks careened off to the side instead of striking the humans. He appreciated any and all shelter. Tav wasn't going to argue about what made a good defense and what didn't. The rocks didn't hit them. That's all that mattered.

When the rolling ceased and the rocks stopped falling, Tav asked the question on everyone's mind. "Was that finally the big one? Are we done building? Only smaller aftershocks from here on out?"

Jen sniffed. "I hope so." She moved closer to Tav. "I'm so tired of being afraid of tomorrow and tomorrow and tomorrow."

He laid his head on top of hers, but gently. "I know, Jen. I know."

Luke added his opinion. "I think that had to be the 'big one.' Professor Orton called for it today. Look at what we passed. Look at what passed us. I'm fairly sure the worst is over. In the morning, we walk back to camp and start living again."

Chay shook her head. "Living how? Where? I'm still in school in Santa Clara. I doubt this reached all the way there. Maybe a small shock. The university should still be there. But for you all…what are you going to do?"

Tav shrugged. "Pray. Move. Find where God wants me…us"—he hugged Jen—"and go there. I'll work where He puts me."

"It'll take time. Maybe the Knights can pool our resources—"

A horrendous crack exploded above them. Boulders came crashing down, stopped by the remains of the SUV. Some crushed it further. Some bounced off and went around. A substantial pile gathered above them.

Water rushed down the hill. The four grabbed arms. Tav screamed above the torrent, "Hang on!" The runoff from a stream whose banks had been destroyed cascaded over them. The rockpile provided partial shelter, but the water dragged at them, tearing them away from their perch. Tav held both Luke's leg and Jen's waist. He would not let go of either.

And still, the water poured over them. Gallons and gallons of water threatened to choke them, drown them, even as they clung to life. Rocks groaned under the weight and power of the stream, now a tsunami of mud and debris. The flow pushed against them. Tav felt Luke ripped from his grasp even as he clung tighter to Jen. He screamed against the torrent, "Luke!" In horror, he watched the river of mud swirl his brother down the hill and away. He buried his head in Jen's shoulder and screamed. "Luke!"

* * *

SATURDAY MORNING

Dawn brought an end to the rumbling. Tav uncurled from his place beside the remains of the crushed-out hulk that had been their SUV. He rose to a sitting position and stared down the hill. The swath of liquid destruction had scoured the landscape. Isolated mangled trees stood buried in mud. Boulders piled up forming fence-rows down the hillside. The wasteland filled his eyes. But nowhere, as far as he could see, was there a sign of Luke. Gone. His brother was gone.

Jen and Chay came to sit beside him. Jen stared him in the face. "Tav. Are you with me?"

Tav continued to gaze down the hill. "I'll never see him again."

Jen's face contorted into ugly tears. Chay put her hands over her eyes. She refused to look at anything. Tav's voice cracked. "If I hadn't—"

Chay slapped him hard. "Stop that! Stop right now! Luke did not blame you. Don't you dare blame you, either."

Tav didn't feel the blow. He turned and stared at Chay. Her shoulders sobbed. She repeated through hiccups, "Don't you dare blame yourself." She lifted her head skyward, and the tears pelted to the ground. "Blame God if you have to. But not you. We need you. We need you to help get us out of here. Back to camp. We can't get there alone. You have to help us. Which means you need to want to live."

Jen lowered her head but joined Chay in supplication.

"Please, Tav. We can't make it on our own. We need you."

Tav stared blankly from woman to woman. He tried to hear their words, the meanings behind them. Pointlessness ate at his soul. What mattered?

Luke mattered. And what Luke would want mattered. He would want them to live, to make their way back to camp, and to keep going. He would expect it of Tav. He would feel like Tav, too, were the places reversed. But they both expected the other to carry on.

Tav nodded. Once. "We'll go." There would be no sense in tracking after Luke. Nothing survived in the valley. Gone. All gone.

He struggled to his feet, sinking deep into the muck and mire. The three Knights dug themselves free and slogged up the incline. Every step had to be won against the sludge. First one foot, then the other, had to be pulled free from the filth and made to step into a more stable footing. At times, they found one. Other times, they sank deeper. The three heaved and strained and hauled each other forward. Shoulders screamed in agony. Backs strained to the breaking point. Knees and legs lugged forward, always forward.

An hour, and they'd gone a hundred yards. Survival required they keep going. To stop meant to be cemented in place as the clay dried around them. Shoes were sucked off their feet. They debated shucking their clothes. Discretion won. That and the need for warmth if they topped the hill. If.

Another hour of swimming in the mud, and the slope leveled out. The ground became more firm beneath their feet. Tav's legs came out of a hole with relative ease. He could breathe in a normal fashion. No more fighting the river of sludge. He pulled Jen, then Chay, out of the last mudhole onto flat land. The group rolled over and lay on their backs, gasping air into exhausted lungs. Still felt nice. Still meant life. They could stay still forever.

But there were many miles yet to go to camp. Tav, Jen, and Chay climbed to their feet and labored forward. Their clothes turned to shards of brick as they fought forward. Every step pained bare feet, every motion cut at them.

Another hour. Tav swiped his nose to flick the sweat off. "Time to stop." He sank back on his haunches. "I'm done."

Jen didn't comment. She slipped to the ground and lay still. Chay joined her. The women looked to Tav. He shook his head. "I got nothing. I'm done. We're done." He settled to his rear, crossing his feet in front of him. He leaned forward and stretched his arms out in front of him. "I've got to rest. Sleep. Something. Anything but keep moving."

Chay rolled onto her back, her knees bent. She gave a grief-stricken hiccup. Jen curled into a fetal position opposite Chay. No one argued. No one spoke. Nothingness surrounded them. And took them.

* * *

Addison and Quinn came over the hill. Addison saw the three silent, unmoving figures. His heart lurched. He dashed ahead of Quinn to reach the downed Knights. Breathing. Breathing mattered. Were they?

Yes. In. Out. Chests rose and fell. Quinn reached his side. Addison looked around frantically. "Where's Luke? They should all be together? Where is he?"

Quinn held out his hand. "One step at a time. We have these three to revive." He kneeled between Tav and Chay and began stretching out limbs, looking for signs of trauma. Little moans and groans gave an indication of deeper wounds than the outside presented. But nothing explained the lack of consciousness. Except deep exhaustion, maybe.

The mentor eased each body to a comfortable resting position and covered them with survival blankets from his pack. He raised an eyebrow at Addison. "Wait here with them, or go back to camp for more help?"

Addison motioned to the sleepers. "I'll stay here. You'll be faster." He smiled, straight-lipped. "Thanks for giving me a choice, though."

Quinn shrugged. "You deserve to choose." He turned and began sprinting away. "I'll be back."

Addison sat beside his brother. "I know you will." He lay a hand on Tav's shoulder. "He'll get help. We'll get you back to camp." His voice choked. "You'd never leave him. Not if there was a chance." Addison raised his eyes to the sky. "Oh, Lord. Please. Let him be alive and lost. Bring him back. But please don't let him be…" He trailed off. He couldn't say it. "Don't let him be gone. Not forever."

He swiped away the tears threatening to drip into his ears. "I know it's not forever. But don't let it be for now, either. Please. If there's any room in Your will. Please."

Addison moved his hand from Tav's shoulder to Tav's chest. He wanted to feel his brother breathing. In. Out. It's all that mattered.

An hour later, Addison heard before he saw the rescuers come over the hill. Quinn drove his van up to the injured sleepers. BB, Grace, Wendy, and Kenmore all scrambled out to transport the wounded. They were able to maneuver Jen and Chay into the van without waking them. But Tav came alert as soon as his rescuers took hold of him. He struggled, trying to break free. "No! I can't! I have to—"

Addison calmed him. "It's okay, bro. It's okay. We got you. We got the girls. Everyone is safe."

Tav stared at Addison until comprehension dawned in his eyes. Followed by horror. "I lost Luke. I couldn't hold him. I tried. The water—"

Addison shushed him as the others picked him up. "It's okay, Tav. It's okay. You did all you could. We know." Tears poured off his chin. "I know you did. You'd never leave him otherwise."

Addison assisted with the lift, then climbed in to sit beside his brother. He continued to weep with Tav. "I know you did all you could."

Tav closed his eyes. "It wasn't enough. It wasn't. I

failed. I lost hold of him. The river pulled too strong. It tore him away from me. I tried, Addison. I tried."

Addison reached down and kissed his brother as the van jostled over the hill. "You did all you could, Tav. I know. We know. No one blames you."

Tav drifted off into sleep. "I tried. I tried."

Addison squeezed his shoulder. "I know you did, big brother." He smoothed the hair on his head and looked up at Wendy. Tears drained off her cheeks onto her shirt. She whispered, "There's a chance."

Addison closed his eyes. "God…only You can bring him back. Please. If there's a way, please."

They rode the rest of the trip in silence. When they reached the camp, BB, Wendy, Quinn, and Kenmore lifted the sleeping warriors from the van and onto cots under the shade. They would rest comfortably until they were ready to rise. And face the agony of losing Luke.

* * *

Tav woke. His mind tried desperately to make sense of where he might be. He didn't remember having a cot by the washout. Nor were there tents. Or trees. Or voices beyond his own, Jen's, and Chay's. But he heard Ben talking. "Dad is bet-ter to-day. Bet-ter than yes-ter-day. He will get well."

Grace assured him, "Yes, he is stronger. And he will get back to himself." She lowered her voice but held the same joking lilt. "More's the pity."

Micah's voice answered in complaint. "Now, wait a minute. I resemble that remark."

"You certainly do."

Tav sat up. Hallucinating? Or… He gazed around the area. Camp. He was in camp. "We made it!" He looked over at two empty cots. His eyes widened to agonized saucers. He whispered, "Jen. Chay."

Before horror could take him, Quinn walked up and smiled. "They're fine. They took a little walk accompanied by Wendy and her mom. No one wants to let them out of sight."

Tav sighed and lay back down. His body approved of not moving. His mind… He flew back to a sitting position, prepared to dive out of bed. "Luke!"

Quinn clapped a heavy hand on Tav's shoulder. "Rest, Tav. We've sent people looking for him. They'll find him."

Tav stared at the ground. "No, they won't. I lost him, Quinn. I couldn't hold him and Jen and Chay. The dam broke, and I couldn't hold him."

Quinn interrupted. "The dam didn't break. It overflowed. Like a tsunami. The earthquake altered the water level, and the dam couldn't hold the water back. It sloshed over like a bathtub when a child jumps in it."

Tav shook his head. "I still couldn't hold him. I tried, Quinn. I tried." Misery ate at his gut. And poured out over his eyes.

Quinn squeezed Tav's shoulder. "That's what you've been saying since we got you back here. We know you'd do your very best, son. And you did." Quinn paused. "God has plans for Luke."

Tav drew in a sharp breath, held it, then let it out in a tiny whistle. His voice tremored. "I know. I have to trust Him. Even now. Even when…" He trailed off, unable to finish.

Quinn shook Tav's shoulder. "Even when it hurts. Even when it makes no sense." The big man motioned toward the bed. "Try and rest more if you can. We're going to need every voice later. We have to decide what to do next. Sleep."

Tav lay back down. He settled into the sleeping bag. "Take care of him, God. Tell him I love him. Tell him to save us a place." Tears erupted once more. Tav buried his head in the mound at the head of the cot and let his sorrow empty from his chest. It would take a long time.

* * *

SUNDAY

Luke teetered toward the door of the ramshackle doublewide trailer. The back had slid down the hill and rested precariously on the edge of the boulder that had stopped its slide. Windows were busted out. Curtains quivered with the stirring of the earth, their cheery gnomes a macabre counterpoint to the destruction around them.

The wounded man balanced on his left leg. His broken foot would bear no weight. Maybe there might be a device inside that could help him. Either way, he could go no further.

The door stood half off its hinges. He knocked anyhow. He jolted when the door yanked open, and a woman threw herself into his chest. "Richard Dean! I was so worried about you."

Luke pressed backward against her embrace. "Whoa! I'm not Richard Dean."

The woman stepped back, stared at him, and then dropped her eyes. Her shoulders sagged. "Don't. Please. Don't start this again. I can't take it. We worked so hard the last time."

Luke hopped to stay upright. "I don't know—"

"—what I'm talking about, right?" The twenty-something woman sank down in an upholstered barrel seat. She motioned for Luke to sit across from her on the couch with three legs. "You're going to tell me you're not Richard Dean, my husband and the father of our child." She pointed to a bundle of blankets at the far end of the couch. It breathed. "You'll even show me a license with a name you'll insist says other than Richard Dean. I'll read it, and it will say Richard, but you'll insist it says Doug or Fred or whatever name you're trying to use."

Luke eyed the woman closely. "But you know better?" His voice carried incredulity. What was with this crazy woman? He leaned forward on the couch to look into her eyes. *The eyes always tell the story.*

"Of course." She sighed. "It's pathetic. I don't know why you play these games. You're my husband. I know you didn't want to be, but here we are. Please, don't make me have to hit you over the head again to get you to remember."

Luke raised his eyebrows. "How did that go?" *Watch your words.*

"You suddenly remembered who you were. And you went to get help."

Luke didn't reach for his ID strapped to his leg. Just like Quinn insisted. He eased his ankle out in front of him. "Can we do anything about this? It's killing me."

The woman sprang to her feet. "Richard! Why didn't you tell me you were hurt?"

"I figured the standing on one foot might be a clue." Pain laced his voice with sarcasm. Not what he wanted, but he'd ask forgiveness later. After they did something to stop the throbbing.

"Well, it wasn't," the woman snapped at him. She disappeared into a room on the side of the trailer. Luke felt the structure shift. He yelled, "Don't move! Come back!"

She slipped her head around the corner. "Calm down. I'm only going into the…"

The trailer groaned. The woman dashed back to the living room. Her eyes widened. Her face paled. Her mouth formed a tiny "o."

Luke nodded. "Yeah. We both shouldn't move more than necessary." He eased the bum foot to the front and massaged it as best he could. He didn't remove the boot. Too great a chance of never getting it on again. He weighed his options, then took a chance. "Don't hit me, but what's your name?"

She gave an exaggerated sigh. "Valance." She sneered. "And yes, my parents were scientists." She sat on the couch opposite Luke.

"Nice name." He motioned to the pile of blankets. "And the baby?"

"Are you really going to play this game? You're going to pretend you don't know our son's name is Devon?"

"Right. I forgot." You can't forget what you don't know. But she probably still had a two-by-four handy.

Valance picked up a blanket and wrapped it around Luke. "What happened to you? You left three days ago to get food from town." She put the baby on her shoulder. The smell of infant soaps and lotions wafted from the pile.

Luke grew still. "Three days? Which day, exactly?"

"Friday. You should have been back before now. And where are the supplies?"

Luke stared at the floor, then held Valance's eyes. "I need you to hear me. If Richard Dean went to town on Friday, he's not coming back. The town flooded. The dam broke. My friends and I left Acorn Friday at noon. We made it as high as the Sentient Junction, then the quake burst the dam. I got washed away from our group, down the Banks gully. I've been working my way back up since." His voice softened. "If your husband survived, he would have come up the same way. I'd have seen him."

Valance's eyes lost their focus. She stared into space. After a moment, she came back to herself. "That's quite a story, Richard Dean. It doesn't get you out of being my husband or being Devon's father."

The trailer creaked and shifted. Luke rose to his good foot. "We can't stay here. We've got to get out of this trailer and to higher ground." He held out his hand to Valance. "I know a place where you and Devon will be safe." He waved his hand to encourage her to take it.

"Where will you be?" Valance's eyes narrowed with suspicion.

"There as well. The campgrounds at Table Mountain. We've got a group of survivors there with food and supplies." *Lord, help her hear me. And agree to come. We can't stay here, no matter how crazy she is.*

Valance picked up the blanket bundle. Luke heard an infant squeak. He smiled. "How old?"

"Three months." Valance soothed the small head and kissed it.

"Precious." Luke drew in a deep breath. Survival just got harder. The five miles to camp may as well be twenty with an infant and a bad foot. But the sooner they started, the safer they would all be. Especially Devon.

He studied the layout of the trailer. The kitchen was still at the safe end. "Do you have any food at all here? For the baby, even?"

"I'm feeding him myself. And we've got crackers and dry fruit."

"We'll take whatever you have." He laid a hand on her arm. "But only what's here in the front room. Do not go to the back for anything."

Valance nodded. "I hear you." She handed the baby to Luke and went into the kitchen. She began shuttling things from cabinet to countertop and into a bag.

Luke unwrapped the bundle to peek at the complication to his survival. Devon made squeaky yawning noises. The boy opened his eyes and stared into Luke's soul. Luke lowered his gaze and prayed, *Father, protect this child of Yours. Help me get him to safety. And sanity. And help Valance see the truth. Your will be done in all things. In Jesus' Name, amen.*

Valance came back with a sack. She smirked. "Trade you." She held out the bag of food and waved her hand at

Luke.

Luke kissed the little head then handed Devon back to his mother. He accepted the sack of food without looking in. He would trust God to multiply whatever they needed. Sure, he would.

Luke cut the cording from the cushions on the couch to use for a backpack. He wrapped the food inside the blanket Valance had given him, along with the other throw blankets in the area. He glanced at the woman as he worked. "You have anything I could use as a crutch? At this end of the trailer only."

Valance gave him a straight-lipped smile. "You're in luck. Your crutches from last summer are still here." Once she finished strapping Devon into his front carrier pouch, she moved to the closet and pulled out a pair of crutches.

Luke accepted them. "Thanks." He immediately leaned on the crutches to give his good leg a break from supporting all his weight. He made an adjustment to the height. "I must have been shorter then."

Valance sneered. "You've always been the same height. Playing with the holes doesn't change who you are."

Lord, what is it going to take? Touch her, please. "I guess." Luke settled the crutches under his arm, took a few practice steps, and declared it good. He returned to bundling the supplies and blankets. It would take them at least two days, maybe three, to reach the encampment. Nights would be chilly if he couldn't find dead wood to burn.

Luke lowered himself to the couch one last time and pulled out his SAT phone. He keyed the mic and called, "Anyone. Does anyone hear me?" He grimaced. "Is this thing on?"

No response. *Okay, Lord, we do it Your way. Show me what it is, and I'll do it. One step at a time, I know.* Luke put the phone back in his pocket.

Valance cocked her head. "Cell phone? You think a cell phone—"

"—satellite phone. And yes, it worked before. It's probably lost its charge. But it was worth the shot." He stood with effort. "Let's go."

Valance exited the trailer first, and Luke followed. She asked, "Which way are we going?"

Luke motioned up the hill. "That way. The camp is at Table Mountain. Up the hill and over about five miles."

"Wouldn't down be easier?" Valance settled the weight of the straps across her back.

"There's nothing down to help us. We were there. The place is all but destroyed. That was before the dam broke. Now, there will be nothing. Up is our only hope."

Valance stared down the hill for several moments. Her voice softened and tremored. "Are you sure no one would survive?"

"I won't say no one. God can save anyone." Luke studied her a moment. "If you mean Richard Dean who went into town…no. I don't think he survived." Luke didn't voice the concern someone would walk off and leave a family in the situation where he found Valance and Devon. Unless… "When did the trailer lose the back-end support? Which quake?"

"The one last week. Tuesday or Wednesday, I think."

"And Richard waited until three days ago to go for help? He…I…must be a real slouch to leave you alone for so long."

Valance shrugged as she walked. "Like I told you, I had to hit you in the head so you'd know who you were. That's when you left for town." She grimaced. "Don't go asking me lots of questions about where you were and what you were doing before. I'll have to hit you to make you remember. And neither of us will like it." She smirked at him.

Luke dropped the line of questioning. Better to save his breath for walking. And make sure she never picked up a stick.

They toiled for an hour before Luke called a halt. Devon wailed his displeasure, and Luke's good leg protested all the climbing. He pointed the crutch to a spot off the mudslide area. "There. We can take a break there."

Valance made her way to the flattened area and melted. She crossed her legs and sat. Luke stumbled over to the area and debated how best to lower himself to the ground. In the end, he collapsed, facing away from Valance and Devon. He could hear the sound of the infant suckling at his mother's breasts but needed no visual to add to his imagination.

Valance chuckled. "You can turn around, Richard Dean. It's not like you haven't watched me feed Devon before."

Luke's face burned. "Maybe. I'd prefer not. Since coming back from the valley, I've changed a few perspectives."

"Change back. You're my husband. Devon needs you." Her tone came out flat and hard. Wind whistled down the gully with nothing to stop it.

Luke remained calm and what he hoped sounded reasonable. "I accept Devon and you need help, and I'm here to give it to you. I'll be here as long as you need me."

"Is that the extent of the changes?" Again, the sneer. She was a hard one. Or had a hard life.

He raised his eyebrows. "That remains to be determined as we go, I guess." Luke leaned back against a stump and closed his eyes. *Lord, look after Tav and Chay and Jen. And Addison and BB, wherever they are. Father, please let them make it out of the valley. I know You have Your will. I know Your will is perfect. But in this lifetime, I need my brothers. Please keep them alive. In Jesus' Name, amen.*

Thirty minutes passed before Valance declared, "Okay, we're done here. You can turn around."

Luke cleared his throat. "You covered up?"

Valance laughed. "Would I do that to you? Given your

'changed perspectives?'"

"I don't know. And why I asked."

She sighed. "Yes, I'm covered. Are you happy?"

"Ecstatic. We should go." He struggled to his foot and crutches, settled the pack, and led the way up the hill once more. Valance followed a foot or so behind him.

"How far will we go today?" She wrapped one hand under the baby to make him easier to carry on the incline.

"As far as we can. It's only five miles, but with the baby and my bum foot, it could take us two days. We can't travel at night. Too risky." Luke hobbled ahead. Crutches on an incline were problematic at best. He'd do better to crawl. But he couldn't give up that easy. Not yet.

"You mean we'll have to stay out in the open?" Valance caught Luke's arm and nearly brought him to the ground. "With no house? No tent? Nothing?"

He wavered, caught his balance, and "Watch it!"

"Don't yell at me!" The woman glared at him.

"I'm sorry. You grabbed me. It almost knocked me off my foot." And forced him onto his bad one.

Valance's face drew into a mask of fury. "Don't ever raise your voice to me, you hear me, Richard Dean? I will not be addressed in that tone."

Luke lowered his head. "I'm sorry. I promise to do better."

They began walking again. Valance eyed Luke sideways. "That's twice you said you're sorry. Must have picked that up in the valley. You never apologize for anything."

"New perspective. I should have been doing it all along. Bad manners on my part." Maybe it explained her manners. Or lack thereof.

"Humph." Valance stared at the ground. She turned her gaze and looked at him with curiosity in her eyes. "Why didn't you yell back?"

"What would it have accomplished?" Luke dug his

crutches in the dirt and swung himself forward.

"Never stopped you from doing it before." Valance kicked a small rock in her way.

"I unlearned it on the trip up." He gave her a straight-lipped smile. "Almost like I'm a totally new person."

Valance nodded with approval. "I like the new you. Very different."

Lord, this is not what I need now. Okay, maybe it's what she needs. To see there are men who will treat her with respect. I don't know how many Richard Deans she's gone through. Make me the last, please? Help her out of this game she plays. Show her the truth of Your love for her. I'm with Chay, Lord. I love her. I want to marry her. I plan to marry her. Don't let Valance get the wrong idea. Please? I'll do everything I can to make sure I don't give her any excuse to think differently. Watch my tongue, Father.

They climbed another hour, took a break, climbed an hour, took a longer break. Luke estimated they covered maybe two miles. The sun sank in the valley, disappearing behind the far mountain range. Luke spotted a level clearing and limped toward it. "I think we can set up camp over here."

"Camp? What camp?" Luke detected fear in her tone.

Luke shucked the pack from his shoulders and dropped it to the ground. "If I can find dry wood, we'll have a fire. We'll lay the blankets out, bundle Devon, and have a place to stay warm and dry. Sleeping under the stars is fantastic."

"You've never been the outdoors type, Richard Dean. You even hate yard work." She sneered, happy to remind him of his failings.

Luke crawled on all fours to gather as much dry wood as he could find in the immediate area. He did not want to travel far afield to find it. "Another perspective I changed. As long as the ground is soft, it'll be fine."

His foraging led to a small pile of kindling and a few larger logs to burn overnight. They might be a little green, but they would still give off heat. Any smoke would act as a beacon if there was anyone around to smell it. He could always hope.

Once the fire curled to life, Valance passed out a share of the crackers. Water bubbled along the gully, running crisp and clear. Luke sampled it and decided it would be safe to drink. Take the chance or die of thirst. Survival is all about choices. He lapped from his hands, then nodded to Valance. "I think it's fine. We have to chance it."

Valance sipped at the water. "When did you become the expert?" Still the sarcasm.

"When I came back from town." Luke scooted on his backside back to the fire.

The woman followed him. "Lot of learning in a short time, Richard Dean. I'd almost say you were a different person. Except I know you're not."

Luke shrugged. *Lord? Up to You.* He handed out the blankets, giving Valance all but one. He suggested, "Put several of them under you to keep the cold out. The fire will warm you at the top."

Valance curled around Devon to cradle the infant. Luke sat upright, tending the fire. He watched the stars. Not far off, Tav and the others were watching the same majesty. Luke hoped. Within God's will, Luke and Tav would join up again. Life without his brother was impossible to imagine. Grief and fear gripped his heart. He closed his eyes. *Please. Please.* There were no other words.

Valance's voice interrupted his prayers. "Who are you thinking about?"

"My brother. And my friends." Luke stared into the fire, afraid to let Valance see his eyes.

"You don't have a brother."

Luke's eyes flashed open. He spaced each word. "I have a brother. His name is Tav. Taylor Alexander Vaughn. He's waiting for me at camp. He's alive, and God will bring us back together."

Valance's eyes widened, and her jaw dropped. She

worked her mouth to say something, but Luke interrupted her. "I know what you want to say. Don't. Just don't. I have a brother. Two brothers, in fact. They're real, they exist, and I will see them again." He stared her down.

Valance studied him for several moments, then waved him off. "If that's the fantasy you want to hold on to, fine with me." She snuggled closer to Devon. The infant chucked and cooed.

The night moved on, and the stars made their inexorable path through the skies. Luke drifted into an uncomfortable dream, sitting propped against a boulder. He jerked awake to find the fire smoldering but still alive. He blew on it to bring it back to a life-giving crackle. Valance wheezed in her sleep. Devon snuffled and squeaked and kicked and tossed covers…whoever coined the term "Sleep like a baby" had never seen one. Luke took a chance, dragged himself over to the infant, and scooped him up. He shifted back to his position and cradled the little man closer to the warmth.

Luke smiled at the baby. "There. Now you won't wake up your mama. And you'll stay warm. Just no ringing the dinner bell, got it?" Luke hummed a praise chorus as he rocked the little fellow back to sleep. He held him close and whispered, "I'll introduce you to Uncle Tav when we get to camp. And Uncle Micah and Uncle Addison and Uncle Quinn…he's the big, burly guy who taught us everything we know. There's Uncle BB and Ben is too young, so maybe he'll be your brother. And there's all your aunties, Grace and Jen and Chay and Wendy, who's actually my sister. Did you know that? I never had a sister growing up. But we found her…well, she found us…a year or so ago. So now I have a sister. And you'll have another auntie. You'll never be alone again, little man." Luke looked up at the lightening sky. "If you bring us home, Lord. I swear it."

"Swear what? To who?" Valance sat up groggy and confused.

"Swear to the Lord in Heaven Devon won't be alone anymore."

Valance's eyes snapped. "Alone? He's not alone. He's never been alone. If you were any kind of father, he'd never have to worry about it."

Luke sucked in his upper lip, prayed, then said, "I'm not his father, Valance. Just like I'm not your husband. But I will make sure you're both taken care of. I've said it before, and I mean it. Richard Dean, whoever he was, may have abandoned you. I'm sorry that happened. I won't replace him. But I won't leave you stranded, either."

Valance glared at him. He held her eyes. Stand off. Valance looked away, then snorted. "You'll say anything to get out of your responsibilities, won't you? You're Devon's father, my husband, and you will be 'til the day I die. You got that?"

Luke breathed hard but said nothing. *Lord, she's all Yours.* Devon let out a wail. Luke gazed at the little one. "Feeding time? Back to your mom." He passed the baby to Valance, then turned his back.

Forty minutes later, Valance announced, "All done."

"You covered?"

"Of course."

Luke turned, then snapped his head back to look away. His face burned. "That is not a joke. Have a measure of self-respect."

He heard the lilt in her voice. "I have no problem seeing myself."

"Respect I do." Luke closed his eyes. *Lord, help me. If I have to walk backward and cover her myself, I will.*

"I was only joking, Richard Dean. Having a little fun."

"It's not a joke to me." Anger replaced embarrassment. Frustration replaced anger. Discouragement replaced frustration. *How do I deal with this? I'm committed to purity.*

Guard your thoughts. You walk in a fallen world. Jesus walked among the street people, yet without sin. You can do the same. Guard your thoughts and your heart.

Luke lowered his head. Thank You, Lord. I'll remember. Give me the strength to honor You in everything. Guard my mind and my actions. And I will, too.

Valance heaved an exaggerated sigh. "Fine. I'm covered. Honest." Luke turned around. Valance had her shirt in place. She sneered at him. "Happy now?"

"Yes." He stood. "We should break camp and head out. We want to cover as much ground as we can."

"And get to your imaginary camp?" Valance came to her feet. She lay Devon down and helped Luke wrap up the meager belongings. She packed the baby into his carrier, and they set off uphill once again.

The landscape seemed determined to defeat their efforts. Luke and Valance were reduced to crawling along the inclines, battling to make every inch it seemed. They'd barely been at it half an hour when Valance stopped. "This can't be the way to go. It's ridiculous. You're not taking us anywhere to safety." She sank to the ground and placed a sleeping Devon on a pile of blankets.

Luke sat and looked at her. "Why would I be going this way if it wasn't to where we could get help?"

Valance snapped, "Maybe you're trying to kill me and Devon. Get us lost and take off somewhere. Back to town, likely."

Luke's jaw dropped. "Why would I come back from town to get you lost so I could return? By your way of thinking, I should have stayed there!"

"But you said it got destroyed."

"All the more reason your thinking is wrong. Why would I lose you to go back to a place that doesn't exist?" He couldn't keep the frustration from his voice. "Think, Valance. Either I'm leading you where I believe it's safe, or I would never come to you in the first place." He held up his hands. "Which is it?"

Valance waved her arms in the air. "I don't know!" she

shouted as loud as she could.

Which woke Devon. He added his cries to the argument, but on which side was a mystery. Mostly, he voiced his displeasure.

Valance ignored the cries and walked away a few feet. Luke picked up the wailing child and soothed the boy as best he could. He jiggled and rocked and bounced the baby, repeating, "Shh, shh. It's okay. Your mama's just upset. It'll be okay. Shh."

Five minutes of his ministrations, and the boy slowed his crying into little "sup sups" of hiccups. Luke put the child on his shoulder and patted his back. "There you go. It's all right."

Valance turned to face Luke. She wore a smile he mistrusted. She blinked twice. "Of course, I trust you, Richard Dean. You wouldn't let us down. You're my husband. You're Devon's father. You'll always take care of us." She stepped close to him and drew her finger down his cheek. "You love us. You're taking us to a place safe."

Valance took Devon from Luke. She kissed her son. "See? Daddy loves you. He takes good care of you. You know your daddy."

Luke closed his eyes, drew in a long, deep breath, opened his eyes. "Let's keep going."

They began to fight the hill again.

* * *

Evening brought them to another hilltop. Yet it was only one among many, and the gully disappeared. Luke's eyes widened as he realized his roadmap had disappeared. Now what? Now where? He sat in despair. Valance sat beside him. "Which way, Richard Dean? We're out of the gully. Now, which way?"

Resolve melted in him. He stared into space, seeing nothing. He'd been so sure. Climb the hill, follow the wash, and they'd be safe. But this wasn't like anywhere he knew. Worse, they hadn't passed the crushed car. Maybe he'd climbed the wrong ditch? Did he really have any idea where they were?

Valance repeated, "Which way now?" Fear crept in around her voice. She must have sensed his confusion. "Richard Dean. Answer me."

Luke stared at the sky. "Lord? Which way? What do I do?"

Valance mocked, "Give me a break. You? Praying? You hate God. You said only an idiot or a fool would ask him for anything."

Luke ignored her. "I need help, Father. We need help. Show me which way to go, please."

"Like he's going to do that? What do you expect, a sign in the sky? A roadmap to appear in the dirt? You're pathetic. And to think I trusted you. You're nothing." Valance smacked him on the head and shoulders. "You are nothing!"

Luke fended off the bulk of the blows, resisting the urge to grab her hands or arms. And all the while, he prayed, "Lord God, show us how to get to camp. You are able. You can. Please."

Valance stopped swinging her fists. She mimicked his voice. "Show us how to go. Please. No one is listening to you. No one cares about us. I trusted you, and you're a failure. A zero. Less than a zero."

A magnificent raven swooped from overhead and landed on the ground. It pecked at the dirt for a moment, then hopped along a path only it could see. Luke watched, then stood to his feet. He turned to Valance. "I got my sign. Are you coming with me or finding your own way?"

Valance's mouth dropped open. "You're following a bird? That's your sign from God? You're pathetic." She gathered the blankets around her, pulled Devon out of his carrier, and laid him in her lap.

Luke hobbled forward a step. "God used ravens to feed one of His prophets and keep the man alive. I'll trust Him to do the same with us. You can come with me or find your own way. It's up to you."

Valance's eyes narrowed to slits. "You would abandon us?"

"It's your choice. This is the way I'm going. You can come, or you can sit and wait for Richard Dean to save you. But I'm leaving." His tenor came out harsher than he wanted, but truth remained truth. "Take it or leave it."

The raven hopped a few paces further over the hill. Luke raised an eyebrow. "What's your choice?"

Valance screamed, a guttural, wrathful expression of frustration. When she finished, she jostled and bounced a wailing Devon. "Mommy is sorry, baby. We're following a crazy man. Shh, baby. Shh." She brushed past Luke and stalked ahead of him. But behind the raven.

Their messenger took flight but stayed close to the ground. When he did lift off, he flew into a tree ahead of them, landed, and squawked. No missing where he had gone. The trek continued uphill, at times on all fours. Luke slung the crutches over his shoulder. He would need them when they stopped climbing. The rocking motion put Devon to sleep. At least one of them was content.

The path climbed higher and higher until it evened out. The raven landed again and hopped several paces. It fluttered, gained altitude, banked right, left, and soared high, disappearing from view.

Valance scorned, "Now what? Your precious bird is gone, and we're still lost. Now what?"

Luke waved her off. "Listen!" He heard voices in the distance. Laughing voices. Shouting voices. Voices of men and women and children. Luke broke into a wide smile. "It's the camp!" He galumped down the hill on his crutches toward the sound. Valance followed him at a more reserved pace. Luke yelled for all he could, "Tav! Addison! BB! Quinn!" His headlong dash brought him to the Knights' tents and the arms of his brother.

Tav grabbed Luke around the middle and shouted,

"Luke! Praise God! I thought we'd lost you!" He hugged his brother hard, chest-bumped him equally hard, then hugged him all over again.

The crowd of Knights gathered to spin Luke around and embrace him. They left no one out but Micah. He waved from his bed, tears streaming from his face. "Luke!"

Mialma danced and pranced and raced from Luke to Tav to Micah to Ben and back again. She even licked the hands of everyone in the circle, just so no one would feel left out. Kenmore and Mrs. Nance stood on the outside of the circle.

Valance walked into the circle carrying Devon. She stared wide-eyed at the crew, delight and amazement on her face. Luke pointed her out. "This is Valance. The baby is Devon. Last name Dean." He could not stop beaming nor hanging on Tav. He'd never let him go again. Never.

Quinn stepped forward. "Welcome, Ms. Dean." He gave her a grave smile.

She demurred. "It's Dennis, actually. Valerie Dennis. And this is my daughter, Deena." She sneered, then laughed. "Who names their kid Valance?"

"Electrical engineers," Addison offered.

"Physicists." Chay threw in her two bits.

Jen smiled. "Interior decorators." Luke smiled with relief. Trust the Knights to have his back, even in something so simple.

Valerie scowled, then her eyes softened as she looked at Luke. "Luke hit his head, and he's been spinning this tale of being Richard Dean for three days now. I didn't want to argue with him." Her tone reflected condescension of the worst kind.

Luke's jaw dropped. Words didn't come. He couldn't even stutter. He could only stare at Valance. Uh, Valerie. She touched his cheek with her hand. "I couldn't make you understand I wasn't your wife. You were so insistent." She breathed in and raised her eyebrows. "A little too insistent at times. But since you got cracked on the head, I let it go. No harm, no foul." She smiled at the congregation of Knights. "He swore he knew of a camp off to the west, but I'd heard you were over on Table Mountain. I had to pretend to follow him, all the while leading him this way. It finally worked, and here we are."

Luke raged inside. How dare she? He'd been the one who led them here. He'd been the one who kept them alive. He'd been the one…

Smirks on the faces of his buddies. For or against him? Hard to say. Quinn stepped forward and took Luke's arm. "We'll get you checked out by Doctor Stevens. I'll go with you."

Valerie shook her head and waved him off with her free hand. "There's no need. He came out of it when we got over the hill. I think he's fine. They won't find anything."

Quinn smiled tight-lipped. "We'll get him checked out anyhow. Don't want to take chances."

Devon/Deena let out a wail. The child had been ignored too long. Grace held out her arms. "Let me hold her." She stared into the bundle. "Oh, you are a cutie!"

Mialma investigated the squirming bundle, nosing the blankets and trying to lick the baby's head.

Valerie beamed. "Yes, she's the light of my life. She's probably hungry."

Grace motioned to the tent. "You can feed her in there. More privacy."

Valerie shrugged. "I don't mind. It's cooler out here."

Luke wondered at the double meaning. Considering her stunt earlier, it could go either way.

Grace, however, would have none of it. "We have impressionable young men here. It's best if you stay inside." She raised her eyebrows. "You understand, right?" The inflection on the "right" left no room for argument.

Valerie sighed. "But breastfeeding is natural. It shouldn't have to be hidden."

"Granted. But out of respect for others, I'd appreciate if you would step into the tent. We have diapers and wipes available for you. You'll be more comfortable."

Valerie glared but got up and moved into the tent. Luke sighed. Quinn chuckled. He kept his voice low. "Little conflict on that?"

"More than a little. She's not stable."

"I get the impression. No one doubts you." He glared at the rest of the Knights. "Right?"

Nods and, "Right. Absolutely" followed. No snickers. Luke relaxed for the first time. Quinn pointed to the foot. "What happened?"

"Got it caught in hole. It's busted up." He leaned on the crutches. "But that hole kept me from being swept completely away. With my foot caught, I couldn't go anywhere. Nearly drowned, but I wasn't going anywhere."

Quinn shook his head. "You boys are impossible. Let's get you to Doctor Stevens." He placed a hand of direction on Luke's shoulder. "And make sure there's no brain damage."

Luke sneered. "Thanks for the vote of confidence, Boss."

Grace held up one finger. "You didn't change the baby's diaper, did you?"

Luke shook his head. "No. I know anatomy. She told me the baby was her son. A boy. Never once did she say girl." He glared at his brother. Tav looked up, down, around, his eyes wide with innocence.

Grace Cheshire-catted a smile. "That's what I thought. We'll see you in a bit."

Luke and Quinn hobbled off to visit the doctor.

* * *

Later in the evening, the group met all together as one again. Micah sat in a chair, Wendy on the ground by his feet. BB sat on one side of his father, Ben on the other. Mialma sat under her master's chair, protecting him. Tav, Luke, and Addison perched on a log together as brothers should. Jen and Chay sat in proper chairs. Quinn, Grace, and Mrs. Smothers sat in metal bounce-back chairs, comfortably rocking. Wendy's brothers had gone to play baseball with the other teens. Kenmore and Mrs. Nance left to stay with relatives who had fled Acorn before the quake. Valerie fed Deena in the tent. Quinn whittled on a piece of wood. Mrs. Smothers hummed to herself. A more contented group could not be found. They were together, and all was right with the world.

At camp. There were still decisions to make. Where to go from here? Living at camp might be fun, but made it hard to make a living. Luke waited for one of the Knights to bring a motion to the center. No one seemed so inclined, so he did. "You know, we need to figure out what comes next."

Mick quipped, "Beside the fire and the s'mores?"

Wendy patted his leg. "Stop. I think Luke wants to be serious."

"Which is why I suggested the fire. We do better when we have a fire. We can't get up and hit each other as easy." Luke knew Mick was only half-kidding.

Wendy scowled. "I'm going to put you back to bed if you don't behave."

Mick smiled. "I'll behave." He used his good arm to lift the bad one and drape it around Wendy's shoulder.

"Sure you will." Wendy turned to face Luke. "You had a point to make?"

"Just this is great and all, but we do need to come off the mountain and go into the valley to work. Jesus led Peter, James, and John off the mountain, even though Peter wanted to stay there."

Quinn leaned forward. "Have you thought what that looks like?"

"No." Luke shrugged. "I can't figure out where would be safe to set up. Do we all live together? Do we split up?"

Mick interrupted again. "Does Wendy marry me?"

Wendy looked up at Micah. "Are you asking?" Her

voice trembled.

The group became silent. Luke wondered at his friend's choice of time and place. But this was Mick. You never knew.

Mick held Wendy's hand. "If you're saying yes. If not, then no." Luke heard the vulnerability in his friend's tone. Luke hurt for the fear the man must be feeling.

Wendy leaned in and kissed Micah tenderly. "Yes, I'll marry you."

Mick shouted, "Hallelujah!" His eyes erupted with tears. "So you know, I already asked BB and Ben. They both said yes, I could ask you." He pointed with his chin to BB.

BB stood and pulled Wendy to her feet. Ben stood as well and took Wendy's hand. Together, BB and Ben asked, "Will you marry Dad and be our" BB took over, "Friend and guardian." Ben added, "Mom and friend."

Wendy's voice shook. "Yes. Proudly. Happily. Humbly."

An Andres group hug followed, with Micah looking on from his chair. Luke's eyes narrowed as he read the pain in Mick's face. He knew. Mick wanted to be in the middle. His disability prevented him from participating. At least now. Mialma stood in for him, lapping up all the pets and kisses she could nose her way into.

Which was why Mick asked now. With his friends and sons around him.

Hmm. Mick obviously didn't have a ring. But Wendy still said yes. Were rings overrated? Maybe.

Luke caught Chay's eye. She narrowed her gaze and scowled at him. Maybe not. Different strokes. She might want a more private venue. Which he would provide. When he could.

He cleared his throat. "Now we've had our interruption, so can we get back to the subject at hand? What are we going to do next?" He decided lighting a fire would be a good thing. Just so they had something to toss rocks at.

Made for great punctuation of sentiments. No breeze to blow smoke into anyone's eyes, either. He stacked the logs and lit the wood. And sat back to see where the conversation would lead.

Eyes naturally drifted to Quinn. He didn't look up from his whittling. "Who's asked God what He wants?"

Chay raised her hand. Grace raised hers. Tav raised his. Quinn gazed around at the three. "And?" His knife on the wood provided the only sound.

Chay spoke first. "And nothing. It's not He's not there or not listening. He's short on answers right now."

Tav nodded. "That's what I'm getting. Plenty of assurance He's with me. But nothing that looks like direction or guidance."

"Hear, hear." Grace chimed.in.

Quinn stared into the fire. "Maybe we're asking the wrong questions. You're asking what He wants you to do. His answer hasn't changed in two thousand years. Live for Him. Be His witness. Die for Him."

Quinn stretched. "The question you need to ask is where does He want you."

Tav dipped his head to the side. "I've asked, too. And I get the sense of community we have here. But we can't stay here."

"True. What does that leave you?"

"Going back to what's left of Acorn or moving to a place like Galt, or Blendon, or Santa Clara, even. Leaving this area is hard. Acorn needs to be rebuilt." Tav stopped. "Or does it? Do we leave and move on? Or stay with those who want to restore and rebuild the town?" He stared at Quinn. "That's where I'm not getting any answer."

Quinn picked up another piece of wood and began whittling it down to shavings. As all good whittlers do. "Maybe there's no one perfect plan. Maybe God is saying, 'You choose. I'll be with you no matter what. Up to you what you do or where you go. It's all good.'"

Luke cocked his head. "Would He say that? I mean, what about His perfect plan?"

Quinn chuckled. "You really think you can mess up God's perfect plan? If you could, it wouldn't be perfect, would it?"

Their mentor let it sink in. "You're not robots or automatons. You have free will. Make a choice based on the best information you have. God will honor it or move you where He wants. He's interested in your heart and your head. Unless you feel a strong inclination to go one place or another, pick one and go."

Micah's eyes narrowed. "Is that what you do?" He reached out and scratched Mialma's ears with one hand and held Wendy's hand with his other.

"When it comes to it, yes. With no other leading but to serve Him wherever and whenever I go with my best information and gut feeling."

Luke tossed a stick into the fire. "Can I ask what you're going to do?"

"You can ask. Doesn't mean I'll tell you. I want you boys and girls to think for yourselves. Make your own decisions."

Tav spoke up. "We will. But it's been amazing being together. Almost like the first church, living together, having all things in common. I like this. It feels right."

Luke studied the eyes around the fire. Most seemed in accord. Others, maybe not so much. It would be good not to railroad anyone into doing what they didn't want. He crossed his legs and looked at Mrs. Smothers. "What is your plan?"

Wendy's mom shrugged her shoulders to her ears. "I will stay with Wendy and Jen. The boys will live with me. I can't continue to live without help. I know." Early-onset Alzheimer's. How long did she have? Where would she go?

Micah held out his arm as far as he could. "You'll come live with us. With Wendy and BB and Ben and me. The boys will be old enough to make their own decisions. They can live with Peter and Kevin. Or with us." He looked to Wendy for confirmation. She nodded and held her mother's hand. Mialma woofed her approval.

So Mick would have to have a huge house. Lots of moving parts. And would need lots of help. With the college underwater and debris, it could be months or years before Luke, Tav, and Addison could finish their degrees. If ever. Or they could move to another town and another college. And leave Mick to deal with all those kids on his own?

Quinn threw his shavings into the fire and put his knife in his pocket. He took Grace's hand, squeezed it, and humphed. "I know an eight-plex. It's in Galt. Two, three, and four-bedroom units. It's sitting empty. Needs a little renovation, but nothing major. I'm sure we could purchase it for a nominal price. It would give everyone who needs it a place to live until you decide where and what you want to do. Anyone interested?"

Nine hands went into the air. Chay glanced around the circle. "I'm still in school in Santa Clara. I've got a place to live." She eyed Luke. "You could come there and finish your degree." She corrected her offer. "All three of you could come."

Luke felt the air rip out of his chest. Leave the nest? Leave his brothers? The Knights? Break up the band? For Chay?

Why did he question this? If he loved Chay, he would happily follow her to the ends of the earth. Right? He realized Chay waited for an answer. The longer he hesitated, the worse it looked. He punted. "I'll have to think about it. I don't want to lose my credits if I can help it."

Disappointment colored Chay's face. She gave him a straight-lipped nod. "I understand."

Did she? Did he?

Quinn suggested, "Let's sleep on it. We're all exhausted. We can discuss it more tomorrow. I'm ready to call it a night." He glanced at Grace. "If you'll check on our visitor. I expected her to come out by now."

Grace's eyes narrowed. "Agreed." She stood and walked to the tent. "Valerie? Everything okay in here?" She poked her head under the flap.

"Quinn!"

Everyone who could jumped to their feet. Mialma barked and raced into the tent. Grace disappeared into the tent, then came out carrying baby Deena. The infant slept content. Grace's eyes burned. "Valerie is gone. She cut a hole in the tent and left."

Luke groaned. "I'm so sorry I got us into this mess."

Mrs. Smothers held out her hands. "Let me hold her, please."

Grace surrendered the child. Mrs. Smothers smiled. "It's been too long since I fostered a baby. I knew there had to be a reason I came up here. You said there would be children I could care for." She beamed at Wendy. "And here she is."

Quinn asked, "Any note? Anything saying she's coming back?"

"No. She didn't take anything, either. I'm guessing she'll look for a new 'Richard Dean.'"

Luke lowered his head and shook it. "Is she crazy? Or a mistress of manipulation?"

Quinn scowled. "She'll use anyone and anything to get what she wants. Even a baby."

Mrs. Smothers cradled Deena to her shoulder. "Do we look for her? If this precious child is to have a future, we need to say we did all we could to locate her. And give her the chance to reclaim her child. Deena isn't lost property you can claim after three months." She sighed. "Acorn used to be the county seat. With it destroyed, who knows where we can go for guidance."

She raised her eyebrows. "We have a more pressing issue. Do we have formula? Bottles? We'll have to hope Deena will take the new milk."

Wendy climbed to her feet. "I'll canvass the neighbors. I know there are infants in the camp. Someone should have food to spare."

Jen rose as well. "You go east, I'll go west."

Tav pointed to Addison. "Let's see if anyone saw Valerie leave. Or if she's still in camp."

Addison climbed to his feet. "Sounds good." He grinned. "I'd rather look for Mom than babysit the little one."

Luke chuckled. "Yeah, you're great at looking for women."

"Except my track record isn't good at finding them."

"I'm not sure you want to find this one. And if she calls you Richard Dean, run for your life."

Addison tossed a woodchip at Luke, then walked off.

* * *

Tav scoured his area of the camp, looking for Valerie. No one had seen her. Or they'd seen her but not talked to her. Or talked to her, but she didn't talk back. He came on his final contact, a young man working on his SUV engine. Tav approached him. "You got a problem?"

The man looked up. "No. Just tuning her up. What can I help with?"

Tav leaned against a tree. "I'm looking for a woman."

"Aren't we all?"

Tav chuckled. "Well, a specific woman. Young, maybe early twenties." He held his hand up. "About this tall. Dark shoulder-length hair. Uses the name Valerie or Valance."

"You mean Vickie?"

Tav sighed inside. "That might be her."

"What do you want her for?"

"She left something behind I think she might want."

The man shook his head. "She said she didn't have anything. She said she'd been kidnapped, ran away from her kidnapper yesterday, and ended up here. My brother took her to Galt to find the sheriff."

Tav stared off to the side. "Strange. We have a sheriff here. Sheriff Knott. He's just up the hill there."

The man shrugged. "I mentioned that, but she wanted to speak to a higher-up."

Tav held out his hand. "Tav Vaughn."

"Kershon Bailey."

"Did your brother plan to spend the night in Galt? It's two hours away."

"Yeah, that was his plan. He is going to pick up supplies for us and see what the housing situation is. Much as we like it here, we do gotta get back to some kind of life."

"I hear you." Tav hesitated. "Is he bringing her back?"

"Why would he? She said she got stranded here. Didn't want to be here. She couldn't wait to get started. What'd she leave?"

Tav shook his head. "Her baby."

Kershon's jaw dropped. "Her what?"

"Baby. Three-month-old daughter. When your brother comes back, will you let us know? We're over nearest the perimeter of the camp. West side."

"Sure will. I hope my brother uses his head."

"You and me both. But she's quite the storyteller."

"If she left a baby here, she definitely spinning wild yarns. I'll let you know when Weston gets back tomorrow."

They shook hands, and Tav returned to the encampment. Addison had completed his rounds. "Nothing. No one's seen her."

"I hit pay dirt. Found a guy whose brother is driving her to Galt."

Quinn raised an eyebrow. "Really?"

"Yeah." Tav smiled without mirth. "According to Vickie"—he drawled the new name—"she'd been kidnapped, escaped, and ended up here. She wanted to go to Galt to inform the authorities." Tav held up his hand to ward off any protests. "I know. We have a sheriff. He's not 'high enough' for her. Guess she's looking for the FBI or the like."

Luke growled. "Or the like is right. A fast trip away from any responsibilities."

Tav scanned the area. "Where's the little miss?"

Quinn explained, "Unlike her mother, we do feel Sheriff Knott is high enough. Rather than face a kidnapping charge against us, we're reporting the baby abandoned. We'll keep her here with us, but she will be evidence against Valerie or Vickie or Valance or whatever name she chooses to use. Wendy found formula and bottles so we can keep her fed and clean."

Grace stepped out of the tent. "And loved. We will certainly provide the little one with all the love a child deserves."

Wendy came down the hill carrying the baby, Jen in tow with supplies. Wendy transferred the baby to Mrs. Smothers, who waited with outstretched arms. Jen announced, "We have blankets and diapers and formula and bottles to last us a week at least. Then we'll have to decide what to do."

Quinn nodded. "We'll have to decide what to do about all of us by then. We may have shelters up here, but the work is in the valley. We need to be up about our Father's business."

The Knights returned to their tents. And their prayers. Tomorrow would be decision day. For all of them.

* * *

TUESDAY

Morning came with cool breezes and more tremors. But slight ones. Aftershocks that wouldn't cause property damage but still rattled nerves and brought back harrowing memories.

Tav woke first in the tent. He slipped out, stood and stretched, and immediately wrapped his arms around his chest. Cold. They needed a fire.

He lit one and started the coffee. He muttered, "I'll be happy when Mick takes up his duty again. I never realized how tedious this gets." He sniffed. "Like he has nothing else to do with his time. Lord, bring him all the way back to us, please. Heal him. In Your will. Always in Your will."

Deena voiced an opinion from the Smothers' tent. Feeding time. Did the baby do anything except eat? And poop? He couldn't remember from Addison's infant days. He'd been too busy being his four-year-old self to care about the requirements of babies. High time he learned. If he and Jen were going to be together…

Jen and him. Why didn't he ask her last night when Mick asked Wendy? It would have been easy. He wouldn't have considered it stealing Mick's thunder. Or Wendy's moment. Nothing said he couldn't ask today. It was, after all, decision day. What greater decision could there be? He'd do it. Right after breakfast. He'd fashion a ring from the tall grasses, and he'd ask her. He would. He would.

Tav knelt in the dirt. God, if this isn't right, tie my

tongue. Have her say no. Stop us. I want to honor You. Especially with this. This is the rest of my life, Lord. All of it. Don't let me make the wrong choice. I know what Quinn said. And I agree. But this…this is no going back. Direct me, Father. In Jesus' Name, amen.

Before he could rise, a hand grasped his shoulder. Luke knelt beside him. "Lord, whatever my brother is struggling with, give him the answers he needs. Lead him in You, always. Show him Your will and give him the courage and faith to do it. In Your Son's Name, amen."

Tav turned and hugged his brother. "Thanks, Luke."

"Care to share?"

"Jen."

Luke nodded. "I understand. I almost asked Chay last night myself."

"Almost? Why didn't you?"

"She warned me off. I saw it in her eyes."

"Sorry, man. What do you think she means?"

"I don't know. Her offer seemed obvious enough. She wants me near her."

"But not with her?"

"I don't know, Tav. I can't read that far."

"What are you going to do?"

Tav motioned to the ground. "Pray."

"I'll join you." Together, the two men stormed the gates of Heaven.

Tav became aware when Addison joined the prayer circle. Followed by BB and Ben, dragging Micah in his chair. Mialma joined the circle, lying at the feet of her family. Five minutes later, Quinn and Grace entered the group of pray-ers. There were whispered words, there were supplications, there were praises. Wendy and Jen and Mrs. Smothers came in. Chay followed. The circle filled in. And still, they prayed.

Only when everyone sat back on their haunches, opened their eyes, and murmured, "Amen," did they stop.

Wendy crossed her legs to sit beside Micah. Jen joined Tav, slipping her hand into his. Chay remained across from Luke.

Quinn asked, "Where is Deena?"

"Asleep in the tent. She's warm, she's dry, and her tummy is full. We should have a few minutes to talk."

Quinn smiled. "What more could an infant want?"

Tav quipped, "A mom who cared."

Wendy corrected him with heat. "She's got more moms than she can shake a stick at right now. She'll always be loved."

Tav remembered Wendy had been abandoned by her mother—his mother—when Wendy had been younger than Deena. He understood her fire.

Quinn gazed around at the Knights. "Decision time. Who is doing what? Going where?"

Micah spoke first. "I'm in favor of the idea of the eight-plex. Since none of us have housing except Chay, it will make sense to start with. Gives us a place to go until we are ready for our next move. Whatever that is." He smiled. "And I can see my bride-to-be every day."

Ben cautioned. "But no kis-sing. On the cheek on-ly."

Micah shook his head. "I hear you, Ben. We'll keep it holy."

Tav looked to Quinn. "Are you in favor of the complex? You, of all of us, have more opportunity to move where you want. Would you really want to neighbor up with us?"

Quinn raised his eyes. "I wouldn't offer if I didn't want to." He ducked his head to the side. "I've come to like this family arrangement. You're the sons and daughters I don't have. I could live like this the rest of my days."

Tav's heart burned. He choked on his words. All that came out was a lame, "Me, too."

Luke tapped fists with Tav. "Goes for me as well. This is the family we don't have otherwise. Where else can we get this kind of closeness and support?"

Addison sniffed. "Oh, say it. Where else would we find love like this? Come on, guys. We love each other. Admit it."

Quinn held out a fist. "Are there any objections?"

Mrs. Smothers raised her hand. "What about Peter and Kevin? Will they be allowed to join us, too? To just live with us? Or would they have to agree to be Knights?"

Tav shook his head. "The Knights are different than just living with your mom and sisters. No one is ever forced to make that choice."

Mrs. Smothers sighed a bit. Then she hardened. "They will toe the line. I'll make certain of that. No more partying around."

Grace laughed. "I think we should take this one vote at a time. Once we know who wants to join us, we can set out rules of conduct."

Addison added, his voice dry, "Yeah, like no loud country music. Rock and rap are okay, but none of that twanging stuff."

Woodchips flew across the campfire and landed on Addison. He held up his hands to ward them off. "Fine! I yield." Mialma didn't know what the excitement was about, but she barked to be in on it.

Quinn cleared his throat. "Let's get back to the decision at hand. How many will want to share the complex?"

Mrs. Smothers said, "I'll need to have two units. So, I vote yes twice."

Tav put his fist in. Luke did the same. Addison joined. Wendy looked at Jen. Jen nodded. They both put their fists in. Micah, BB, and Ben cast their lot. Grace and Quinn voted yea. All eyes turned to Chay. She lifted her chin. "I'm in Santa Clara."

Grace made one appeal. "But you still need a home base. You could have your own apartment."

Chay glared at her mother. "No coercion, right?"

"Just an offer."

"I'll go back to Santa Clara."

Tav hurt for Luke. But maybe this was God's way of saying, "Not yet." Or "Not her." Either way, Luke would have to deal with the loss. He eyed his brother to gauge his reaction and saw peace. Good man. Luke walked away from the circle. Maybe he needed time.

Quinn smiled. His eyes sparkled. "That's six houses. Maybe we'll remodel the last two into meeting rooms or recreation rooms. Family gathering rooms."

Deena gave out a loud squeal. Mrs. Smothers suggested, "Nurseries."

Wendy laughed. "I don't think we'll need that many at one time, Mom." She got up and retrieved the baby. Micah held up his good arm. "Let me hold her. Just once."

Wendy snuggled the little girl into Micah's chest and wrapped his limp arm around the child. Tav watched Micah's face reflect total awe. This seemed right. Micah needed kids. He deserved kids. *I know. No one deserves anything. But if there's room in Your plan, let them have a family of their own. Besides BB and Ben. In Your will, Lord.*

Kershon came into the camp. Tav greeted him. "What word from your brother?"

The young man scowled. "He's not back yet. He should've been here an hour ago. I need those supplies." He kicked at the dirt. "What do you know about the woman?"

Tav admitted. "Not a lot. She's trouble. Or troubled. I'm not sure which. But my brother found her in a trailer perched on a cliff and rescued her and the baby. She gets here and starts spinning a tale about him having brain damage and not knowing who he is. Told him the baby's a boy, then tells us she's a girl. Which she is."

"What trailer? Where?"

Tav called over his shoulder. "Luke." His brother walked back from the trees. Tav did the introductions. "Luke, Kershon. Kershon, my brother Luke. He's the one who knows Vickie best." Luke eyed Tav with confusion. "Valance. Valerie."

Luke nodded. "Ah, yes. Vickie. I see she's not done with the stories yet."

Kershon growled. "And she's got my brother involved now."

Luke held out his hand. "Sorry for your luck. And his." Luke motioned to a slingback chair. "Have a seat. This will take a while."

Luke explained the entire ordeal with Vickie/Valerie/Valance. When he finished, Kershon scowled even deeper. "Fool brother of mine. Knew he'd get into trouble."

Tav suggested, "I have a young friend who can draw a picture of her for the sheriff's department if you like. Maybe they can alert their counterparts in Galt to be on the lookout for her."

"But if she hasn't committed a crime, why would they?"

"She abandoned her baby. That ought to get a response."

Kershon nodded. "Yeah. I guess it would."

Tav called over Ben. He asked, "Will you draw a picture of Valerie for Mr. Bailey? He needs it to take to the sheriff."

Ben retrieved his art pad from the tent and set to work. In minutes, he had a full-color portrait of Valerie/Vickie and handed it to Kershon. The man said a few unkind words in an approving fashion. Tav raised his eyebrows. "I know how you feel. His talent is exceptional."

"I thought you were fooling around, that he'd give me a sort of sketch. But this…this may as well be a photograph."

Luke nodded. "That's our Ben."

Kershon shook Ben's hand. "Thank you, Ben. I appreciate your help. Maybe I can get my brother out of trouble."

Ben gave a single solemn nod. "I like to help bro-thers. I have lots of them."

Luke put his arm around the boy's shoulders. "Yes, he does. And he has a full-time job watching over us."

Kershon walked away. Tav squeezed Ben's shoulder. "Good job, Ben." He pointed to where Micah sat, perched in his chair. "Let's go massage your dad's legs and arms and see if we can get more life in them. He's making good progress getting feeling back in them."

Ben nodded. "Je-sus will make Dad well. Je-sus told me."

Tav gave the boy a straight-lipped smile. "If God wants your dad to be well, He will make Him that way. But we have to do our part, too. And that's working his muscles to make him stronger."

"I will work on Dad. Je-sus will work on Dad. We will make him strong-er."

"That we will."

Mialma supervised the massage until the interlopers arrived. Kershon and Sheriff Knott stalked into camp. The sheriff had Ben's picture. His eyes were narrow as he approached Tav. "Is this the woman who left the baby?"

Tav nodded, unsure of the vehemence of the question. "Yes, sir. That's her."

Sheriff Knott growled. "Figures. Where did you find her?"

Luke stepped up. "She was in a trailer over off Sequence Gulch. Nothing else around it. If there had been, the quake took it before I got there. Just the trailer hanging off the supports."

"Sequence Gulch? What were you doing there?"

"Surviving the slide."

Sheriff Knott walked around in a tight circle. "Can you take me there? I'd like to search the premises."

"You won't find much. The back half of the trailer hung by a thread. Any one of these aftershocks could send it over the edge."

Knott's eyes narrowed further. His jaw worked tighter. "Tell me everything."

Luke pointed to the chairs. "Get comfortable. And get ready." The men sat. Kershon leaned forward. Knott leaned back and crossed his arms.

Tav's brother took over an hour to tell his story. It would have been shorter, but the sheriff interrupted to ask questions, go back over details, and mutter, "Richard Dean."

When Luke finished, the sheriff stood. He lowered his eyes, then looked up and asked, "Can I see the baby?"

Tav popped into the Smothers' tent to bundle Deena away from Wendy. She stuck her lower lip out in a pout. Tav grinned. "I'll bring her back. I promise."

He carried the infant out and handed her to the sheriff. The man gazed deep into the tiny face. Deena opened her eyes and gazed up at Knott. He lifted the child to his shoulder and cradled her for several lifetimes. He kissed the little head, then handed her back to Tav. "I'll trust you to keep her safe until I can make arrangements to care for her."

Tav cocked his head. "You're going to take her?"

Knott cleared his throat. "She's my granddaughter. Valance is my daughter."

Tav's gut twisted. He could only respond, "Oh."

Knott snorted. "Yeah, oh. She's got issues. I didn't know she was pregnant, much less she'd had the baby. She disappeared a year ago." He looked at the ground. "Probably when she found out about expecting." He shook his head, then looked at Kershon. "We'll locate your brother. Valance will use him until she finds someone else, then she'll drop him. I'm guessing he'll come back here this evening."

Knott shook Tav's hand, then Luke's. "I appreciate what you've done for Deena. And for Valance. Saving her from the trailer and getting her here to safety? I owe you."

Luke shrugged. "I was saving both of us. All three of us."

Tav hoisted the baby to his shoulder. "We'll take good care of Deena until you're ready for her." He grinned. "Don't wait too long. You might not get her back. We have a host of women here who are ready to adopt her."

Knott laughed for the first time. "I hear you. I'll make sure you all get visitation privileges."

The sheriff turned with Kershon and walked out of the camp. Tav glared at his brother. "Kidnapping the sheriff's daughter and granddaughter? What were you thinking?"

"Survival. Tell me you wouldn't have done the same thing."

"Truth."

Deena squeaked, then squawked. Mialma snuffled at the blankets. Tav grinned. "Time to get you back to Auntie Wendy. Crying babies belong with women."

Wendy came out of the tent. "I heard that remark. I should make you keep her."

"Hey…she's the sheriff's granddaughter. Only the best for her. That means I'm out."

Wendy sneered at him. "Nice try. But give her to me."

Tav surrendered the baby. Reluctantly. Wendy disappeared into the Magary tent to care for the infant. Tav went over to sit beside Micah and work the man's muscles. "How's it coming? Any more connections being formed?"

Micah lifted his good arm to shoulder height. The left arm he could move out away from his side nearly a foot. "It's coming." He motioned to his feet. "I'm more worried about walking again." He breathed hard. "How'm I going to provide for Wendy if I can't walk?"

Tav wanted to slough off his friend's concerns. Wanted to say, "You work a desk job. What's the big deal?" But he couldn't. He understood. He'd had enough experience when he tore up his knee—twice—to know the anxiety of "Will I ever walk again?" Then there were the months with Addison and the same questions. So much of their self-worth remained tied up in the question, "What do you do?" Rarely,

"Who has God made you?" Tav gripped his friend's arm. "You'll provide for her the same way we all provide for anyone. With God's help and grace."

Tav raised his eyebrow. "Have you set a date?"

Micah pursed his lips. "I know the standard is to put it off a year or two to plan a perfect wedding. But Wendy is more concerned about her mom still being able to come rather than all the formalities. And with the living arrangements, the sooner we get married, the easier it will be on both of us."

Tav grinned. "Better to marry than burn?"

Micah huffed. "I was thinking about all the coming and going from her house to mine." He ducked his head. "But yeah, it did enter my mind."

Tav patted Micah's chest. "You will have many a chaperone to make sure you stay on the straight and narrow, my friend. I'm sure Ben will be chief among them." Mialma woofed to voice her support.

Micah groaned. "I bet you're right." He cocked his head. "Have you talked to Jen yet?"

"About making it a two-fer? No. About getting married? Yes. Just not gotten to the official question."

"What are you waiting for?"

"Time and place, man. You stole my thunder with asking Wendy in front of everyone. Now I have to come up with something romantic and private."

Mick grinned. "Sorry 'bout that, chief. Totally spontaneous."

"Sure you were. Having BB and Ben stand up and ask her to be their mom and friend? Nice touch, by the way." Tav nodded. "Wise, too. How did you convince Ben?"

"I didn't have to. He asked me. Wanted to know when Wendy could be his mom like I'm his dad. I had to explain that one."

"And he agreed."

"He's excited and keeps asking when she will come

live in our tent. I have to remind him she has to live with her mom for now to help out Jen. But soon. Soon, she'll come live with us."

Jen's voice called from across the way. "Are you boys working or talking?"

Tav called back, "We can do both. Unlike some people."

Jen's voice arched. "Yeah? Who?"

Tav thought fast. "Luke." He looked around for his brother. Luke had wandered away when the sheriff left.

Jen walked up to join them. She embraced Tav. "Nice save." They kissed warmly. He heard Micah clear his throat, hum a few bars under his breath, then say, "Uh…breathe. Come up for air. Break, or I call Ben."

Tav and Jen broke. Tav warned Micah, "Watch it, Knight. I know where you sleep."

Micah grinned. "You and everyone else." He looked to Jen. "Did you need anything besides Tav's company?"

"No. Just wanted to make an appearance. And ask when you think we'll move down the mountain?"

"It depends on how fast Quinn can secure the apartment building. Knowing him, maybe by the end of the week."

"And you think this is a good idea?"

"We voted on it. Yes."

Jen smiled. "Just making sure." Her eyes gleamed. "I love the idea of being close to you. Even with Mom between us."

Tav looked at Micah. Micah raised an eyebrow. Tav stood and took Jen's hand. "Let's take a walk."

Jen dipped her head. "Certainly." She grinned at Mick. "Bye, Micah."

Micah waved with his good arm. Tav led Jen to a spot overlooking the valley beneath. He held her hand. She eyed him, her eyes sparkling. "Yes?"

"Jen, I need you to understand me. I've thought about

what this moment would look like for a long time. But I never thought it would be as…as scary."

Jen stepped back half a step. "Scary?"

"Have you ever wanted something so bad it hurts? You think if you want it that much, maybe it's not good for you? And so you ask God about it, and you don't know whether to hope He says yes or no?"

Tav took both her hands. "And He says, 'Do what your heart desires.' But you know your heart, and you don't trust it to make a good choice. So you ask Him again. And He says the same thing. 'Do what your heart desires.'" Tav looked into Jen's eyes. He opened his soul for her. "So I'm asking. Will you marry me and be my life partner and my wife?"

Jen looked at the ground. She spoke barely above a whisper. "I do know about asking God for your heart's desires. And being afraid of the answer. So you couch the question. 'If this happens, I'll know the answer is yes. And if the other happens, it'll be no.'" She lifted her gaze to meet Tav's eyes. "And you just gave me the yes answer. Yes, Tav, I will marry you and be your life partner and your wife."

Tav sealed it with a kiss Ben would have been proud to break up. They embraced and kissed again. And again. And…

Tav broke it off, breathless. "Okay, that's enough. For now. We need to get back to civilization."

Jen's eyes twinkled. "And chaperones."

They held hands all the way back to camp.

A crowd had gathered when they returned. The Knights, plus Mrs. Smothers and her sons Tim and Ury, waited. And watched. In total silence.

Tav lifted Jen's hand in triumph. "She said yes!"

Cheers and whoops and laughter greeted them. Wendy ran out and hugged her sister first. "I'm so happy for you!" Mialma ran around in little circles, barking.

Tav saw tears trickle down Micah's face. Luke stepped

up and grabbed Tav. "Congratulations. It's great." Tav read both pain and joy in his brother's face. He clapped him on the back. "Your time will come. Hang in there."

Luke nodded. "I know. God has His plan."

Tav led Jen over to Micah's chair so he could wish them well. Micah hugged Jen, then shook Tav by the shoulders. "Well done, Knight. Well done."

Quinn laughed. For the first time in a month, Tav saw his mentor with a genuine smile on his face. "Fantastic! I'm pleased for both of you. All four of you." He kissed Jen, then Wendy, and shook hands with Tav and Micah. "We'll have a father-son talk soon, you hear me?"

"Yes, sir. Absolutely."

Grace beamed. She embraced Mrs. Smothers. "We have so much planning to do!"

Jen's mom nodded. "And I know who will help me with everything." She smiled. "I'm so happy I have you all to help. I know Jen and Wenders will be well cared for." She looked off and whispered, "When I'm gone."

Grace assured her, "You're not going anywhere anytime soon."

The woman nodded. "I already am. I can tell." She brightened. "But that's for another day. Today is celebrating."

Ben jumped up and down. "Celebrating. Break out the marshmallows!"

Quinn grinned. "Right. And the good chocolate."

A voice came from behind the tents. "What are we celebrating?"

Everyone froze. All eyes turned to look as a figure stepped out from between the tents. Kurt Andres stepped into the clearing. He walked over and stopped in front of Micah, BB, and Ben. His face appeared solemn. "Hello, boys."

Micah stared, unable to speak. Ben grabbed his grandfather and chortled, "Pop-dad is here! Pop-dad is here." Mialma walked up and sniffed Kurt's hand. She kept all four feet on the ground, however. A little unusual, but Tav ignored it.

Micah's voice came out barely above a whisper. "Where have you been? We searched for you. We thought you were buried deep under the rubble."

Kurt pointed to a bench. "May I sit?"

People moved to make room. Tav noted Quinn's face lost its unfettered joy. Replaced by suspicion. Regret? Maybe a little. The man swallowed it swiftly. He gazed at Kurt, waiting as they all were for an answer. The lab lay opposite her owner.

Kurt glanced around the ring of Knights. "I doubted you. Okay, I didn't believe any of this would happen. I thought you were being led astray. When the quakes started happening, I still didn't believe it. I didn't want to believe it. I wanted you to be wrong."

Micah nodded. "We all wanted to be wrong. None of us wanted any of this to happen."

"I thought you did. I thought you were convinced you had a word from the Lord and were going to hide up here until he came back."

Mick's eyes softened. "I told you it wasn't like that." He hesitated. "Where did you go? We looked for you."

"When the quakes began happening, I left the office by Uber. I hitchhiked to the hills." Kurt lowered his eyes. "I've been living up in a fifth wheel with a family who gave me a ride."

Tav studied Mick's eyes. He saw the hurt, the confusion. Micah asked, "Did you know where we were?"

Kurt gave a half-shrug. "Everyone in camp knows where you bunch are. If there's a problem to be solved, your names are the first to be suggested."

Tav watched Micah draw in a deep breath. "You knew, and you didn't contact us? Didn't try to let us know you were alive?" Pain laced his friend's voice.

Kurt hedged. "I spied on you. I knew what happened

around here."

"You knew I'd been injured and didn't come help?" Micah made a wide circle. "My friends—my family—saved my life. They're the reason I'm going to walk again. They're the reason I'm breathing. And you knew?"

Kurt held up his hand. "You need to understand. My pride hurt. I was wrong, and I couldn't admit it."

Micah exploded. "Your pride? And that justifies leaving me dying? Where were you when Ben ran off? When Wendy and Addison went after him? Where were you when the mob from town came? Where were you—"

Kurt raised both hands. "I was wrong, Mick. I admit it. I was wrong. I'm sorry. I want to start over. With all of you. I need you to forgive me and give me a second chance."

Tav remained silent. He had more than a few words he wanted to throw at Kurt Andres, but Micah seemed to be managing fine on his own. And it was, after all, Mick's dad. He would make the ultimate choice.

Micah swallowed hard. He pulled himself to lean forward in the chair. "I forgive you. But I'm not the only one you hurt." He motioned to BB and Ben, then to the remainder of the Knights. Tav noted Micah made a point to start with Quinn.

Kurt lowered his head. "I know. I hurt all of you. And I'll do my best to make amends where I can." He glanced from person to person but seemed to brush past Quinn. He landed on BB. "I'm sorry, BB. I'm sorry, Ben. I should have been here for both of you, and I wasn't. I'll make it up to you."

BB's voice snapped, "How? How do you make up for abandoning Dad when he needed you most? You're his father. Is that what fathers do?"

Kurt stared off to the side. "No, they don't. I was wrong. I admit it. I want to make it right." He held Micah's eyes. "I have the cabin up at the lake. It's got four bedrooms. Plenty of room for the three of you. And you would be close to a town where you can get the medical treatments you need. I've checked, and it's still in perfect shape. I'd love it if you three would come live with me. I can help you get settled. We could be family again."

Micah held his father's eyes. "You know I'm engaged to Wendy? Did you see that, too?"

Kurt nodded. "I did." He dropped his eyes, then looked sideways at Micah. "I'm happy for you, of course. But we can discuss it later."

Mick's eyes bore holes into his father. "I don't know if there's anything to discuss. If there is, it gets discussed in front of the family." He circled the group with his hand. "The whole family."

Kurt looked pained. "Mick, let's not start a fight. I came to apologize and offer you and the boys a place to live. You can't stay at the campgrounds forever. Even with all the supplies you stockpiled."

Micah growled, "We gave those supplies to the town and to the campers here. We didn't stockpile any of it for ourselves. I told you in the beginning. It turned out to be a hollow gesture because we did it before the last one hit. But we did what we could." He closed his eyes, opened them, breathed out slowly, and then said, "I appreciate the offer. But the boys and I have a place to live."

"In Galt? There's no work in Galt. And you'll need to be where you can get help."

"I'll have help. And there's work everywhere. With all the rebuilding needing to be done, I'm sure there will be plenty to do. Even for a cripple like me."

A collective psychic lurch passed around the circle. Every Knight stood ready to jump Micah for the use of the insult. But Kurt would be the one to verify or deny the pejorative.

Kurt let it stand. He looked at Quinn, then at Micah. "You're choosing Quinn over me? I know all about the apartment complex. And I know it's in rough shape."

Micah held his head up. "I'm choosing to honor my word, sir. I'm a Knight of the Octagon, and we stand by our commitments." *Unlike you who took off when I was a kid. I needed a dad then, and you were nowhere to be found. But that's past history. This is about now.*

Kurt frowned. "You really have become a cult, haven't you? I thought there might be hope you'd get past it when the earthquakes ended."

BB started forward, but Micah waved him off. "It's okay, son." He stared hard at his father. "We are not a cult. We are a band of men and women who have committed to following Christ the best way we know how. And part of that is being true to our word. Scripture commends those who 'swear to their own hurt and change not.' Who make a promise and stand by it. I made a promise to Quinn. What kind of man would I be, what kind of example would I be to my sons, if I changed my mind with the first 'better offer' that comes along? No, I'll stay with the man who stood by me."

Micah turned to Quinn and eyed him. "And don't you say anything."

Quinn held up both hands. "Not a word. Except—"

"Not a word. Right." Micah wouldn't let the man speak. He looked back to his father. "We have space for you to come live with us if you like. Same as we have before. You'll have a room of your own and a place to stay when you're in the area. Will you accept my offer?"

Kurt shook his head. "I don't think so. Not now. Not right now, anyhow. You've obviously got things to work through. I'll check back with you in a few years." Kurt rose and walked back over the hill.

No one breathed. No one moved. Ben broke the tableau. He stood up, walked over to Quinn, and hugged the man. "Pop-dad. I love you."

Quinn rubbed Ben's head. He looked off to the side, then held Micah's eyes. Tav waited. The mentor's voice came low. "Are you sure? You don't owe me anything."

Micah's voice was fierce. "I owe you everything. And if I didn't, I'd still come with you. Not because I have to. Because I want to." Mick grinned. "You owe me a father-son talk, remember?"

Quinn shook his head. "You boys." He looked around the group, opened his arms wide, and declared, "My family." Mialma ambled over to plop beside Quinn.

The Knights put their fists in the circle. Tav pronounced, "To family." All fists went in. All thumbs raised. "Carried. We're official."

Unanimously.

If you enjoyed ***Knights of the Octagon,*** sign up for Colleen Snyder's newsletter to keep up with new books and projects. It will also give you a place to talk to the author directly. And she loves to talk to her readers. Trust me!

Emails will NOT be sold, shared, or used for any other purpose. Promise.

Go to: **colleensnyderauthor.com** and leave your email to sign up.

Also connect with her at Facebook, **Colleen K. Snyder, Author.**

Coming in Spring, the next chapter in Knights of the Octagon:

Micah keyed the phone on his van. "Yes, Wendy."

"Quinn's been sent away." Her tone belied this as a typical pronouncement.

"What's different?" His fiancée was never this agitated. Not over the phone.

"Grace says he's been sent off with no forewarning. And no return estimate. He got a call, picked up his away bag, and left."

Micah turned the van toward home. Council meetings could wait. Quinn being sent out required attention. Immediate attention. "I'll be back home in twenty minutes. Round up the Knights." He numbered them in his head. Tav, Luke, Addison, all brothers. BB and Ben, Micah's sons. Grace, Quinn's wife. Wendy, Micah's intended, and Jen, her sister, Tav's fiancée.

"There's nothing we can do about Quinn being gone. Calling a round table isn't going to change anything." Wendy sounded more frustrated than angry.

"No, but we can make contingency plans in case he doesn't get back in the next two months."

"What plans? He was supposed to stand in as a father and walk Jen and me down the aisle."

Micah nodded, realized she couldn't see a nod, so voiced, "I know. We'll need to make other arrangements. We are getting married, Wenders. You and me, Jen and Tav. Quinn being gone isn't going to change that."

It would. Quinn being gone changed everything. Saying it didn't was a lie. He assured his fiancée, "We'll work it out. Round up the others. I'll see you when I get home."

He disconnected her number then connected to Tav.

His closest friend answered. "You heard."

"Wendy called."

"I talked to Grace, and she admitted this is different. He didn't give her any information. Nothing."

Quinn's trips away weren't unusual. The "office" manager could be counted on to disappear, then reappear some couple weeks later. But his wife always knew something. Even when she couldn't share, she knew. To not know…

Micah chewed his lip. "Okay. I'm on my way home. I'll skip the council meeting and meet you all at the quadrangle."

"We'll have the troops assembled and a fire in the pit."

"Great. See you." He disconnected the phone.

Crash!

The van slammed sideways. The side airbag deployed. Another crack and the front end connected to something solid, shredding the engine compartment. The front airbag exploded then deflated, collapsing Micah's lungs. The van careened like a billiard ball off the side bumpers. Micah's head jerked forward and sideways and came to rest against the steering wheel, now a foot deeper into the driver's section. His left shoulder had dislocated with the impact. His hip felt mashed. Sirens screamed in the distance.

Someone peered in the shattered remains of the window. Micah grunted to let them know he was alive. The figure cursed soundly then disappeared. Micah leaned back against the seat and breathed. Blood flowed from cuts on his face and hands. Everything hurt. Everything would hurt worse before it was over. But he was alive. That's what counted. He whispered, "Thank You, Father. Watch over the other driver." Micah hesitated. "Unless he was the one swearing. Then he really needs to be watched over."

A helmeted head popped in the window. "You okay? You alive? You hurt?" A figure jerked at the door, vainly trying to pry it open.

Micah forced air into his lungs and responded, "No. Yes. And yes. But I'll live."

The figure at the door yelled over his shoulder, "Get the jaws! We've got a survivor." Foam settled on the engine, extinguishing any remnants of flames. The rescuer demanded, "Who's your ICE?"

In Case of Emergency. Micah gave him Tav's number. Maybe he should have given him Wendy's. But in the event of an emergency, Micah trusted Tav to handle things better. At least until Wendy and Micah were married. Then they were on their own.

With practiced efficiency, the rescue crew extricated Micah from the remains of his van, got him on a stretcher, and loaded him in an ambulance. He heard the paramedic on the phone. "CRMC. Right. Twenty minutes. You can meet him in the ER."

The man nodded to Micah. "Your people are on their way."

Micah felt the bite of a needle in his arm. Before the drug could take effect, he had to know. "The other driver. Did they make it?"

"There was no other driver here. Someone must have pulled them out and took off with them. It was just you here."

Micah's mind retained two facts. Quinn was gone. Someone had crashed into him then fled. Making sense of the facts would require a brain functioning far better than his was now. Micah closed his eyes and let darkness take him.

* * *

Fifteen hours later, Micah rested at home in his living room. Rested was a misnomer. He would rest if half the people in attendance went home and left him alone. Tav paced the floor in front of the couch.

"This isn't coincidence. Someone was gunning for you."

Micah started to shake his head, then thought better of it. Not that thinking hurt less than moving, of course. Both were equally painful at this juncture. But he protested, "We don't know that. Hit-and-runs happen all the time. Look at the call sheets downtown. More people leave than stay."

Tav wasn't having it. He glared at Micah. "You said he swore when he heard you were alive."

"People swear for lots of reasons."

Luke, Tav's younger brother, threw in, "Like you would know. Your potty-mouth jar has never had more than a dollar in it."

"Okay, but I hear it enough."

"Not from this bunch."

"Truth." One of the Knights' codes was purity in thought, word, and deed. Word and deed were patently easier than thought. But the jar only held the penalty for words. And yes, it was almost always empty.

Micah cleared his throat. "Can you all take this somewhere else? I'd like to close my eyes." He smiled at the assembled Knights. "Not that I don't appreciate your concern. But go home."

BB, Micah's eighteen-year-old adopted son, nodded. He stood and made a shooing motion. "Go. I'll wake him every two hours like the doctor said. And I'll let you all know if he needs anything. We'll be fine."

Ben, Micah's twelve-year-old adopted son, nodded once. "Dad will sleep. We will take care of him. Thank you for helping. Go home now."

Tav laughed. "Ben has spoken. We've been

dismissed." He squeezed Micah's good shoulder. "We'll check in later."

Micah grumbled. "I'm sure you will."

Tav exited, followed by Luke, Addison, Jen, and Grace. Wendy brushed Micah's cheek with her lips. "Rest, Mick. I love you."

"Love you too, Wenders."

Wendy hugged BB and Ben, then followed the others out. BB closed the door. Micah shut his eyes and let out a groan. BB chuckled. "I wondered how long you could hold that in."

"Not much longer. Thanks for sending them home."

"They love you. And they worry about you."

"And I love them. But from a distance would be better right now."

"I hear you."

Mialma, Ben's black lab support companion, came out from under the kitchen table and took her place beside the couch. She stretched, then curled up beside Micah. BB laughed. "Too many people for you, Mia? Especially with Tav wearing holes in the flooring."

Ben frowned. "Tav was worried. Why is Quinn gone?"

Micah pointed to BB. "You explain it."

"Hurts to think, huh?"

"You could say that."

BB's voice moved away from the living room. Micah guessed he was taking Ben to the kitchen. "Quinn had to go on a special job. We don't know how long he'll be gone. It was very sudden. Tav is worried about Quinn being gone so close to the wedding."

Micah heard Ben's confident, "Quinn will be back. He will not let Wendy and Jen down. He will come to the wedding. I know Popdad. He will be here."

"I hope you're right, buddy."

"Jesus will bring Popdad back. He will not miss the wedding. I will ask Jesus, and He will send Popdad back."

Micah murmured, "Faith of a child. Lord, make mine like his." He slipped into peace.

* * *

Did you miss the first books in the Knights of the Octagon Series? Find them here:

It's life or death. Can they pull together to survive?
Dumped from a raft in the middle of God literally only knows where, four friends are stranded in the wilderness. No cellphones. No maps. No food. Three pocketknives, a compass, and each other are all they have.
Until two shadowy figures lead Micah and his friends to a stash of survival equipment scrounged from the river. Who are these mysterious benefactors? What do they want?
Then rescue comes with a catch. Micah and his friends can wait four days to be taken to civilization or join a real-life quest for a million dollars. The Magary treasure hunt— going on its fiftieth year with no winners—has seen deaths before. With a murderer in the field, will the men become victims?
Is the reward worth the risk? Can the Knights work as a team to not only survive but find a treasure no one else has found? Where is God in their search? In their lives?
Join the Knights of the Octagon on their first adventure.

Also find:

Knights of the Octagon: MIA
Q is missing.

Quinn Magary, patron, supporter, champion of the Knights of the Octagon, is missing.

Five days late from a three-day personal assignment, and no one can find him.

Then Grace Painter, another member of the Knights, disappears without warning.

The remaining Knights—Tav, Luke, and Micah—vow to find their friends and mentors.

Then someone runs Tav off the road. And Micah is nearly murdered at Grace Painter's worksite. An innocent lunch date becomes a conflagration as a shadowy figure blows up the restaurant.

Dead bodies appear. Knights are battered, kidnapped, and left for dead. Who is after them? Why? What can they do to end the attacks? And above all, where are Quinn and Grace?

Join the Knights for their next adventure in:
MIA

ABOUT THE AUTHOR

Colleen K. Snyder has always had a passion for writing. She authored two previously published books: *Journey to Amanah: The Beginning* and *Return to Tebel-Ayr: The Journey Continues* (B&H Publishing). In 2020 she published the first book in the *Collin Walker* series: *Verdict at the River's Edge*. There are now seven books in the series. She lives on a "ranchette" in California and is the juniorest ranch hand. She serves on her church prayer team, and exercises a ministry of intercessory prayer. She has worked as a factory line worker, pharmacy technician, USAF missile systems analyst, janitor, nanny, teacher, accounting manager and anything else the Lord required. Her son, Bear, and his wife Krystal, their two daughters, Mara and Kaylynn, and her daughter Katie all live in Ohio.

Colleen's story is for His glory, always.

Read on to learn more about Colleen's books in the *Collin Walker* series.

The Collin Walker Series

Seven books of action and suspense for your reading enjoyment. Follow Collin Walker as she follows the Lord into murder, intrigue, mayhem…you know, Life.
Available on Kindle, KindleUnlimited, and in paperback.
(Also hardback, but why??)